GOODBYE, HELLO

Visit us at www.boldstrokesbooks.com

By the Author

Transitioning Home

Hands of the Morri

Goodbye, Hello

GOODBYE, HELLO

by

Heather K O'Malley

2025

GOODBYE, HELLO

ISBN 13: 978-1-63679-790-8

THIS TRADE PAPERBACK ORIGINAL IS PUBLISHED BY
BOLD STROKES BOOKS, INC.
P.O. BOX 249
VALLEY FALLS, NY 12185

FIRST EDITION: MAY 2025

CREDITS
EDITOR: CINDY CRESAP
PRODUCTION DESIGN: SUSAN RAMUNDO
COVER DESIGN BY TAMMY SEIDICK

Dedication

To my father. Thank you for everything.
You will be deeply missed.

And as always, to Kaye

CHAPTER ONE

K elly Matheson sat on her bed streaming a ridiculous romantic comedy and tried to relax from her studies. Nursing school was hard, and she was still finishing up her other general ed classes. After this semester was over there would only be one year left in her schooling, and she was so looking forward to graduating. She wanted to get to work and was trying to look at all of her options, including possibly going back into the military.

She also wished she had a girlfriend. The only relationship she'd had at school only lasted a semester before they graduated and moved on with their life. That was over a year ago, and she missed the companionship. She heard that finding dates was easy on campus, but that wasn't her experience so far. There were too many people who just didn't mesh with her and her sense of humor. Dating was rough and had been mostly hit or miss since she'd graduated high school. Somedays it almost felt like she was cursed.

She thought of her high school girlfriend, Teresa McCune. They had been together for most of their senior year, and honestly, Kelly had been getting ready to propose to her before Teresa broke it off with her. They didn't talk that summer and they both went in different directions in life, Teresa to college and Kelly into the army. She wondered what ever happened to her? That was the last time she had been in a relationship that felt right and she was missing that right now.

She shook her head and brought her attention back to the movie. Her plan had been to de-stress and not wool-gather over the past. She was where she was and she would be fine with that, as if there was any other option available. Besides, there were other dating options that could help fill her time while she looked for someone more permanent. She just had to keep herself open to possibilities that presented themselves and take the chances offered. She sighed as she focused back on the movie.

Her phone rang.

It was her mother. Kelly almost never spoke with her mother anymore so that made the call even more confusing. What could she want? Kelly answered, "Hi, Mom."

"Hi, Kelly. I'm afraid I'm not calling with good news. I wanted to let you know, your father passed away. I just got the call a little while ago myself. Apparently, he had a massive heart attack as he was leaving the doctor's office and there was nothing they could do."

"Oh God! What the hell? How? Why? Mom, are you okay?" Her father was dead? Shock began to set in.

"No, I'm not okay." Kelly could hear how flat the affect was in her mom's voice and it wasn't that big of a surprise all things considered. Her parents had been together for a very long time.

"Is there anything I can do? Do you need anything?" Kelly wished she were there in person. Maybe she could have been able to do something.

"Not that I can think of right now. Your brother is taking care of things with the funeral home, and we'll have to wait to see if there's going to be an autopsy or not. I'll call to let you know when the funeral is planned when we get it worked out."

"Thanks, Mom. You aren't worried about Aunt Kate raising a fuss with my being there?" Aunt Kate had been getting on Kelly's case for serving in the military. She couldn't wrap her head around it and tried to just avoid her as much as possible. Nothing had ever given her a clue to why it was an issue.

"If she raises a fuss at your father's funeral, I'll show her what raising a fuss is all about. But I think she'll be able to contain herself."

"Do you want me to come out there early to help out? I can arrange it with the school, and I don't want you to be there all by yourself. I can leave tonight easily enough." Kelly was already starting to run down a packing list and what she would need to pack. The military had prepared her to move rapidly when there was a need.

"Don't worry about me. I'll be fine. Besides, your brother is here, and I know that you and Tim don't get along great. When we get closer to the funeral, come on out. It'll be better that way."

"Okay, Mom, if you're sure, I can wait." Not going and doing something felt antithetical to Kelly but it was her mom's call. She could use the time to talk to her professors and arrange for a leave of absence. She was going to be useless in classes until at least after the funeral. Something else occurred to her. "Is Carrie going to come out as well?"

"I'm calling her next. Your brother was visiting when I got the call, so that's why he already knows and is making plans. But once we're done, I'll be talking to her. I'm sure she'll come out. She was her daddy's little girl."

Kelly firmed her lips and nodded, trying to not let her irritation through. She and her younger sister didn't get along well and this was sure to open new lines of tension between them. But she wouldn't start anything because there was no way her mom was doing alright with this. Sure, her dad had been fighting against lung issues and had just been in a rehab facility to deal with his semi-regular bouts of pneumonia and bronchitis. But for him to pass from a heart attack…that was a surprise. "Okay, Mom. I love you. Does anyone know what happened? I thought he was still in that rehab facility and supposed to be under care."

"I love you too, Kelly. And we don't know yet for sure. Your brother is talking to them and trying to see what happened. I imagine he'll tell me once he knows. As for the rehab place, he got out a few days ago and was going in to see his regular doctor when this happened. I'll keep you updated as we learn more. Talk to you soon."

The phone went dead in her hand. She fell back against her chair and stared at the far wall, not seeing anything. Her father was dead. A blanket of numbness fell about her.

Her father was dead. The whole thing didn't feel real. However, it wasn't like her mother to joke about such things. This situation was sudden and it wasn't. He had been under hospitalized care for a month as he'd been having a harder and harder time breathing. In his condition, if he had gotten a bad case of bronchitis again it could have been fatal. He'd been in his early sixties and these lung issues had been persistent for the last several years. He was diagnosed with advanced COPD and needed permanent oxygen, so Kelly had started thinking she needed to be ready for this development, especially when he went into the rehab facility. She had planned for the worst and still hoped for the best.

She'd known it was a possibility, but the last thing she ever expected was this phone call. It didn't seem real, more like a bad joke. If it'd been a call from her brother, then maybe it would have been just a terrible joke. But never from her mother. No, it had to be true, and she would just have to adapt to a world where her father was gone. How could she even do that? Right now, she could barely think.

The tears caught up to her.

She sobbed for the loss of him. He'd been a good father when she was young. Their relationship improved as she grew older and they had more to say to each other. He was the first person she told when she signed up for the army. His pride was quite evident when she graduated from medic school. He told everyone about it, and the memory of it made her face warm. He was the first she told about her plan to transition. He'd supported her choice to not reup and leave the army so she could pursue school. They had been so close and she had shared so much of her life with him. And now, he wouldn't be there to be proud of her getting her degree and working toward becoming a nurse practitioner. He was gone.

It felt like there was a great empty hole expanding in her chest. How would this feeling ever get better? She wanted to sit there and do nothing else save cry, which surely wouldn't help anything. She wanted to lament the passing of her father, but her mother had continued on after her parents died when Kelly was in middle school. And her father had continued on when his grandparents died.

Continuing on was possible, so it would surely be better after time had passed. Right? Maybe there would be a little bit more closure after the funeral. It was all that she could hope.

God, she realized she needed to talk to her mom about the funeral. How was she supposed to dress? Would she be allowed to show up dressed as she usually did or would she be forced to play the part again? The black would be easy enough to manage, but her mother had been rather adamant about her not showing up dressed like she usually did years ago. She had balanced that by dressing rather androgynously or slightly masculine, but it was never comfortable. It was playing the part of the dutiful son when she would rather be wearing leggings or even a skirt. Her father tried to talk her out of caving like that, but she had anyway just to make her mother happy. Why had she ever agreed to do that?

Would she have to wear a suit to the funeral, like she used to wear to church? That was back before she started her real-life test six months after returning from deployment to Afghanistan, when she realized that she was transgender and started her transition. She was finally growing truly comfortable in her own skin, generally wearing whatever she wanted to, whenever she wanted to. Hell, she even had her gender confirmation surgery so she was sure she would draw more attention if she had to dress drab than she would otherwise. However, she would do whatever she had to in order to go to her father's funeral. If it meant that she had to wear a suit and tie to be allowed in, then she would do so. It would be uncomfortable and make her skin crawl, but she would be there. That was the important part.

Maybe her mother would reconsider her ultimatum that she only show up dressed as she approved? Maybe the loss of her husband would help make the gap between them close, or at least lessen to a place where understanding could happen. Kelly had some hope things would improve between them, because honestly, it seemed like her mother took Kelly's desire to transition personally, as if her mother believed sincerely that she had failed somehow at raising her. Kelly didn't understand the issue and just hoped it would fade. Her father had been more bemused about her transition, not really understanding it but accepting that she felt like she needed to go through the process. He had accepted her even as her mother had not.

Did she want to show up dressed like herself and possibly further antagonize members of her family? No. She couldn't do that. It would be disrespectful to her father. If her mother didn't relent in her proclamation, then she would arrive dressed in drab, if only for the funeral. She would have to go out and buy a damn suit if that was the case. That was something she didn't even want to think about. It might even be her last trip to visit her mom and see her siblings if she would have to live that farce.

That brought a new wave of tears. Her brother and sister were both against her choice as well, aligning themselves with their mother's position, not that she cared about their positions, because in the grand scale of things, it was her life. Tim didn't want others to know, because of how it might reflect on him. And Carrie seemed offended by her choice somehow, but as they had never really talked about it, she wasn't entirely sure what Carrie's issue was. Maybe it was no longer being the only girl in the family? It wasn't like they had talked over things, as they had never gotten along, even as kids.

No, she would need to talk to her mother and try to find some way to make this work. If she put her hair into a low ponytail, it might pass muster, but there was no way in hell she was going to cut it. And she still had some clothes that she kept to wear home, the few times that she visited. It hadn't been as frequent of late, because hormones and clothes had altered her appearance quite a bit, which caused her mother to fuss more about her appearance. At this point, she would look like the woman she was wearing a suit rather than anything else. Hell, even her grandparents were moderately okay with her appearance. She had visited them a few times as herself, so it wasn't a generational thing. But she would play the game to be there, just so she would have the ability to say good-bye to her father. That was what mattered.

She looked around her dorm room with an unseeing gaze, looking far more inward. Telling the administration and her teachers that her father died was an important first step. It wasn't like she could focus on her schoolwork at a time like this. No, she would tell them and that would be it. She was thankful that she'd worked ahead of where they were in the textbooks. Her training as a medic certainly put her ahead in several of her nursing classes.

She needed to send a message to her English teacher, because she wasn't in the headspace to discuss literature or even take notes right now, and that was her first class of the morning.

She sent off the email to her English professor. She then sent one to her advisor, letting them know what was going on and asking what she needed to do.

She headed to the bathroom. Her face burned a little with her crying and her eyes felt puffy. She filled her hands with cold water and rubbed her face. The chill brought her back to the here and now, so she could more easily think. There were things she had to do, and she should get them done to ensure she didn't fall behind in any of her classes. Emailing her professors would be easy. She could copy paste the message into each of the emails. None of the syllabi talked about bereavement leave, and that was something she needed to find out about.

Oh man...what if they wanted proof? She would have to keep an eye out for the obituary so she would have something she could show them. There were sure to be people who would abuse the system otherwise, and she didn't want to be thought of as one of those people. Email first, proof when she could get it. It was the only way. Hopefully, they didn't require a copy of the death certificate. God, this whole situation sucked. Here she was needing to worry over bullshit when she had bigger issues to deal with, such as her dad being gone. But that was life, at least to her experience, always mixing issues when even just the one problem was more than enough to deal with.

She looked in the mirror, gazing into her own eyes. Her blue eyes looked bleak, with wet tendrils of brown hair framing her face, which seemed paler than it usually was. Right...she needed to deal with the email first. She could breakdown later after she arranged for a respite. Tears filled her eyes as she turned away and headed back to her room.

CHAPTER TWO

K elly was glad that she didn't have a roommate. She was grieving and didn't want to subject anyone else to her private suffering. She had woken up crying last night and again this morning, and that wasn't something she wanted to talk about with anyone. This was her pain, her grief, and she would need to be the one to go through it. Maybe if she had a girlfriend, it would be different, or even any close friends, but right now she just wanted to be alone with her pain.

She had informed her RA, but that was as far as she wanted to deal with other people right now. Handling this on her own made sense to her, and she would keep doing it. Part of her was aware that this wasn't the healthiest of choices but it was what she wanted to do.

After hearing back from her teachers, she knew she would be allowed a small sabbatical to go to the funeral and mourn her father without having to worry about any class assignments during that time. One teacher wanted a copy of the obituary as proof of her father's death, but she hadn't heard anything about the obituary coming out yet and so had nothing to send her. Doing the assigned reading kept her occupied and ensured she wouldn't fall too far behind, but she wasn't sure how much of the material she would actually able to recall at test time. She read the words, but her thoughts weren't focused on them, and she would find herself crying at the oddest times.

That morning, she went down to the cafeteria later than her usual time. She got some cereal and coffee. She ate mechanically, barely tasting the cereal. The coffee helped with some of the muzziness she was wrapped in but not all of it.

She headed back upstairs. While in the elevator, she gave herself a sniff. While not rank, she smelled of sweat and decided a shower would help. It might even help her wake up even more. To be honest, so much of her wanted to go back to sleep and sleep until this whole nightmare was over. It would be nice for all this to go away, but her father would still be dead.

She wiped the tears gathering at the corners of her eyes with the palm of her hand. This all felt like so much to deal with. It was almost like she was drowning in it. Why did her grief have to feel like it was rending her on the inside?

The hot water felt good and she stayed under the stream for a while, letting her hair get saturated. She wanted to stand under the stream of water and just be. The heat was comfortable enough for her to just sit in the sensation and feel it over her whole body. She was able to stay in the moment and without any thoughts about her dad or anyone else running through her head as the water trickled over her. Just focusing on getting clean seemed like enough for her right now.

She dried herself then wrapped herself in her towel and returned to her room. She sat on her bed and stared at the opposite wall, unsure what to do. She needed to get dressed but should it be in her pj's again or should she put daytime clothes on? Probably daytime clothes, because she needed to clean out her car so it would be clean when she headed back home. It had to be done so she might as well get to it.

She was nervous about the trip because she would have to deal with her siblings and her mother. Tim and Carrie both had issues with her decision to transition and she had been hearing about it ever since, mostly in passive-aggressive remarks. Add to that the fact that she and Carrie had never gotten along well even before transition, and there were likely going to be several scenes she could frankly do without. Her brother took being older seriously and challenged her over her identity, or at least he still had as of Christmas. They did very little to make her feel welcome.

Her mother seemed uncomfortable with the idea of transition, thus Kelly had gone from being the well-thought-of middle child to the black sheep rather quickly. Despite the pain that caused, her response was to keep the peace, which was almost a default action for her at this point, and so she had been going back home in drab for a while. She loved her family and did it for them, but oh, how it pissed her off. She did it for them because she didn't want to have to fight over things. Home was supposed to be the place where they had to take you in, but so far, she felt like she had to perform in order to be even remotely welcomed.

She had bitched about it with her dad about five months ago, before his emphysema took a seasonal turn for the worse. She remembered sitting in his relaxation room/man cave where he often watched some game or other. It had been basketball then, and he had only partially paid attention to the game while they spoke. She'd been complaining about the situation as usual. "I'm just frustrated by this, Dad. I'm trying to be me and I feel like the others can't or won't accept that. And I look so different, how can they act like my transition isn't real?"

"I raised you to be true to yourself. Maybe you need to decide if you're dedicated to this path if you are so easily dissuaded." He paused and took a few breaths before continuing. "Stop letting your mother run you over and take charge of your own life."

"I try, Dad, but I can't bring myself to do it, to say anything. I don't want to hurt her."

"Then you're letting them force you into this position. They will never change or adapt to this new you if you keep letting them run all over you." This wasn't the first time they'd had this conversation.

"I'm just not sure what to do. Mom is literally the only person I'm doing this for. I don't care what Tim and Carrie think about it."

"Didn't you tell me you transitioned for you? Maybe you should take your own feelings and desires into consideration for a change. Besides, you look like a young woman wearing men's clothes awkwardly. I think it draws even more attention to you." He coughed a few times, a ragged sound that had Kelly crouch down next to him. He had an oxygen canula in his nostrils to help him breathe. He waved her away. "It's just a cough. I have them all the time."

"That didn't sound good, Dad."

"Tell you what. I'll tell my doc about this cough when you tell your mom about how you really feel."

Kelly wiped tears from her face at the memory. She had chickened out and not talked to any of them about her clothes and how she was practically forced to dress. It still felt like too much, and she was scared of what might come of such a conversation. That fear was keeping her silent. Since she hadn't been able to summon up her courage and have that conversation, maybe she was to blame for her father not getting seen earlier? Or maybe he was just stubborn. Her father was where she had gotten her stubborn streak from, after all, so he might have just been avoiding the doctor for other reasons and it wasn't her fault at all. She dearly hoped it wasn't.

Kelly dressed by rote, putting on comfortable daytime clothes. She sighed and rubbed her face. Right, she was going to clean her car. She didn't want to do it. All she wanted to do was sit in her room and mourn, but it would keep her mother from fussing at her. It was easier to drag herself out of her room so she could clean the car than put up with her mother calling her car a mess. There were plenty of things she felt guilty about and didn't need to add to them. She was about to head outside when her phone rang. She snatched it up and answered, "Hello?"

"Kelly? It's your mother."

"Hi, Mom. What's up?"

"Your brother talked with the funeral home and has things set up for this coming Saturday, so come on home. It's only a few days in advance, but it will be nice to see you."

Kelly felt her breath catch. This was the moment where she needed to ask the hard question, how to dress. However, it was hard to push the words out of her mouth. This was going to rock the boat and she desperately hoped for the best. "Come home as me or as I usually come home?"

Her mother sighed heavily, and after a silent moment that felt like an eternity said, "Just come home in whatever way is most comfortable for you. I just want my family here."

Kelly could hardly believe it. Her mom was letting her come home as she was? This would be cause for celebration at any other time. The likely cause of this change in policy was too somber for that. "You know if I come home as me there will probably be fights between Tim, Carrie, and I."

"Your father just passed. I want my family here. If they try to fight with you, I will take care of it. So long as you don't antagonize them, I will take care of it. I just need my kids home with me right now."

Kelly stared at the phone in her hand as if it had grown a chicken head or something. Was this truly happening? "I have no intention of fighting with them, Mom, because you're right, we lost Dad and that's more important. I just expect them to raise a fuss about me if I show up dressed as I normally do."

There was another long pause that grew more uncomfortable as it stretched out, before her mother said, "I'm sorry you felt that you had to hide yourself from me and us."

"No, Mom, it's fine," said Kelly, trying to wave away the guilt that was in her mother's voice.

"No, it's not, but I don't want to talk about that right now. Are you ready to come home?"

Kelly gave a quick look around her room. She already had a bag packed, but she would need to repack it with clothes she would far rather wear. "I just need to pack and clean my car."

"Just pack. You can clean the car here. There'll be time enough for that tomorrow. Are you set with your classes?"

"Pretty much. One teacher wants me to send her a copy of the obituary before she'll excuse my absences, but has tentatively given me leave."

"Seriously? Of all the stupid...that is supposed to be out sometime tomorrow. Tim talked with the person at the funeral home about it. They handle getting the details that the family wants over to the *Register* so it can be published."

"That's good. I should be able to find a link over at the *Register*'s website and turn that in."

"Just get yourself packed up and make it home. I think Carrie is coming over tomorrow, and Tim and his family are coming over for dinner tomorrow night. The church has already dropped off some casseroles, so it's going to be easy food for a bit, which is good because I don't even want to think about cooking."

"That'll be nice. You don't need to be worrying about cooking right now. Grief is a big enough thing to be concerned with."

"True." She could hear her mother sniffle a little. "How are you doing?"

Kelly decided to take a chance with this new, more open mother and share more than she had planned. This was new territory and she was unsure. "Crying a lot. You?"

"Same. Thankfully, he had a Last Letter ready. That helped me get into various programs, emails, Facebook, and the like, plus some of his accounts. Your father was always good at being prepared for things." Kelly could hear her mom sniffle a little more.

"That's good. You being cut off from anything you might need right now is not a good thought. Dad always was one to be concerned with being prepared."

"Your dad was a good man in so many ways."

Kelly wasn't sure how to reply to that. This new emotional space she was sharing with her mother was awkward and hard to talk through. She needed to wrap her head around this over the drive home. "Well, let me get going so I can get packed up. The sooner I leave the sooner I can get there and help you work through some of the casseroles."

Her mother laughed. "You drive safe, Kelly. I want you to get here in one piece."

"Will do, Mom."

CHAPTER THREE

Kelly looked at her bags. Her mom was actually letting her come home as herself. Her giddiness almost broke through the grief making her smile and then she felt it slowly fade into a frown. Being happy over a decision that likely came at the expense of her father didn't give her any joy. Her mother probably felt like she wanted to have her family all together, and it wouldn't do if Kelly was frowning with more than a sense of grief. She just couldn't truly smile when she was in drab, and she had the pictures to prove it.

With a shake of her head, Kelly tried to clear that thought out of her head. There was no reason to be like that. She honestly didn't know why her mother was acting like she was, and Kelly should just take the gift for what it was, a chance for her to have the conversation she told her father she would have. Maybe this one-time grace could be moved to a more permanent situation if things went well. She just wanted to be herself in all areas of her life, and this was literally the only area where she wasn't herself. Hell, she had started her transition in the military, and they let her be who she was. Her grandparents accepted her the way she was. Maybe, just maybe her mom and siblings would let her be herself. It was a decent hope.

She got out her drab bag. It was great to be able to replace those clothes with things that were more her. Unpacking was simple. Now she needed to get clothes that would be comfortable and look good. She pondered what to take.

The decision was fairly simple. She needed to pack mostly comfy clothes, similar to what she was wearing, and then something appropriate for the service. There was no way she would be out of there until Sunday afternoon at the earliest, so she would need to be ready for church as well. Hopefully, no one would make a fuss over her at church, but then again it had been over five years since she had spent any time at the church, and then it was as a kid, so maybe people's memories would be foggy. That should be fine. Or maybe her mother would let her stay home…yeah, that was unlikely so she better pack something that would work.

She had a dress that would work for the funeral, so long as she also wore leggings against the cold. And she was sure she had a skirt and blouse that would be nice enough for church. It wasn't the most thrilling of outfits, but it would work. She looked down at herself, in her leggings and comfy college shirt. At least it wasn't her PT shirt, which she still had and used when she worked out. The clothes were good when she needed something durable, and they would certainly be good enough to show up in.

Honestly, she had a lot of leggings and baggy shirts. They were nearly mandated clothing on campus. Almost every girl wore that combination. Besides, when comfort was the name of the game, they certainly fit the bill. She packed several different pairs of leggings and tops that worked well together, along with a few sweatshirts. She would carry her dress separately so that it wouldn't get wrinkled in her bag. The last thing she wanted was to show up at the funeral all wrinkled. She owed her dad at least that if not more. She wanted to look good and all put together while she was at the funeral. Once her toiletries and makeup were packed, she zipped up her bag.

She should take some of her books. Having to repeat any of this would set her back more than a semester, since the classes she needed weren't offered all the time. Passing was important. She wanted to get into nursing and then get the training to become a nurse practitioner. She didn't want to put up with the rigors of medical school, and from what she had heard, nurse practitioner was the next best thing. She already had a step up on her classmates from having worked in the medical field in the army. Now she just needed the training and paperwork to take her to the next step.

She needed to clean out her car, because while her mom seemed to have changed some, it wasn't like she had changed all that much. A tidy car was its own reward, or something like that was what her mother always said.

She picked up her things and headed out to the common area of her dorm. She spotted her RA sitting on one of the couches watching the floor TV and made a beeline to her. "Erika."

She looked up from the TV. "Yes?"

"I'm gonna be gone a few days. I'm heading home for my dad's funeral."

"Are you gonna be okay?" Every time they had met up since she had informed her that her father had died, Erika had asked that. Kelly figured that it was just part of her job. If so, she was doing her job well.

"I will be. Spending time with my mom will help." And to her surprise, Kelly actually meant that. Maybe this declaration by her mother was the start of something good? She'd considered not going home anymore, but did so for her father. So, this was an encouraging development.

"Okay. When you get back you let me know if you need anything, even if just an ear. It's what I'm here for." Erika caught her eye and held it.

"Thanks, Erika. I should get going." She nodded in acknowledgement of what Erika was trying to do. She was facing this alone so far and planned to keep it that way, which might or might not be a good idea. She might talk about her feelings with her mother. Maybe.

"Take care."

Kelly hustled down the stairs, happy to have some sort of direction. Since the call with her mother telling her about her father, she had felt adrift, unsure what to do, and every action felt like it had to be deliberated and thought over. It was almost like a kind of paralysis. She managed to get a few things done, such as emailing her professors and talking to the school about her need for grief time, but not much more than that. However, simple things like knowing whether she was hungry, or needed to use the bathroom seemed to be debatable items in the overall scheme of things. Her main urge had been to sit and wallow in her grief, to feel it most keenly, but that wasn't helping her take care of herself. Nothing had worked so far, yet this call to come home galvanized her into action and now she wanted to get on the road and get moving.

She'd never been in a rush to get home ever since her transition, because wearing drab boy's clothes was never motivating and having to deal with the wrong pronouns was a pain. Between the discomfort of the clothes and the tightness of the binder she wore to better convey a flat male chest, she hadn't wanted to go home and have to endure all that. It had been wearing away at her, reducing her desire to be home at all. But now she was being welcomed home as herself and that made all the difference. Going home and talking to her mother appealed to her, whereas before it was more of a dread. She had done what she had to to make her mother less uncomfortable with the situation by taking that discomfort onto herself. Maybe now she could stop that and just be. It would be a nice change of pace.

Kelly made her way into the parking lot and cleaned out her car. Her enthusiasm for going had flagged since the call with her mother. Questions arose as to what she was heading home to and she wasn't sure what to do. She told her mother she was going to drive home, and so that was what she needed to do. A part of her was reveling in her mother's allowance, but a part of her dreaded it. What if she got there and her mom changed her mind? At least she would have a few days to sort that out if she had to. But she wanted to see her father off dressed as herself. Was that a selfish wish?

"Fuck it. It'll be what it'll be. All I can do is take her at her word." Kelly exhaled heavily, got into her car, and settled into the front seat. "I'm doing this for you, Dad."

She was soon on the road, headed toward her parents' house. Right, there was only one parent now. Tears gathered at her eyes and she sniffled a few times as thoughts about her dad arose. She wiped her eyes and focused on driving, turning her radio on. If she was going to make this drive without having to pull over to cry several times, she would need to distract herself. After a short while, she was cruising down the road and eventually began to sing along to the radio.

She tuned the radio to a classic rock station where a lot of the songs were favorites of her father's. That caught her a few times and tears welled, but it wasn't until "Modern Love" by David Bowie came on that she felt her control begin slip. She pulled off on the side of the road. Her dad had loved this song. He was a huge Bowie fan and had gone to see him during his Glass Spider tour. He loved to tell that story. Tears filled her eyes as she sang the chorus loudly, almost drowning out the radio. When the song finished, she turned off the radio and wiped her eyes, trying to regain control of herself.

She just stared ahead of her, not thinking, or at least trying to do her best job of making that happen. Would every time she heard that song bring her to tears? Would his favorites haunt her until she no longer wanted to deal with the grief that music would bring? She breathed deeply a few times, trying to calm her turbulent emotions and wiping tears from her eyes. No, the grief was too fresh for her to even know that. It had been a few days since she had gotten that phone call, and she barely remembered the first day at all. After a few weeks, she might be able to see things differently. Right now, she was in the deepest parts of her loss and had to remind herself that things could and would get better down the line.

She had a drink of her water and her eyes burned a little after crying. She changed the station, hoping this one wouldn't bring her any surprises like that one had. Kelly drove on, listening to modern alternative rock, something she was fairly certain her father wouldn't have listened to. Or at least, it wasn't something she had ever heard him talk about. There was a drive to make and she needed to be focused more on the road and less on her pain.

CHAPTER FOUR

Driving into the old neighborhood brought back memories. She remembered her dad teaching her to drive on this street. She also remembered sliding in the snow and almost hitting someone's car when she wasn't driving carefully the winter of her senior year. Her dad had actually laughed at her for that, once he was sure both Kelly and the car were okay. It was also where she had walked in the dark, trying to decide if joining the army was the right decision for her. She had asked a lot of questions of herself walking this street and come to some answers. Not all the answers, as there seemed to always be questions that she needed to discover.

Realizing she was trans was one of those questions. Being shot at and rushing to patch up people had made her face a lot of questions, including questions about herself. Realizing she was a she, wasn't easy. Because she started on that path, she had been transferred from her unit within an infantry battalion to the medical unit for the headquarters, where her job was less about patching up soldiers on the line and more about seeing and screening patients. She hadn't been completely upset, since she had still found her work fulfilling. She received training in several different medical areas, which helped make her sure that the medical path was what she wanted to stay with.

She had answered that question and made the choice to follow her answer to wherever it led, and now she felt like she was in a whole different world. Things made more sense than before, and she felt more fulfilled by things. Sure, she cried more often, but that almost felt like an improvement to how she had been before. Feeling anything was better than the damping down of emotions she had lived with before transition. It felt like she was living a whole life now and not just a part of one.

Kelly smiled when she spotted the house. For all that the reason for coming home was sad, she was excited to be coming home as herself for the first time. Her mother had said she never understood, so Kelly had made the choice to be out and herself everywhere but around her family just to make it easier on them. Maybe that had been the wrong choice, given that her grandparents seemed okay with her as she was, but things had changed now and she hoped it would all go well. She parked her car and just stared at the house, trying to get her courage up to head in.

It was a two-story house with a big picture window behind which was the living room and a two-car garage on the other side. That space was mostly used for storage rather than cars at this point. There were the windows of the big room over the garage, and the ones for her parents' room and the bathroom with their little deck and walkway to the big room. She looked at the front windows and then sighed at herself for sitting there thinking about the house. Kelly grabbed her things before heading to the front door. She tried to open the front door and failed, so she knocked on the door.

Her mom opened the door after a short wait and it was clear when her mother registered seeing her. Her mother's eyes widened in surprise so Kelly just smiled and said, "Hi, Mom!"

There was a very brief pause where her mother was clearly thinking something, before she replied, "Come on in, Kelly. How was the drive?"

"Good. There was little traffic at this time of day which made it a pleasant trip." She stepped into the house and looked around. It was just like it had been when she had last been here over Christmas, though the decorations were all gone.

"That's good to hear. Take your stuff upstairs and then do whatever. I have to run an errand to pick up some notice cards to let people know what happened. You can help me with them tonight so we can get them out into the mail in the morning."

"Sure, Mom. I'm not behind your car, so that should be fine." Kelly turned to face the stair up to the second floor where the bedrooms were. Something occurred to her, and she turned back to her mother. "Were you waiting for me?"

Her mother was quiet for a moment, shifting slightly. "Yes. I was worried because there are some terrible drivers out there. That and I wasn't sure you still had a key."

"I made it just fine. The drive was easy. And thanks." Kelly was fairly certain that her safety wasn't the only reason she had stayed. She'd wanted to know what Kelly looked like, and clearly, she had surprised her mother with how normally she was dressed.

Her mother smiled and gathered up her purse. "I'll be back in a few. Do you need anything?"

"No, Mom, I'm fine."

Her mother bustled outside and closed the door behind her. Kelly just shook her head and headed upstairs with her luggage. Her mother had reacted better than Kelly had expected but was still a touch stiff in her conversation. Maybe things would be better when her mother got more used to seeing Kelly dressed in her regular clothes, college student casual. Maybe.

She entered her room and looked about at her decorative choices of the past. She didn't mind the posters of sexy women athletes in attractive action poses, because she had never lost her desire for them. There were a few pictures of cars and stuff that she had used to want but had since outgrown. It was weird, like a window to a past she didn't miss. Puberty had been hard and things had come up she just dismissed as her mind rambling until after her time being deployed. But then again, it wasn't like puberty wasn't tough for everyone, especially when seen from a distance. There were so many changes to your body and mind it was amazing that anyone got out of there in one piece.

She tossed her bag onto her twin bed and hung her dress up in the closet. Inside, in a nice dress bag were her old dress uniforms she had worn a few times back in the service. They had looked good on her, and she had her old male one as well as the female one she had gotten to wear after she had transitioned. So long as she stayed fit and able to do her job, the army had basically let her transition without too much fuss. Of course, there was the inevitable jumping through hoops and proving yourself, it was the army after all. But she'd been able to become herself while she was serving and that felt like a huge blessing to her. It had been hard work to keep her physical fitness up to standard as she had lost muscle mass, but she had managed it through lots of hard work.

Kelly pulled out one of her textbooks, wanting to get some reading in. She went downstairs, to be available if her mom needed anything when she returned from her errand. Her mother had said something about helping deal with notice cards to be sent out. That seemed odd with all the phone calls and the obituary would be coming out soon. However, she would help with that task if her mother needed her. Helping her mother was something she used to do when she was younger and continued into her teen years. She hadn't done it much since returning from the army, because it had been uncomfortable lying about herself. However, that wasn't an issue at the moment and she was glad to get back to familiar things. The lack of discomfort was refreshing.

She'd already covered a lot of her basic nursing classes from her previous training from the army, and was happy those credits had transferred. It made school a good bit easier since she could take more medical classes than some of her contemporaries and it made getting into the nursing program easier. The nursing program was competitive, and she had discovered that she was as well. The army version of that discovery had been going for Soldier of the Month, and other challenges like the Expert Medic Badge that she had pursued. She was much more motivated to excel after her transition than before and she liked it. It made her stand out.

She lost herself in reading and made note of important sections with a highlighter. She was aiming for being near or at the top of her graduating class because she wanted to look good for prospective employers and because she wanted to get into a nurse practitioner program. It helped that the program that she was in was a good one and well respected. The program had been the major reason she had chosen the school she had. That and the fact that the school was close to home, because she had missed her family despite the fact that the occasional visits had been hard for several reasons.

Her eyes teared a little as she remembered how proud her dad was of her going to college. She certainly wasn't the first, as both Tim and Carrie had gotten into college while she had been in the army, but it meant that all three of them had made it. Since she had been unsure of her plans after getting her degree, she hadn't taken advantage of the Green to Gold program that would have helped her move from enlisted to officer by letting her go to college and get her degree. She wasn't sure if she would be able to tap into that program, but there was always ROTC and she could just sign up again if she felt compelled to get back into the army. It wasn't her first plan of action, but as she had learned, plans changed. Better to have the option rather than not. Besides, it would give her a stable job while she waited the five years needed before she could even apply to a nurse practitioner program, and that was appealing. There were other factors as well that she kept at the back of her mind.

She headed into the kitchen for a drink. She was being pulled in several different directions and she just wanted to put her energy into only one thing. Degree first, nursing job second, the rest of her future third. She tried to remember that, but it was difficult when things happened to throw her carefully worked out plans into a whirl. Her father passing was one of those things. It felt like something important had been pulled from her and now there was just a gaping hole.

Tears began to fall. She missed her dad and lamented that she never dared to playfully call him daddy, like Carrie still did. It was an opportunity lost. She could almost picture the surprise on his face if she had been brave enough to do so. She missed his advice, since that would certainly have helped her figure out her future. She just missed the presence of him. She enjoyed just spending time with him and not necessarily doing anything. Watching movies and listening to him complain when the story got too implausible. Having a few beers as she had talked about her life and what she hoped it would become. Tears dropped onto her shirt and she sniffled. She missed him and wished that he was still here.

Thankfully, there was a box of Kleenex near at hand, which she made use of. There was no question in her mind about her mother grieving. Despite their issues, it had always been clear her parents loved each other. Kelly might not be pleased with her mother for several different reasons, but she was pleased to know that her parents had been happy together for a long time. Love could last, even though they occasionally fought, sometimes quite loudly. They both held opinions the other didn't agree with and it came out at times. Her transition had been one of those bones of contention, and for that she was sorry.

She just sat there and cried about her daddy and how he had loved her for her and not for who she had been before she had become fully herself. She had gone from being a sad unmotivated boy to a driven and focused young woman, and a large part of that journey had been thanks to his advice and support. Of course she would miss him. How could she not, when he had been her rock.

CHAPTER FIVE

The sound of the front door closing startled Kelly from her musing. She blinked up at her mother, who had a few bags in her hands. "Need a hand?"

Her mother waved her down with her free hand. "I got it. You can help me get all the cards in the envelopes and then stamps on them. I called a lot of the most important people who are local to let them know what had happened to your father, but the cards should reach those who are on our Christmas card list but likely can't make the ceremony because of where they live. I didn't want to spend a lot of time on the phone calling everyone and this was the best compromise I could think of."

"I guess that makes sense. But family will be here, right?" Kelly was asking to ensure she was ready to deal with the mix of people that were sure to come to the funeral.

"Yes. I got hold of your grandparents, and your aunt Kate. They will all be making it to the funeral, plus a lot of your dad's friends from work. Then there are all the people from church who will be there. It's going to be a busy day from what is planned. We have the visitation for a little over an hour, the ceremony at the funeral home, and then the graveside service. The church is going to put out a meal for us after the funeral and then it's done." Her mother looked tired just thinking about it.

"That does sound busy. Are you sure it won't be too much?" Kelly was concerned about her mother but had no idea what to say.

These sorts of things were simply exhausting and wore her down. She would try to help as much as she could to make it easier on her.

"I think the day should be fine. Besides, after the service I'm sure your grandparents will want to come over for a bit. I know you won't have anyone there to talk with, except Tim and Carrie, maybe your aunt. So, I'm sorry about that."

"That'll be fine, Mom. The worst will be the visitation. Besides that, the meal should be fun, so we can be together as a family. I can talk to other people at some other time." There was a great deal of false cheer in what she was saying, but she wouldn't mind seeing her grandparents again.

"Even with Kate there?" Her mom's tone was lightly teasing.

"Well, maybe not Kate." Kate had been giving Kelly grief ever since she joined the army. She had some sort of bone to pick with the army or just the military in general and decided to use Kelly as the focus for venting. It was annoying. Kelly generally avoided her when at all possible because she had little interest in trying to defend the military. No telling what would get said about her being trans, since she had either avoided Kate when at her grandparents' or she'd been in drab at other events. Hopefully, she wouldn't get an additional earful over her choice to live her fullest life.

Her mom chuckled. "I'll see if she'll leave you alone this weekend."

"Thank you. It's gotten old at this point. I don't want to be constantly defending the army or the military from who even knows what."

There was a slight lull in the conversation before her mother asked, "So how are your classes going?"

Kelly smiled. This was a simple and comfortable topic and one that she felt was safe. "I'm doing well. The biology class is currently the hardest I have and that one is actually going well. I'm focusing a lot on that one. My nursing classes are going well. I'm still ahead of a lot of the material thanks to my getting assigned to headquarters after I transitioned. That experience is really helping me out."

"I think you'll be a good nurse."

"Thanks, Mom. My goal is to become a nurse practitioner so I can see patients and help people, like I was doing in the army."

"I know that, Kelly." Her mother narrowed her eyes in annoyance. "It's not like I haven't been paying attention while you've been going to school."

"Sorry, Mom."

"You have a good temperament for the job at least. I dislike nurses who aren't patient and try to rush you through things."

"It helps that being a medic came with a lot of work that's similar and let me get a feel for things before I got into college. I didn't have to try things out to see if I would enjoy it."

"I never understood your choice when you signed up, but it makes much more sense now, seeing what you're doing with it."

"Yeah, I always felt a pull toward the medical field. For a while, I wanted to be a doctor, but the nurse practitioners I've met seemed to do a mix of the work of a doctor and the time with a patient of a nurse. That was most of what I wanted, to directly help people. Doctors never get to spend time with patients, which is one of the reasons I made the choice. I think I'm heading in the right direction for me."

"You always were focused in helping others when you were younger." Her mother smiled at her.

"Do you need me to help with supper?"

"No, it'll basically be warm up a serving of one of the casseroles that I've gotten from several people at church. There're even some vegetable dishes that can go with them, so we can manage a balanced meal."

"That sounds good. And easy will be nice." Easy would be good. Grief was exhausting.

"Yes, it will. Let me go put these things in the family room and we can deal with filling out the envelopes so they can go in the mail tomorrow."

Kelly put her book aside, realizing the comment by her mother was more than simply a casual suggestion. As chores went, putting something in envelopes was pretty simple and was easy enough to lose herself in. She would be happy to help her mother with that.

The setup her mother made was simple; she would address the envelope and Kelly would put in the card and close it. It was slow work and things at first seemed fine but grew awkward as the silence stretched.

Kelly wanted to break the silence, but nothing seemed like a good reason to talk, especially if her mother was just fine with this situation. Had Kelly talked too much already? Had she not talked enough? Had she not found the right topic of conversation? There were a lot of possible options and not a lot of answers available to her. To be honest, she didn't want to break the silence because that might mean they would have to talk and after several years of awkwardness between them, it seemed like nothing would break the divide. There had been a few too many painful conversations between them for her to want to make the first step.

"So, have you found a girlfriend yet? You are still into girls, yes?" Her mother finally broke the silence.

Kelly's face heated and she shifted some in place as she put a card in an envelope. "Yes, Mom, I'm still into girls."

"Okay. I wasn't sure if that changed as well. So?" Her mother was still focused on addressing envelopes, but Kelly was sure she caught a hint of a blush on her mother's face. Maybe this was just as awkward for her as it was for Kelly. Playing along might actually make it easier to have other more important conversations later on, conversations that needed to happen.

"I haven't found anybody. I'm a couple of years older than the other students, and that seems like a lot sometimes when I'm talking to them."

"Could it be that your time in the army is making a difference as well?"

Kelly started a little. She had thought it was an age thing and not an experiences thing. Maybe her mother was on to something. "That's…likely. Personally, I'm not there to party or cut loose, because honestly, that was taken care of in my first few years in the army. Now I just want to find someone who gets me and that I get, someone who doesn't mind that I'm working on my nursing degree and take it seriously. There aren't a lot of super-focused people there who are part of my dating pool."

"Well, at least you won't be bringing over these losers like your sister keeps finding," said her mother casually.

Kelly cut her eyes over at her, trying to figure out what was going on here. "Losers?"

"Oh yeah, this last one, his big goal was to be a music producer, but he wasn't taking any classes or working to make albums or anything. All dream and no follow-through. Carrie is great at finding dreamers and not so good at finding doers. Make sure you have someone who has follow-through when you finally find someone."

"Okay. I mean, I'm not looking right now, but if start I looking, I'll try to look for someone who has follow-through." Kelly was sure this was one of the stranger conversations she had had with her mother in a very long time. But at least they were talking. That was a win. Sure, it wasn't anything important, but did it have to be? This was a start and she was glad to have it.

"That's good to hear. I'm sure you'll be fine once you have your nursing degree but extra income is never a bad thing."

"That's true."

There was another brief lull before her mother continued. "What are you doing for spring break? Planning on going anywhere?" Her mother looked over at her and smiled.

"Not so far. I was just going to rest and maybe catch up on some of the classwork I'm sure to miss. I just want to do a good job in my classes because the nursing program is competitive. I want to be the top graduate of my class, because that will make getting a job easier."

"I'm sure you'll do fine. You've always been a good student. Don't forget to have fun though."

"I'll try to have fun, Mom, I promise." Kelly couldn't help but roll her eyes at that. Her mother was telling her to have fun? Where was the woman who had pushed her to do and be more? This conversation was starting to drift into the bizarre.

"Good. You were always good about keeping your promises. Only a few more of these to do. Want to watch something while we eat?"

"Sure. Is there something you want to watch?" Kelly honestly couldn't care less about watching anything, but her mom was clearly trying to make conversation, so she should meet her at least part of the way. If her mother was going to try this hard to fix their connection, then she would do her part as well. It was one of the things she had wanted for a while and had all but given up on.

"I can pull something up if you can get the food ready."

"I'm supposed to know what casserole you want?" said Kelly, in what she thought was a logical point.

"Do you want to pick out something?"

"I have no idea what to pick out, either for a show or food," admitted Kelly. "I haven't watched a lot of TV lately."

"Fine. You put the food in the microwave after I serve myself. Honestly, Kelly."

She blushed a little and kept putting cards into addressed envelopes until there were no more. Her mother put away her address book and stretched. "Right, let's eat."

The casserole her mother was slowly working her way through was a chicken poppy seed casserole that looked good. There were also green beans and carrots as side dishes and some mashed potatoes. Food was soon ready and plated. She carried it out and handed her mother a plate as she was pulling up a show.

Kelly had to admit that today had been not that bad, certainly not as bad as she had feared it might be. Something had clearly changed with her mother, but she wasn't sure what. Not that she was going to complain. She was just happy with the changes that allowed her to be home and dressed normally without getting fussed at. So, she just sat there next to her mother, eating her dinner and watching *Dancing with the Stars*.

CHAPTER SIX

K elly woke late. She usually woke early, but since she had heard about her father, she was sleeping later than usual. It felt like she didn't want to face the world without him. In a lot of ways that was true. He had been her rock and had been there for her, for her entire life, a touchstone to all the events. And now he was gone. She lay there looking at the ceiling of her old room and just sighed as she felt the desperate hollowness of her grief. This wasn't an auspicious sign to the start the day on. She wiped tears that had gathered and sighed again. She needed to get up. There were things to do.

Her muscles resisted as she sat up, dragging out a groan as she moved. Sitting at the edge of her bed, she tried to figure out what was ahead of her day, so she could plan. Primarily, she needed to be ready to help her mom with whatever tasks needed to be done, but outside of that she didn't have anything else to do today. Tomorrow was the service at the funeral home and the burial. Until then, she was left to her own devices, or rather her mother's devices.

That made her realize that Carrie might be coming by, and maybe Tim. It was better that they come over and get the fighting out of the way here rather than at the funeral. She honestly wanted tomorrow to go smoothly and without any issues, so it could be about her father rather than about the fight or argument that occurred between family members. Kate's presence would make that proposition difficult, but she would try to avoid the woman. The last thing she needed was to be poked at over her choice to serve in the military or over anything else. This trip wasn't about her, and she didn't want to make it about her in any way.

A shower and coffee were what she needed, in either order. She opened the door and the very faint smell of coffee that had been tickling her senses became a full-blown assault. She breathed in deeply through her nose to get the full effect. The shower could wait. Coffee beckoned now.

Down the stairs she went, lured in by the coffee. Her mother was in the living room, sitting at the sofa while drinking her coffee. She was also going over some paperwork. "Good morning, Kelly. Did you sleep well? There's coffee in the pot."

"Morning." Kelly was still somewhat groggy and wanted coffee to get her brain and everything up to full working mode. She filled a cup, sniffed the goodness and then leaned back, feeling her eyes open a little wider. She took a sip of the mug and then headed out to the living room.

Her mother just smiled at her and went back to the paperwork. After another sip of the coffee, Kelly felt enough synapses firing to engage in conversation. "What's the plan for today, Mom?"

Her mother regarded her. "Going through this paperwork. I'm making a list of what I need for each account and insurance. In some cases, I'm waiting for the people to send me the paperwork I need to fill out. This is so much just busywork."

"Is there anything I can help with?" Kelly asked after a longish pull of her coffee.

"There are still a few places I need to call and inform of your father's passing. They will likely need a copy of the death certificate, which I'm getting tomorrow. I could have picked it up earlier, but I just couldn't face it. Things would feel too final. Right now, I can almost imagine he's just late coming home."

Kelly came around to hug her mother. At first, her mother seemed surprised and then relaxed into it. After a moment of just holding her, Kelly said softly, "I miss him as well."

"I know. Your father was always so proud of you and all you've done. He was proud of everyone for all they had done."

Kelly felt her face warm and to cover it she went back to her seat and took another pull from her coffee. Her heart ached missing her father, because that was one of the things she would most miss, his belief and support. She smiled tightly. "Thanks, Mom."

"What do you have planned for today?" she asked.

"I don't know. I can always do schoolwork, but is there something you need me to do?"

"I...can you collect your dad's clothes? I can give them to the thrift store, so someone can get some use out of them. The bags or whatever you put them in can go out to the garage and I can donate them next week when things quiet down."

"Okay." It hurt knowing that this practical action had to occur. It felt like removing her father from the house entirely. Still, it was a task that needed to get done. "Is there anything you want me to keep out?"

"No, anything I wanted to keep I've already taken out of the closet. Your brother grabbed a suit he could be buried in so you can just get what's left."

"Okay, Mom, I can do that for you after I have some breakfast. Are any of his clothes in the dirty clothes?"

"Not that I'm aware of. I think he had some stuff with him at the rehab facility that hadn't gotten done yet and they might need to be taken care of. I'm not sure."

"Want me to check?"

"Please. I just want to focus on the paperwork so I can get it done. If I get this done, we might be able to skip probate but I'm not sure." Kelly managed to catch that her mother was starting to tear up. Maybe she needed to give her some space.

She headed into the kitchen. She felt awake enough to make herself some breakfast. She was going over her plan for the day as she got her food together. Taking care of her dad's clothes would be the first thing she did, followed by checking the laundry. Then, if she needed to, she could start a load to take care of the final bits of clothes.

Maybe she should also check with her mother in regards to clearing out the upstairs room, where her dad had all sorts of items he collected. It wasn't quite a full man cave, but it was a space with a lot of her father's things. There was also a little sewing nook her mother had used mostly for mending clothes and letting out hems. She had no idea when it was last used.

She went to the small dining room and ate, looking out the glass doors at the backyard. The lawn had yet to be mowed, but it was still too early in the season to be worried about that. The backyard still had the old wooden playset farther back. She remembered playing on that set, years ago, or even just sitting on the swings and thinking about life. It was a well-loved piece that her father had put together for them and it seemed to be holding together well. Maybe if Tim had kids they could play on it.

The wall hid the part of the deck with the outdoor furniture. Maybe she could spend some time outside, just thinking, despite the cold weather. She was feeling rather melancholy, which made so much sense given everything. Just sitting and thinking was what called to her, but she also felt that she needed to keep busy so that her thoughts and feelings wouldn't overwhelm her. It felt like her father would be there forever, always available to talk to, despite her knowing that everyone died. But when did death ever make sense or happen at an easy time?

She cleaned her dishes and put them into the dishwasher. Time to get to that task. She opened the storage under the sink to grab several trash bags she could put her dad's clothes in. She pondered where to tackle first, underwear and socks in the dresser or the closet with most everything else. She decided the dresser would be an easy start.

The bag snapped open as she flicked it. She pulled out the drawer and paused. This seemed wrong somehow, but it wasn't like her father was going to come back and need any of this. He was gone and his need for these clothes was gone. All she had to do was collect these things and then set them in the garage so they could go to some charity. Someone else would be happy to have these things. Her heart was racing and her breath was tight as she stood next to the open drawers. She sat on the bed and shook her head. The finality of this action brought back the finality of his loss.

She cried for a while, unsure how long. She tried to hold in the sobs so that the sound wouldn't travel downstairs and affect her mother. Her grief at her father's loss hit her strongly, more with his absence than his loss since part of her still expected him to walk in and ask what she was doing. This was an action that set in stone that he was now gone. Nothing she could say or do would bring him back. This was almost like wiping him away from this place, from their life. However, Kelly rationalized that this was just basic housecleaning. This was not removing her father; it was just removing stuff, things that wouldn't be needed and would be taking up space. If her mother wanted to get it taken care of now instead of later, that was her decision. Kelly was sure she would rather have waited, but wait until when?

How long was too long when holding on to the things of someone who had passed? Was there any time limit on that? She got his underwear and socks into the bag. The next drawer down held white T-shirts, under that, shorts. Those went into the bag as well. It was already over halfway full. And there hadn't been any surprises in the drawers, hidden between shirts or something. She was grateful for that. She wasn't sure what she would do if that had been the case.

The hanging clothes filled a second bag. A third bag held his shoes. There was now a lot of extra room in the closet, and it looked empty with the exception of a couple of suit bags. Or rather emptier, as her mom's clothes were still in there and taking up their slightly more than half of the closet. She spread them out a bit so they had more room than before.

Kelly tied the bags closed before she got out a sharpie and wrote *Dad's Clothes* on the bags. She was trying to be helpful, because there was enough stuff in the garage that they might get lost in the mess, which would not be helpful. This way they were identifiable if her siblings wanted some of the clothes before they went to the thrift store. Kelly hadn't wanted any of it since none of it was her style or would work with what she normally wore. Tim might want a few things and he would be welcome to them.

She took the first two bags downstairs and noticed that her mom wasn't in the living room. Once the bags were in the garage, she headed upstairs to grab the last of the bags. That one went out with the others and then Kelly spotted her mom outside, sitting at the table. A break would be nice and she could see what her mother was up to.

After grabbing a cup of water, Kelly headed outside and over to where her mom was sitting out on the deck. "I got the clothes taken care of."

"Thank you, Kelly." She was clearly distracted.

"No worries. I just wanted a short break before I checked the laundry for any of his clothes."

Her mother turned from watching the yard. If there was any redness to her eyes, or signs of tears in her lashes, Kelly made sure not to point any of it out. "I think there might be."

"That's fine. Any other clothes and stuff I'll put in the bags," said Kelly.

"Bags?" Her mother turned to face her.

"Yeah, I figured that trash bags would work best because I didn't see any empty boxes to use to put Dad's clothes in. And if they're going to the thrift store, does it matter what they go in? I'm putting them someplace easy to get to in case Tim wants anything."

"Good point. Thank you for being here, Kelly."

"Where else would I be? I loved Dad and want to be there for him and for you. I love you as well." Kelly's face warmed as she was embarrassed by stating all this out loud. It had been a hard enough thing to even think of lately, with how her mother had treated her, but this change was healing.

Her mother patted her hand briefly. That made Kelly smile. She didn't know what had happened, but things with her mother were better than they had been since she had started her transition. They were talking and dealing with each other openly and honestly. She would happily take that win. "You're a good child Kelly."

"Well, you both raised me to be a good kid, and I think that the two of you did a pretty good job." Kelly smirked slightly.

Her mother turned to look out over the backyard again. "I was worried about sorting his clothes, in case there were any surprises or anything in there."

"There wasn't anything like that. Just clothes."

Her mother was silent again for a moment, then she had a sip of her own drink. "That's good. Does it make sense that I am both relieved and sad by that?"

Kelly knew they had to talk, but now was clearly not the moment for that. And she had no idea how to reply to what her mother just said. She just sat in the cool air and happily cooled off. Packing was hard work.

CHAPTER SEVEN

K elly was reading one of her books for English class when
she heard her mother's phone ring. Her mother answered,
though Kelly couldn't hear the conversation that followed. Her
mother came into the room shortly afterward looking annoyed.
"That was the hospice. There's some paperwork I need to sign. It
shouldn't take too long."

"Okay, Mom. Is there anything you need me to do while you're
gone?"

"Nothing comes to mind. Your brother is coming over later as
will your sister, I hope. She said she would but that never means
anything lately. I think it's because I don't approve of her latest
boyfriend. Anyway, I'll be back shortly, hopefully before they get
here."

Once her mother left, Kelly went right back to reading. Her
notebook for that class sat ready to take whatever notes she needed
to take on what she might have seen.

She was deep into her textbook when the front door opened.
Figuring it was her mother, she simply ignored it in favor of reading.
If her mom needed something she was sure she would say something.
Instead, she got something different. Her sister practically screeched,
"What are you doing?"

Kelly sighed and rolled her eyes. Great, her sister. Just what she
needed. She lowered the book enough to look at her. "I'm reading,
Carrie. What does it look like?"

"What are you wearing?"

She looked down at herself, dressed similarly to what she had been wearing yesterday, leggings and a T-shirt. There was little doubt what her sister meant, but she didn't want to play. "Clothes."

"You look ridiculous."

"You're wearing the same thing as me." Kelly was well aware she wasn't helping to diffuse the situation.

"I am not," protested Carrie. "I'm wearing the right clothes for me. You're dressed in some sort of costume. Has Mom seen you?"

Kelly regarded her sister for a long moment, trying to figure out where she was going with this. "Yes. I've been wearing this all day. Same as what I wore yesterday. She hasn't complained about what I'm wearing."

"She must be horrified by this, too horrified to say anything. What an embarrassment. Why would you wear this?"

"Wear what? These are just my clothes." She knew this conversation was needed but had not expected Carrie to spew such vitriol over it. This was just her clothes and they hadn't even gotten into her identity. This was sure to make things worse between them instead of better.

"You look like a freak."

"Carrie, it's just my clothes. I look fine since we're dressed pretty much the same. What's your issue?"

"You're my issue. You're my brother, not my sister."

"I think you'll find that I am indeed your sister, in all ways. I talked to you about this before I transitioned and you said you understood. Was I unclear? Don't worry. You're still the youngest and Mom's baby."

"You think that's my issue with all this, that I'm not the baby?" Her hands flew up in exasperation.

"I have no idea what your issue is with me because we hardly talk and you never have anything civil to say to me when we do. You've been saying this sort of stuff for a lot of our life so I honestly have no idea what to say to explain to you that this is just who I am." Kelly was tired of this but was sure it was part and parcel of who Carrie was, just her making a fuss if the focus wasn't always on her. Why her transition was in that equation made no sense to Kelly. "Why don't you tell me about your boyfriend instead of us argue about this. That will surely be a better topic of conversation."

Carrie narrowed her eyes and clenched her fists. "What do you want with my boyfriend?"

Kelly set her book to the side and sat up more. "Jesus, Carrie, calm down. I'm just trying to have a conversation with you about your latest boyfriend."

"He's fine. His name is Nigel and he's a drummer in a metal band."

Kelly sighed. Yeah, no wonder her mother didn't approve. That sounded like a potential nightmare in terms of her mother. Other than that, Nigel didn't sound all that bad. "That's nice. Are they good?"

"They have gigs and a bit of a following, so yeah, they're pretty good."

"That's good to hear. Are you doing okay?"

"What do you mean?" Again, there was a suspicious tone to Carrie's voice that grated on Kelly's nerves.

"Dad just died, Carrie. I'm broken up over it and I was just asking to see how you're doing with all of this. That's all. Checking in on my little sister."

"Why the hell are you broken up about Dad? You're just a fake, being something you're not."

Kelly closed her eyes and counted to ten. "I'm broken up because Dad accepted me as I am and not the illusion I was trying to give you all because I was afraid you might not understand, afraid Mom might not understand. Surely that's not that difficult to understand?"

"Bullshit."

"You are literally making my case for not pushing things earlier right now. Believe what you like, Carrie, but I'm a girl and this is how I dress." Kelly hoped that her tone of voice would bring an end to this conversation.

"Dad would never accept you looking like that."

"What can I say? He liked who I became after I transitioned. So do I. Being myself got me more driven, more focused on chasing my dreams, happier in all ways. I became more myself, not someone else."

"Like I said, that's all just bullshit. You're just a freak forcing us to take part in your sick fantasy."

Their mom walked in, catching that last bit of the rant. Her eyes widened and she snapped out, "Carrie Elizabeth!"

Carrie visibly started and turned to face their mom. It did not do to ignore their mom when she got mad. Carrie seemed cowed by the tone her mother had used. Her mother then said, "You do not say things like that to your sister."

"But, Mom, he's not my sister."

"Yes, she is. Your dad would be so disappointed in you right now. He may not have understood Kelly's reasoning, but he supported and accept her in her transition. You may not understand why she chose to do this, but she is your sister and you will treat her civilly this weekend, because I don't need this nonsense while I am burying your father. Am I clear?"

Carrie stood there stunned. Frankly, so was Kelly. It was one thing to act like she was accepting when it was just the two of them. It was another when defending Kelly. Kelly tried not to simply gape at her mother in surprise. This was a turn she hadn't expected.

"I said, am I clear?"

Carrie swallowed hard and said, "Yes, Mom."

"Good." Her mother took a deep breath and let it out slowly before she continued. "Thank you for coming over. Did you get the email from your brother about when the service is going to be?"

"Yes. I'll be there early."

"Thank you. Will Nigel be there?"

"No, he has band practice because they're going on a short tour soon."

"I'm sorry. He'll be missed. Are you staying for dinner? We have all sorts of casseroles just waiting to be eaten. Most of them are really good."

Carrie just stood there looking flummoxed over the whole situation. Kelly sat back and kept her mouth shut. When their mom was like this you didn't want to intervene. You stood there quietly and took the dressing down and complied. Carrie couldn't let it go. "But, Mom…he's just sitting there wearing women's clothes."

"Yes, because she is a woman."

"But, Mom—"

"No buts. Your father made clear his point and that helped make it clear for me. Kelly is your sister, so drop it. She is dressed appropriately for now. I expect both you and her to be dressed nicely tomorrow, mostly to keep Kate from fussing because you know how she is. And you know your grandparents will be there as well, so we want to put our best foot forward."

"But people will talk."

"People will always talk. It doesn't matter what she wears or who she is, there will always be negative gossip about you. You just have to be better than the gossip or else you're only going to make it worse. Now give me a hug. I've missed you."

Carrie went into the hug with some reluctance but then deepened the hug, resting her head into the crook of her mother's neck. Her mother soothed her and Kelly sighed. Apparently, it was a bit much for Carrie to accept that she now had an older sister, at least not easily. And had her dad talked to her mother about this topic? That seemed to be the case based off what her mother said. If her father had talked to her about this, then it made Kelly feel even more like she had failed her father. Was a conversation really something to be that afraid of?

The door opened again and Tim walked in. He looked over things and said, "What did I miss?"

"I'm your sister and Mom wants to make sure there are no fights about this tomorrow." Kelly wanted to get things out first so that Carrie couldn't try to spin the whole situation like she liked to do.

Tim nodded and said, "Right, a united front. So, you're finally dressing like a chick?"

"Timothy!"

"Sorry, Mom. But Kelly said that she was a girl years ago but kept showing up dressed androgynously. I was of the opinion that it was sort of a weird joke because of that. So I take it, it's not?"

"Nope. I was mostly dressing as a guy for Mom's sake," Kelly replied, locking eyes with her brother. "She was uncomfortable with it so I did what I did for her."

"Right. Don't know why you would want to be a girl, but that's another matter entirely. Hi, Mom, Carrie." He embraced both of them. "We need to be at the funeral home early tomorrow so we can take care of some paperwork. There are some things only you can sign, Mom, as the spouse. But otherwise, everything is all arranged."

"Thank you, Tim. That's nice. Did you just come over here to say that?"

"Yes, because you weren't answering your phone. I was growing concerned."

Her mother looked confused for a moment before she glanced toward her purse. "It was on earlier."

"Maybe it ran out of juice?" offered Kelly.

Her mother pulled out her phone and tried to turn it on. "Oops. Sorry about that, Tim. I'll try to do better to keep it charged."

"No problem, Mom. You've had a lot on your mind. Alison and I will be there tomorrow. Do you need a ride to the funeral home?"

Her mother looked over at Kelly, who nodded back. "I have one. Kelly will take me."

Kelly just sat there watching all of this play out. Her sister was giving her a glare, so clearly their animosity was only renewed rather than dealt with. That meant Carrie would be more subtle with her jabs, which might be nice considering. She was more used to blatant barbs, so this might be a good change. And Tim was so focused on his life that he couldn't care less about the antics of his sister. Besides, his wife, Alison, had been a good influence on him. Maybe tomorrow wouldn't be as bad as she had expected. Her mom's position certainly surprised her. That should keep conflict with Carrie to a minimum.

"Oh, before I go. They have Dad's obituary posted on the paper's website and it was in today's paper," said Tim as he was heading out the door.

"Thanks," said Kelly. "I need to send a link to that to one of my professors."

Tim just nodded while Carrie said, "That seems morbid."

Kelly shrugged. "Some people think that if you claim some family member has died it will get them an A in the course. Not sure where the hell that idea started but it's out there nonetheless. Because of that, some teachers want proof if there was a death in the family and that was what was asked for. Thank God they didn't want a copy of the death certificate."

"Oh, and just a heads up. The obit was written by your ex. She works for the paper and has a decent way with words. It's a good obit."

"My ex?" Kelly wasn't sure who that could be referring to. There were a number of people she had dated before.

"Teresa. You two were quite the item in high school if I remember."

Kelly started in surprise. "Teresa?"

Carrie grumbled, "Oh…her."

"Well, that's quite a surprise. I knew she liked working on the school paper, so I guess it makes sense that she got into journalism. Thanks for letting me know. I should go get that emailed off so that I don't have to worry about it."

"Glad I could help."

With that, Kelly headed upstairs, and away from her sister. Tim was a surprise visit and point of view, but honestly, Carrie was being the spoiled brat that she was used to. She got to her room and pulled out her laptop.

Kelly read the obituary before copying the link and emailing it to her professor. It was a good but depressing review of her father's life. He was more than who he left behind or even a listing of the things he had done. It was a good obituary, which highlighted that he had a full life, but it only made her miss her father even more. And it was certainly by Teresa. Her name was there in the paper and everything. Wow…she hadn't thought about her in years. It was a bit of a surprise that she had decided to stay in town and work for the paper. It wasn't a choice that she would have expected Teresa to make.

Thinking back, she wasn't even sure why they had broken up the summer after high school. She'd been planning on asking Teresa to marry her. And then, seemingly without warning, they broke up. Teresa had said that it was her and not Kelly, but Kelly had no idea what that meant. The whole situation had been jarring and confusing. She was glad that she had basic training to occupy her at the time since it meant that she had been too busy to ruminate over the whole mess. How was Teresa doing now? What was she even up to? Maybe she would look her up after the funeral, when she had some time. It would be nice to catch up.

Chapter Eight

Waking up in her old bed was still disorienting. Kelly lay there just staring at the ceiling, waiting for her brain to wake fully. Today was the day. Today they would bury her father. She brought her hands up to her face and rubbed before she groaned into them. Tears began to gather, which she wiped away. No time for crying now. There would be plenty of that the rest of the day.

She needed to get ready but was unsure what time it was and thus how long before they needed to head off to the funeral home. Lying there was kind of nice, but the flood of missing her father hit, and the tears began to roll down the sides of her face. She sat up with of a groan, her body stiff. She probably needed to do some stretching, as she was way off her usual routine. Thanks to the army, she usually started her days with exercise, but since she heard about her father, she hadn't wanted to do anything except mourn him. This achiness was the result.

Despite feeling lethargic, she stood and began to stretch. It generated a good ache, and she appreciated that, since that let her know she was doing something right. Once her basic stretching was done, she did a set of push-ups, sit-ups, and squats. That made her feel more invigorated, more able to face the day even before coffee helped her be ready for more.

Her body felt warm and a little sweaty. She needed a shower before she could deal with people. The water was hot and it was a different kind of warm on her muscles. Once dry, she put on leggings and a T-shirt again. She didn't want to wrinkle her dress before the service. She came downstairs and noticed there was no smell of coffee, making her think her mom was still asleep. Maybe that was a good sign. She looked in the living room and saw her mom was sitting on the couch looking down at a photo, as still as could be. "Mom…are you okay?"

Her mother started then looked up from the photo and smiled weakly. Her eyes were red-rimmed. "Oh, I'm fine. Let me get the coffee started."

"No, Mom, it's all good. I can get coffee started. You're allowed to feel things and not hide in doing things for me or the others. You're allowed to grieve as well. Especially today." It was hard to see her mother suffering. Part of her felt a little guilty for catching her mother in that private moment.

She gave Kelly a faint smile and turned back to the photo. Kelly realized it was likely the copy of their wedding photo she was looking at that always had pride of place on one of the tables. She went into the kitchen, both to give her mom space and because she could use the caffeine. Once the coffee was started, she headed back to the living room and asked, "What do you want me to make for breakfast?"

"Kelly, you don't have to do that." Her mother started to rise, but Kelly waved her back down.

"This is fine, Mom. I can handle it easily enough. Now what do you want for breakfast?"

"I just want some yogurt and maybe some of the cantaloupe."

"Sure, Mom. Will that last you long enough? It's going to be a long day."

"I'll be fine. You have what you want and let me worry about me."

"Okay. I can do that." When the coffee was ready she took her mother a cup.

Her mother took the cup and murmured thanks. After a while, her mother asked, "How are you doing, Kelly?"

"It's been rough. I miss him so much even though I was well aware of what his illness meant. I still thought he'd be around for a lot longer. It just hurts so much."

"You know he was super proud of you. Proud of all you kids. We talked about you in the rehab facility, when he was between treatments. Made me realize that I was acting the fool when it came to you." She looked at Kelly, with a wry smile on her face. She took a drink of her coffee. "I don't understand it, but then your dad never quite understood either from what he said. He just said our job was to love you as you were, not as we wanted you to be. So, I've been trying to do that for him."

"Honestly, Mom, these last couple of days have been refreshing. I can tell the difference and thank you for it. I was just trying to be myself like you both taught me. It took me to different places than I expected. I'm happy to answer questions for you if you want to better understand. Dad asked me some, but ultimately, he just said, okay, this is who you are."

"I'm trying to get there, but I'm not there yet. I just don't understand why you needed to do this."

"I was unhappy with who I was, because everything felt like I was playing a part. Sure, some parts of me were there but I was trying so hard to be a good boy, a good man for you all that I buried myself into a part that wasn't really me. After the year I was deployed, and the couple of close calls I faced, I realized I wasn't being me and I needed to fix that. I started talking with a therapist and realized I might be trans. After that, I just went with the transition. And along the way as I became happier and more me, I grew more driven to do the best I could. It's why I tried so hard to excel at my job toward the end and why I left the army to pursue nursing. It had nothing to do with anyone but me and how I saw and felt myself."

"I guess I can understand some of that. I feel like I have to be someone else at work so that I come across as professional when I would rather call some of the people idiots." They both laughed. "I'm not going to get it today, but let me know if I falter. I want to treat you better, like your father asked me to and like you deserve."

"Thanks, Mom. I'll hold you to that. And if you want to talk about it, I'm always available." Kelly felt tears prickling her eyes. The sentiment from her mother was a great start, but she felt awkward now that it was stated and in discussion. Maybe today wasn't a good day to talk about her transition. She needed a distraction. "I should make myself some breakfast."

"Okay. And remember, we need to leave in a little over an hour from now to get there when Tim said I needed to be there."

"Sure thing, Mom."

She busied herself making eggs and toast. It kept her occupied and she focused on the details of what she was doing rather than dwelling on her thoughts, trying to push past the awkwardness she was feeling. It helped, her whisking the eggs with the fork and putting them into the pan after melting a pat of butter. She got her eggs onto the plate, topped off her coffee, and went into the dining room to eat.

Her father had told her mother to treat her better? Wow. She knew her father loved her and accepted her, but this was a step she hadn't thought he would take since he had implied that it was her responsibility to have the conversation. She was embarrassed by her mom's revelation. She had promised her dad she would have the conversation with her mother and she hadn't. She had chickened out when it came to it. And clearly, he had talked to her mother about his coughing and lungs, which is what led him to go into the hospital and then the rehab facility for his worsening condition. He likely caught pneumonia that ultimately weakened his heart before he went in, or likely was suffering from it already. It might have put a strain on his system leading to the heart attack. She felt like she had failed him for avoiding the conversation with her mother. But now was most certainly not the time for a more in-depth conversation.

At least she was talking to her mom now, though it was just as uncomfortable as she had expected it to be. Just doing that was something. She was doing as her father had asked, later than maybe he had wanted. Her chest grew tight as she thought about him. The prickles at the corners turned to tears. She missed him so much and she had tried so hard to be a good child for him and her mother. Maybe this was a start to a new relationship between her and her mother. If so then it would be something she had wanted for a while now. She wiped her face and finished her meal.

After putting the dishes in the dishwasher, she headed to the living room. Her mother had already gone upstairs so she was left to look at the photo of her parents on their wedding day. They both had beatific smiles, eyes only for each other. The photographer had done a great job capturing them. Her father was dressed in a nice suit that she had packed up yesterday. Based on the stories he had shared, her father hadn't wanted to get a tuxedo for the wedding. He had said it didn't feel natural to him and he would have nowhere else to wear it. Her mother was in a gorgeous white wedding gown that had sleeves of lace clinging to her arms and the rest of the dress fitted to her body. It was elegant and only made her mother look even more beautiful. The two of them looked so happy.

She wondered if that would ever be her: happily married wearing a beautiful gown. Maybe not one like her mom's because it wasn't like her family was swimming in money for such things. If it happened, the ceremony would likely be done in some courthouse or somewhere else, with her either wearing a nice dress or maybe her dress uniform. The uniform was likely if she decided to reenlist as an officer. Not that she had any other prospects at the moment. School took up the majority of her focus right now and she was okay with that. There had been various dates with people, but they never worked out in the end for one reason or another. Maybe she was just a difficult person to get to know. She had time to try to find someone because as far as she was concerned the time wasn't right for her to get involved with anyone.

She realized she needed to head upstairs and get ready. She needed time to get her makeup on and put on her dress, plus the heavy hose she planned to wear to help with standing in the cold. She smiled at the photo of her parents and her heart was buoyed by how happy they looked. That was more the kind of memories she would rather have of her father, happiness. He was a happy man most of the time so it was an easy thing to picture him with a smile on his face. Maybe if she could hold on to that feeling, of his happiness, she would be able to make it through today without completely crying and doing a number on her makeup. That wasn't even considering what sort of cheap shots Aunt Kate would take. It was a good thing she wouldn't be in her uniform today, because that would simply goad the woman on.

She could do this. Besides, she would have her family around her, and that would help. And she would also be there for them. That is if Mom's détente between her and Carrie held.

CHAPTER NINE

K elly came downstairs in her dress, carrying her purse. Her mom looked up from the couch, her eyes widening a little. She braced herself for whatever the comment would be. She had hoped the last two days would have helped but maybe it was too much too soon. Her mom said, "You look good."

"Thanks, Mom." She felt a rush of euphoria but was still wary.

"I wasn't sure what you were going to be wearing, but you look quite well put together. That is a lovely dress, very appropriate."

Kelly wasn't sure what she felt about that because what else would she wear? Then again, it wasn't like her mother was all that familiar with how she routinely dressed. The situation between them was improving so she should take every success as a win. "Thanks."

"Are you driving?"

"I can if you want me to. I cleaned out my car and everything just in case. I'll need directions or at least a name for my Maps program to work."

"Isn't it called an app?"

Kelly's cheeks warmed and she rolled her eyes. "Yes, Mom, it's an app. That still makes it a program on my phone."

"I can tell you how to get there," said her mother, picking up her purse and coat.

"Fair enough." Kelly pulled on her coat.

They walked out to Kelly's car. The radio blared to life when she turned the ignition and she quickly reached over and turned it off. "Sorry, Mom."

"That's okay. I used to like my music loud as well." She grinned at Kelly who blushed in response.

She pulled out of the driveway and followed her mom's directions through the town to the funeral parlor. They parked and headed toward the front. Wasn't Tim supposed to be here by now to help, since he'd been the one who had done a lot of this stuff in the first place?

Inside, they were met by a woman who was dressed nicely. "Welcome to Holmes Mortuary. How can I help you today?"

"I'm Deborah Matheson. My husband Arthur has his funeral today and my son Tim said you needed my signature on some things."

"Yes, Mrs. Matheson, I have the paperwork in the office. We're also still setting things up for the visitation and the service. Once we're done with the paperwork, I'll escort you to the rooms set aside for your visitation. The service will be at our chapel at the other end of the hall." She gestured in the different directions showing where things were going to occur.

Kelly stood in the foyer rather awkwardly, unsure if her mother wanted her in there with her or not. The funeral home was nice, done in dark wood and a rich burgundy wallpaper. It seemed somber, with faint classical music playing at what seemed like the edge of hearing. There were brochures on the table for various funeral services, but she wasn't interested in that. Even though she was aware of how easy it was for someone to pass away she still had that young-ish sense of invulnerability. She didn't like thinking that all things passed away, though this situation certainly made her aware of it.

Before the temptation to read the pamphlets grew too strong, Tim walked in with his wife Alison. Kelly liked Alison, because she had helped Tim become less of an ass over the two years of their marriage. Granted, Kelly had been more of an ass as well back then and had gotten better over time so maybe it was just his being with someone that enabled Tim to grow as well. And yet he was still occasionally an ass, as the other day had shown. Maybe growth wasn't as easy as she thought.

"Hey, Kelly, how are you doing?" asked Alison.

She gave a shrug. "It's about as okay as I can be right now."

Kelly was surprised when Alison gave her a hug. She tried to relax into the hug, but its unexpectedness made her still, and stilted. Alison gave her an understanding look when she let her go and moved back to Tim. Kelly was trying to decipher it when Tim said, "Is Mom inside dealing with the papers she had to sign?"

"Yes. She wanted to get here early enough to take care of it. I'm hoping she'll be done soon."

"No Carrie?"

"No Carrie. I'm sure she'll show when she wants to."

Tim nodded. "I told her what the schedule will be. Hopefully, she'll show before everything gets started. It would be best to have us all together when things start."

Kelly shook her head. "She's a bit spoiled and will likely show in the middle of us doing something."

"I hope you're wrong."

"Me too," said Kelly. "Of course, it would be just like her to show up and prove me wrong."

Tim laughed. "Yeah, that seems to track. She loves to tweak you for some reason and always has."

"You two have always had a rough relationship?" asked Alison.

"Pretty much. We just were never all that close despite only being a few years apart. It is what it is." Kelly almost wanted to say more, but she was focused on the fact that she was going to say good-bye to her father soon. Honestly, she didn't have the bandwidth to deal with Carrie and her bullshit right now. She just wished that things would go smoothly for a change.

"I know you've tried to work things out, but you both have such different points of view that there's no way for you two to see eye to eye." Tim shrugged. "It's kind of like you and Aunt Kate with the whole military nonsense."

"That's an understatement." Tim being that perceptive, wow, things must have changed more than she expected. Kelly was impressed. Maybe she needed to look at her siblings again in this new light.

Kelly wasn't sure what to say to her brother. There was too much distance and too many experiences between them for her to have an idea how to reconnect. The option of two brothers going to the movies and then grabbing burgers had died well before transition. It felt like there was an uncrossable gap between them, especially since her transition. It was a stupid situation to be in but one that was very real. She was able to give him a smile which he returned.

Before things got too awkward, their mother came out of the office and smiled at Tim. She then looked around and asked, "Any sign of Carrie?"

"None yet. Is there anything else I need to take care of?"

"No, all the paperwork is done. Thank you for dealing with setting this up, Tim. I just couldn't face it after your father died. It was all just too much."

"Of course, Mom. It's what I do."

Kelly felt a pang of annoyance and relief. That used to be her position, the one who took care of things for her mother while Tim had been busy with his own life. That all changed with transition, and she was now used to feeling like the black sheep of the family, the dirty secret no one wanted to share. Now she wasn't sure where she stood because things were good-ish now and possibly getting better, but would that hold? There was no way of knowing and the uncertainty was uncomfortable.

They stood there a few moments in silence, just waiting for someone to come out and take them to the next step. Shortly, someone came from the back and said, "Everything is ready for the viewing. Would you like to come this way and have some time before others arrive?"

Her mother nodded and followed the gentleman, leading the way for the rest of them. They were shown to a room that was mostly open with chairs along the walls. It was the back half of an expanded room with an opened casket at the far end. "We have this space set aside for all of you. If there is anything you need from us, please ask."

He left. Her mom moved first, heading toward the casket for her moment with their father. Alison moved off to the side and set her coat and purse on one of the chairs in the other half of the room. Tim followed her. Kelly just watched her mother, unable to hear anything being said. Tears prickled and she got out a handkerchief to dab at her eyes. She had borrowed one from her mother, who had a collection of nice ones with embroidered butterflies on them. She dabbed at her eyes and hoped that the tears didn't just come rushing out. She was sure it was still too early to be crying.

What the hell could she even say to her dad? Sorry she'd failed? They'd talked about having difficult conversations and she'd accepted the fact that she and her mother were no longer going to be close rather than push things toward a different outcome. Her father had done the hard work and broached the subject with her mother, not Kelly. She'd said she would do this, but still had needed her father to do the thing. Even now, it wasn't like they had had a conversation about the differences and difficulties of her new life. Maybe they were too similar, had too many traits in common to try something different. Maybe she could broach the topic tonight, after all of this. Or was it too early? Maybe tomorrow after church would be better. Yeah, that would be soon enough.

Avoiding awkward conversations had been a big part of her life. She hadn't wanted to tell her command about her desire to transition, but it was a necessity, especially when she told the therapist she was willing to take that step to start her transition. She hadn't wanted to tell her parents about it either. Hell, she hadn't wanted to talk to her parents about being deployed to a combat zone. Anything that might bring out a conflict was generally avoided until there was no other real option. She needed to do this, because she had promised her father and she had let him down.

Her mother had moved over to talk with Alison while Tim was by the casket. Tim's shoulders were hunched forward, his head down, and Kelly was sure he was tearing up. Her tears prickled again and she dabbed them away. She knew she was going to cry when she went up and said her good-byes. It made her glad for the waterproof makeup she had chosen to wear.

And then Tim walked away from the casket.

It was time.

She took a deep breath and let it out slowly. Her heart began to beat stronger, or maybe she was just aware of it more. She walked up to the casket and looked down. His corpse looked good. They had clearly given him makeup to look like there was still a touch of life, but since she was aware of it, the illusion didn't work as well as it might have otherwise. He was also dressed in a nice suit, tie done up right, as opposed to how her father usually did it, in a way that made it just a little bit crooked. These things made him look not right. There was something vital missing.

He was so still, stiller than he ever had been in life and that threw her, adding to the unnaturalness she was feeling. But it was his face and it was clearly him. She started talking before her nerves made her want to run away. "Hello, Daddy. I'd hoped we'd have had more time, but your lungs and your heart got the better of you."

She rested her hand on his chest, right over his heart. "I love you very much. I'm sorry I haven't talked to Mom yet. I'm going to get to it, tomorrow, I promise. I let you down by not getting to it sooner, and for that I'm sorry. I'm also sorry for not being the child you wanted. I know my transition wasn't what you expected, and to be fair I didn't expect it either. I tried so hard to be a good son, but instead you got a daughter."

His body felt wooden under her hand, almost like she had rested her hand on a table, or some other piece of furniture. It felt wrong to her. She pulled her hand back and could feel the tears start to spill over. "I love you, Dad, and I'm so glad we were able to connect again after transition. I know it wasn't easy for you, but you did it. I'm grateful for all the conversations we had and the wisdom you were able to share with me. I learned so much from you that I can't even put into words. You were and are my hero."

She wiped at her tear-filled eyes with the handkerchief, hoping that her waterproof mascara and makeup would last through this. "I love you, Daddy, and I'm going to miss you."

She leaned down and kissed her father's cheek. It was an act she'd never been brave enough to try while he was alive. Her tears flowed over, and she wiped even more as she walked off. It was too much. Her heart ached and all she wanted to do was curl up and cry some more in private. Her mother's arms came around her and she sighed and relaxed into them. She cried a bit longer, comforted by her mother, and then pulled away. She wiped her eyes with the handkerchief and gave a wan smile to her mother. "Thank you."

"You're welcome, Kelly." Her mother squeezed her hand. "Why don't you head to the restroom and get yourself sorted?"

Kelly just nodded and headed toward the door. Carrie was over by the casket having her moment with her father. She exited the door and began the search for a restroom.

CHAPTER TEN

Kelly came back to the room and spotted her grandparents talking with her mother. These were her dad's parents. Her mother's parents had already passed away when she was younger and she could barely remember them. She had last seen her grandparents over the winter break. They were both aware of her transition, and Kelly had worn far more androgynous and feminine clothes around them. She wasn't sure why she felt they could take her transition better than her mother could, however that seemed to be the case. Whatever the reason, she was grateful for it.

As she neared them, her grandmother spotted her and broke into a smile when they locked eyes. "Kelly, it's good to see you again. You look wonderful."

Kelly hugged her grandmother. "Thanks, Grandma. How are you doing?"

The smile on her grandmother's face faded. "About as well as can be expected. We knew your father had lung issues, but he always downplayed how bad they were. This has been a shock even knowing he was sick and went into the hospital. Especially since it wasn't his lungs but his heart."

Kelly's mom said, "He kept trying to be strong and not let anyone worry about him. I only knew how bad it was because I talked to the doctors myself. He thought he would get better again this time, despite how bad his emphysema had gotten. Everyone was so focused on his lungs that I think we all forgot his heart."

"Well, Arthur was always like that, downplaying things. He never wanted anyone to worry about him. Did he ever tell you about the time he broke his arm and came in trying to hide it?" said her grandfather.

Her mother said, "No. This is a new story for me."

Her grandfather smiled, his eyes looking up to the past. "Arthur was playing in that big tree we have in our backyard. He was just climbing like a fool to see how high he could reach. From what he told us, everything was going great on the way up. It was on the way down that his shoes slipped on the bark and he came tumbling down. He must've been in shock when he came inside with his arm held in his shirt like it was some sort of sling. I was in the kitchen getting something to drink when he walked in. I asked, 'Arthur, what's wrong with your arm?' He said, in the least believable way possible, 'Nothing.' Yeah, he was always that way."

Kelly and her mother smiled at the story. Her mother said, "Arthur hated being fussed over because of some health issue. He always tried to power through colds, the flu, bronchitis, and even when he got walking pneumonia. It was infuriating actually."

"Thank you for calling us when he went into the hospital. It helped us prepare more for today." Her grandma's smile was watery as her eyes teared. "Arthur probably wouldn't have bothered to let us know."

"You're absolutely welcome. God, that was so annoying when he did that. It was almost as if he didn't trust anyone to do the right thing with that information, even when the right thing was to take care of him." Her mother dabbed a tear from her eye with her handkerchief.

Kelly had never known this about her father. It helped her to understand some of her own choices in terms of health. "Wait, Dad never liked to admit he wasn't feeling good?"

"Your father always tried to be strong and show that he was just fine. I'm not surprised about the story with his broken arm because it's so very him." Her mother smiled and gave a fond humph.

"I had asked Dad about his cough a few weeks ago as it was starting to sound rougher to me, compared to usual. He said he would tell you about it."

"He said something about his cough being worse lately when we were at the ER prior to him getting admitted, but that was about it."

"So, you mean he could have gotten treatment about two weeks earlier if he had just said something?" Kelly was confused and unsure what this meant. Why would her father have done that?

"Your daddy was stubborn about certain things, his health being one of them."

Kelly had no idea what to say. This wasn't something she'd ever expected to hear about her father. She walked off and sat heavily in a chair. Was her reluctance to talk about issues the same as her father's? If so, was that something that absolved her of the guilt over not talking to her mom? She could almost hear her therapist's voice in her head, "It may absolve you of the guilt, but talking to your mother about a problem you have with her is still something you should do."

Carrie came over and glared down at her. Kelly groaned softly before she cut her eyes up toward her sister and asked, "Yes?"

"What were you talking about with Grandma and Grandpa?"

"The fact that Dad was terrible at telling people he was sick or feeling bad."

"Oh that. Yeah, I figured that out years ago, especially when he got bronchitis or something. He would be coughing and saying he was fine all at the same time. It's hard to miss something like that."

Kelly bristled. She'd noted the same thing but hadn't translated it into anything more than a quirk. "I knew he did that, but I didn't think it was a pattern of behavior that he had his whole life. Grandpa talked about how Dad fell out of a tree and broke his arm and tried to hide that his arm was broken."

Carrie rolled her eyes before muttering, "Boys."

Kelly gave a short laugh. "Absolutely."

Carrie narrowed her eyes and leaned in. "Why are you agreeing?"

"Because boys are weird and often don't make any sense." Kelly certainly knew that after spending time with the infantry guys. They always did ridiculous things to prove how tough, or strong, or agile they were. It had been confounding and she had never understood it.

"But you're a boy."

Kelly scoffed. "Not hardly. I just played one on TV."

Carrie gave an annoyed huff and walked off. Kelly watched her go with some degree of pleasure. Her sister was being annoying. She saw that the receiving line was starting to form since there were already people starting to gather. She stood between Tim and her sister. One of the people from the funeral home opened the door and people began to come in. They started saying their condolences first with their grandmother and moving down the line. Some of them were so heartfelt and sincere that her breath caught in her chest and she could feel her eyes begin to water. All she could do was smile and say thank you as the line kept moving while memories of her father ran through her head.

There was a lull in the line, and she took the opportunity to dab her eyes with her handkerchief. She wasn't sure what she was supposed to think or feel about this because the condolences faded into a background noise, not as much a balm for her soul as a constant reminder he was dead. It was only the sincere ones that seemed to make a difference and register with her. So many of these people were just being perfunctorily polite since this was just a socially agreed-upon position to show that you missed the person who had passed, whether you did or not. Then again wasn't that how people talked to kids when something happened, a kind of talking down to them as if they didn't understand all that was going on. It seemed to be true no matter the age of the kid.

It made her feel good to see so many people here. Her father had been loved by, or at least acquainted with, a large number of people. He hadn't lived a particularly long life yet it was obvious he had lived a rich one. Kelly hoped that when her time came, she would also have a large number of people care about her death.

The person across from her was familiar in a different way. She recognized the face but the hair or something was different. Not the color, dark blond, but maybe the cut. It was bugging her as the attractive young woman spoke. "Hi, Kelly, I'm so sorry for your loss. Your dad was always nice to me."

Recognition took a few seconds before she began to smile. She knew who this was now. "Teresa? Oh my God how long has it been?" Her mind raced and she tried to think how long it'd been since they had last seen each other.

"I think it's been about seven years since then. I mean we broke up and then you joined the army of all things. And now look at you, things certainly have changed since then." Teresa tracked her eyes all over Kelly, taking in the entirety of her.

Kelly searched Teresa's face to see if she meant anything bad. Teresa seemed sincere in her feelings and her appearance made something unclench within her. "I'm so happy you're here. This is such a surprise. We have to catch up."

"Absolutely." Teresa gave her familiar and earnest smile that Kelly had missed. Teresa walked on, saying her condolences to Carrie, then moving off amongst the other people here for the visitation.

Kelly shook her head in some disbelief that Teresa was here. After their breakup, she didn't think she'd ever see her high school sweetheart again. Things had been confusing at the end for several reasons. But it was clear that things had changed a great deal with both of them and maybe the situation was different than it had been before she decided to join the army. She smiled to herself and then went back to the receiving line. This was a positive development. Once this was done, she would have to go and talk to her. It was imperative.

CHAPTER ELEVEN

Teresa stared at the assignment on her screen with a sense of disbelief. She was doing the obituary for Arthur Matheson. Seriously? She looked over the information and saw when he had passed and why. Mr. Matheson was a good man. He had always been kind and polite to her whenever she came over to the house to see Kelly, or when Kelly brought her over there. His passing made her sad.

There was another person she hadn't thought about in a long while, Kelly. He'd been her last boyfriend, because she realized she wasn't interested in guys and wanted to date girls, but it wasn't easy to do that in high school. There'd been no one who caught her eye that she felt comfortable asking out. Kelly had been the boy who felt the least terrible to be with, and so she had agreed to go out with him. After dating most of their senior year, she couldn't stand herself, so she broke it off with him, especially when Carrie let slip his surprise for her. He'd been good to her, so she wondered how he was, despite her being shitty to him in the end.

She needed to stop wool-gathering and work on the obituary since she was on the clock. There was a lot of information from the funeral home, and she read it over a few times, as she began composing in her head. Mr. Matheson had been active in several civic organizations and other activities until he had gotten sick, so she wanted to make sure to mention that. It was the last picture of a man she knew and she wanted to make it an accurate and compelling one.

She had been working on obits for a while now and they all had a certain flow and pattern to them. She mentioned his passing, his activities, who he was survived by, and then the details of the funeral. It would go out first online and then be published in the paper. She was glad she'd been able to do this much for the man who had been kind to her.

She got to work on her next obit.

At the end of her day, she was still thinking about Mr. Matheson, and about Kelly. Despite their breakup, they'd been friends who had drifted away from each other. She still missed him and his occasionally sardonic comments about things. Her appreciation of sarcasm came from being around Kelly and his way of speaking, which had helped when she got to university and started dating women. She had found some seriously sarcastic women who made Kelly seem tame.

The drive home wasn't all that long. Her apartment was only a few miles from the offices she worked in. Being the low person in the office, she did the obituaries and other small fluff pieces that filled out the paper. Other reporters covered the more exciting stories, like city council meetings, local events, and filled out articles they got from other sources. It was journalism, but she felt stuck. She wanted to do more, and her editor told her she just needed to wait, and that when the time was right, she would be moved to other articles. All she had to do was remain excellent in her work and things would happen. Some days, that was harder to believe than others.

It was still frustrating writing only these smaller articles. She wanted to do more but this was where she was. Even if she had gone to a larger paper she would still be dealing with this same issue as she was essentially a junior writer. It was just the way of the working world. She knew she would get to where she wanted to be soon enough if she kept doing the job. Besides, she was sure she could move to another paper if she needed to, at least she hoped so. Jobs everywhere seemed tight.

She pulled into the parking lot of her apartment. She was glad to be home if for no other reason than she could take her bra off and relax. There was a lot that went into looking and acting professional she was annoyed by, but that was a gripe for the workday.

Teresa smiled as her cat, Baxter, rubbed against her leg. His gray and black stripes made him look like an off-color tiger. He even had a little M on his head that she thought was wonderful. He was her baby. "Hey, Bax. Have a good day without me?"

He rubbed against her leg again and then went to his food bowl before turning a plaintive look her way. Teresa laughed a little. "I get it. Someone is hungry. Just a minute, Bax."

Baxter started weaving between her legs as she made her way over to where he ate. She set down the small plate of wet food and said, "There you go, Baxter. Enjoy."

He fell on to the food as if he hadn't eaten in days rather than hours. Teresa rolled her eyes and thought about food for herself. Her mind was still partially dwelling on Mr. Matheson's obit and the fact that Kelly might be back in town for the funeral. He joined the military, but surely, they would let him leave for a funeral of a family member. It wouldn't be humane otherwise.

Did she want to see Kelly? Did he even want to see her? Part of her wanted to see Kelly again and at least explain that there was more to their breakup than she had said. She had no problem admitting she liked women now, and maybe…no, surely Kelly would understand. He had been a remarkably understanding boyfriend and not nearly as pushy or as sex-driven as she'd expected. And there was also the fact that Carrie had spilled the beans about Kelly planning to ask her to marry him.

Breaking up with him had been hard but ultimately the right thing to do. Would he still be upset with her over the breakup? She didn't know and yet a part of her wanted to find out. When she got to school, she dived into the dating scene at her university and had several girlfriends over the course of her time there. Her goal had been accomplished, well, not quite.

She was currently single, but dating wasn't going well because the only options around here were people she had known from high school and had discounted for various reasons. The longer she waited to find someone, the more likely she would reexamine those reasons and possibly waive them, which wasn't something she wanted to do. She had some friends online, but none of them were the kind where she was romantically invested. That reminded her, tonight was her weekly chat with Alex, her best friend. She should grab some food now so she will have eaten before they started talking.

Alex was a former roommate from college who currently lived across the state. While they tried to meet up a few times a year, video calls had helped them stay close. It was nice to see her friend, even if it was only on the computer screen. They usually talked for an hour or two every week, sometimes more and sometimes less depending on what was going on in their lives. Talking to her about Kelly and about the possibly of going to the funeral was sure to be fun. And she wanted to know what Alex had to share with her on this.

She changed out of her work clothes into something much more comfortable and realized that if she wanted to eat before it was time for her video chat, she needed to get moving. There were some leftovers from the other night when she made a pasta bake. That would nuke easily and she could make some garlic toast.

Once her food was ready, she headed out to the living room, took a seat on her couch, and started eating. She ate quickly so she would have no reason to fuss or rush when the chat started. These weekly chats didn't seem often enough to her, since they had been roommates during her junior and senior year. She missed that. These chats were the best thing they could come up with to come close to that time, but she was sure it was just a holding action.

She got her video chat program up and running and waited for Alex to pick up. It didn't take long for her to answer. "Hey there, Teresa. How was your week?"

"Hey, Alex. Not too bad. It got a little surreal today."

"How did that happen? Your town isn't large enough for regularly scheduled surreality."

"You remember me telling you about Kelly."

"The one boy you dated? I recall."

"Well, his father just passed away and I was the one tapped to write the obituary."

"Weird. But then again, you're in a smallish town so that tracks. How many junior writers do they even have?"

"Like you're in a place much bigger. And there are two other junior writers at the paper, so I'm not the only one doing the scut work."

"Fair point."

"So anyway… I was thinking of going to the funeral."

"Seriously? Just so you can see Kelly." Alex gave her a look of disbelief. Teresa just rolled her eyes.

"Not just to see Kelly. His father was rather nice to me so I want to say my condolences to the family. And his mother was nice as well. I still have fond memories of them."

"Alas, that you dumped him so you could go off and date girls," quipped Alex with a grin.

Teresa shrugged. "What? I wanted to date girls and even though he was a great partner he was a guy and I wasn't really into them. I'm still surprised I was even sort of into him in the first place."

"I'm just giving you grief. Do you think it'll be okay if you go?" Alex seemed concerned.

"It should be just fine. Besides, this is a small town. The obits are where you keep track of deaths of friends and neighbors. There will probably be a crowd there as the Mathesons were popular. I mean, they're still popular. You know what I mean."

Alex just gave her a look.

"What?" The look made Teresa feel defensive.

"What do you think Kelly will say after your dumping him so hard that he ran off to the army?"

Teresa gaped at her. Alex smirked a little and said, "Well, maybe the whole situation is not that bad, but you broke his heart according to my memory of you telling me this story. He might still have an issue with you."

"I'm sure it's fine. Besides, it's been seven years since then. I'm sure he's moved on and gotten married."

"Right. That is potentially valid. However, and this is a what if…what if he has been pining for you?"

"Kelly has not been pining for me." Teresa scoffed at the idea.

"You sure?"

"Yes, I'm sure that's the case. We broke up because I had issues and wanted to leave with a clean slate. He was already planning on heading off to the army and so needed a clean slate as well."

"Does that help you sleep at night?"

"Nope. I sleep just fine." Teresa stuck her tongue out at her.

"But seriously, are you okay with seeing him again?"

"I am. I wanted to apologize for the breakup and let him know why it happened. He was a nice guy and really understanding so I think it'll be fine. Besides, he's likely still in the army, so it's not like I'll see him around town once this is over. If that were the case, it likely would have happened already. We likely would still frequent the same places after all."

"Good point." Alex hummed briefly. "I hope the meeting goes well and that you get the resolution that you're hoping for. Or who knows, maybe it will be something better?"

"What better?" Teresa quirked an eyebrow.

"Maybe you'll find a nice girl there into canoodling?"

"I'm sure there are gay girls here in town, but I doubt that I'll find any at a funeral. Besides, seriously, who meets someone at a funeral?"

CHAPTER TWELVE

K elly was glad the receiving line was over. Aunt Kate had made a scene when she saw her in a dress, but Kelly's grandmother shut her down quickly. Kate's eyes narrowed and Kelly was sure she was going to hear more about it at some other point. Thankfully, no one else seemed to care. Seven years was a good amount of time, and she hadn't been back for longer than a few days at a time in that span. Most people edited their own memories or just left well enough alone, choosing to be quiet rather than cause a scene at her father's funeral. Kelly was sure her mom would hear about this, but what could she do except be her true self that her father wanted her to be.

She turned around to avoid Kate and managed to spy Teresa who was in a chair in the back of the hall. She was kind of isolated for what the room allowed. Getting away from Kate and reestablishing an old friendship was a much better use of her time. That is of course if Teresa was amenable to it. She walked over to her. "Hey there."

Teresa started a little. "Hey."

"So…" She paused to allow proper dramatic resonance. "Anything interesting happen in the last seven years?"

Teresa laughed as Kelly had hoped. "Oh, one or two things. I see there have been some changes with you as well."

"Oh, one or two things." They both laughed. Kelly felt glad that her approach to her worked. Breaking the ice after so long was nice.

Teresa had a moment where it looked like she was trying to summon something inside. "Kelly, I wanted to apologize to you."

"Me? Why?" Why did Teresa feel like she needed to apologize to her?

"For not explaining to you why we broke up."

While it was something Kelly had wanted to know for the longest time, it was also a seven-year-old wound that had scabbed over. She didn't need an explanation but wouldn't mind if one was provided. "You don't need to explain anything. It's a lady's right to change her mind at a moment's notice. It was my job to accept what you had to say. You don't owe me anything like that."

"But I do." Teresa paused, clearly gathering herself. "You see, I wanted to date girls in college and having a boyfriend seemed counterintuitive to that."

Kelly blinked at her a few times. This was the reason? "We broke up because you wanted to date girls?"

"Yes."

"I was going to propose to you and you wanted to date girls? I suppose breaking up with me was the better option than cheating on me." Teresa didn't seem surprised that she was going to propose. "You knew?"

"Carrie may have accidentally spilled the beans back then. That made me panic and break up with you before you asked and I would have to say no. I didn't want to ruin things, but I think I did."

"Carrie spilled things?" She took a deep breath and let it out slowly. This was an old wound she had dealt with in therapy so she was trying to be generous about it all. "That makes sense. She was super excited about it back then. And breaking up to date girls, that makes sense as well, as I had noticed you checking out some other girls but wasn't exactly sure why."

"You caught me checking out other girls?" Teresa seemed horrified and recoiled.

"It's not like you didn't catch me doing the same thing. It was just a thing. I don't think it's that big a deal. Besides, we have just re-found each other. So, maybe we can try to let all that go and can get back to friendship and everything is all good."

"Are you sure?" Kelly wasn't sure if she was hearing wrong, but sounded like Teresa wanted to reconnect.

"Yep. No harm, no foul. And I was already planning to join the army so it worked out for both of us. I assume you managed to date girls when you went off to college? Was it all that you hoped?"

"Thank you, Kelly. I did. And it was. I mean, you had a much bigger change over the last seven years than I have. Is Kelly still your name?"

"Yep. I figured it's a good name and one I was used to so I just stayed with it. My middle name is changed to Michelle however. My name is essentially the same."

Teresa nodded. "Kelly Michelle is nice."

"Thanks. I thought so. I'm glad I didn't need to change my first name, though for a while my mom was irritated with me for keeping it because she said it was a boy's name. It might have been, but not recently. You remember how I got teased over my name back in school?"

"Yeah, usually it was that meathead Richard something or other. I can't remember his name." Teresa shrugged.

"Walthers. Yeah, he was a jackass. God, I haven't thought about him in years. What a terrible trip down amnesia lane some of this has been."

"He runs a used car dealership now, just in case you wanted to know."

"What? Really?"

"Yeah, he's the general manager of his dad's used car lot. He's mellowed since school, well, some."

"Do you know all about our classmates?"

"Some of them. Working at the newspaper has made me encounter a number of our classmates in a professional capacity."

"You work at the paper? That sounds cool." Kelly was interested in what Teresa was doing. It was why she'd come over and started the conversation in the first place.

"It's getting there. I'm mostly doing short articles, writing up city events articles, and I do most of the obituaries."

"You wrote my dad's, right? I think that's what Tim said." Kelly sniffled at the reminder about her father. She turned to look at the casket, and she could feel her mood drop. In the excitement of reconnecting with Teresa, she had briefly forgotten about her father.

"I did."

"Thank you. It was really nice. Gave a decent picture of him and what he was like."

"You're welcome. I decided to come because of that, since I hadn't seen you in years. I hoped to see you. Though honestly, this new you is a surprise. I expected you to be in uniform and with a spouse alongside."

Kelly laughed. "Yeah, things have changed a great deal with me. My time in the army was interesting. And I have to say, it's been great to see you too. I've missed talking to you."

"Me too."

"Oh good, there you are." The familiar voice cut into the conversation and Kelly turned to see her aunt Kate. She sighed, positive this was going to be more of the same bullshit that she usually spouted. She didn't need this crap at the moment, not while she was reconnecting with Teresa. That was a far better use of her time.

"What is it, Aunt Kate?"

"So, you're a girl now?"

"Yes, Aunt Kate, I'm a girl. I told you when I started transition several years ago." Why was Kate bringing this up now? She tried to find her mother or her grandparents in the hopes that they could come save her from Kate, but they all seemed deep in conversation. No hope for rescue then.

"I know, but you hadn't dressed like a girl where I could see you, so I thought it was just a phase."

"I was doing that for Mom. She was having issues in dealing with me. Otherwise, you would have seen me dressed more often."

Kate rolled her eyes. "Yeah, your mom would have issues with that. She was always caught up in things like that. Anyway, so this isn't some sort of phase?"

"No. I told you it wasn't before."

Kate waved that off and kept going. "So, this is the real you now?"

"Uhm…yeah." She'd been saying that so why was it so hard for Aunt Kate to get that?

"Good."

"Good?" Kelly was surprised. Kate never had anything positive to say to her.

"Yes. You smile more now, based off pictures I've seen, and it actually goes into your eyes. You look…more alive. That's better than it was."

"Wait, how do you…?"

"I'm one of your Facebook friends, remember? I've been following and just not commenting."

Kelly sighed and told herself that maybe she needed to go back through her friend list and trim some fat from it. Or maybe not. This particular conversation wasn't going exactly as expected.

"You sure you're not going back into the army?"

"I don't know. I might, because then I'll get a bonus and a lot of experience for my career as a nurse."

"Don't do that, it's an imperialistic organization geared toward unending war."

"So you've said. I'll think about that before I decide to re-up, okay? Will that satisfy you?"

"Fine." She noticed that her mother was gesturing toward her. "Gotta go, my mom's calling."

Kelly wanted to thank her grandmother, but had no idea what to say at this point. That whole encounter had been confirming, super annoying, and utterly random, not to mention inappropriate for a funeral. She was annoyed. Turning back to Teresa, she said, "Sorry about that. Sometimes Aunt Kate escapes and her mouth just runs free."

"You're not in the army anymore?" Teresa looked unmoored and drifting.

"Uh…no. I'm in nursing school."

"Nursing school? You want to be a nurse." This only seemed to make the confusion even more profound.

"Well, eventually I want to be a nurse practitioner. I'm going to school at State and have been there about two years. All my basics are done, so now all I need to study is the stuff I'm interested in."

Teresa closed her eyes. She was likely processing that new piece of information to try and understand these changes. She opened them again and sighed. "Everything I thought would be true with you has been turned on its head."

With a chuckle, Kelly said, "What did you imagine?"

"The old you only married and still in the army. I never even imagined any of this." She gestured around, trying to encompass all of Kelly.

Kelly smiled. "Not hardly. I mean, there have been others I've dated, but they never got that serious. Since I've gotten out, there've been a few dates but nothing like that. In a year I graduate because my army training got me a leg up in my nursing and regular classes. So, I'm trying to figure out what to do from there. I can rejoin the army and have the potential to have an interesting career as an officer and still be young enough to have a decent career outside of the military when I get out or I can try to find a job in the area. I'm still not sure which I might want to do."

"You would seriously go back to the army?"

"Sure, it wasn't all that bad. It was interesting work and with what I'm training in, I can go back to the army or any other service I want, because I would likely be assigned to a hospital. That wouldn't be all that bad. And I'd be an officer, which is also not bad. It would certainly be a step up from before. I have to admit the idea is enticing. And then after I get out, I can get a job with the VA and have good government benefits."

"It sounds like you've already made up your mind."

"Not yet. But it is attractive, compared to getting a job in the civilian world. It would likely be more money, but is there more hassle? And government benefits, that does sound good. I'm asking some of the nurses I come into contact with to get an idea of the work options. I'm trying not to jump into anything."

Teresa was about to say something when someone walked into the room and said, "It's time for the service. If people can head over to the chapel. Family, if you can come here."

Kelly gave her an apologetic smile. "I have to go. Will you be going to the burial site?"

Teresa smiled. "Yes. I'll be there."

The smile Kelly gave her was bright and used her whole face. She was looking forward to talking with her more. "Great. Well, see you there."

Teresa nodded. "See you there."

Kelly waved as she walked away. The conversation with Teresa had been comfortable and natural, just like it had been before they broke up. She missed Teresa and enjoyed the ease with which things were going. This was a positive on a day that was mostly negative.

She joined her family and stood next to her mother. Her mother looked at her with a smile. "So did you have a nice chat?"

Kelly's face warmed and she looked away. "Yeah, it was good."

"I always liked Teresa. She's a nice girl. I'm glad she came."

Now Kelly's face burned, as her blush took on a life of its own. "It's not like that. We were just talking."

"Even after Kate came over?"

"Yeah. It was awkward but not that bad. She didn't derail things, just was, you know, annoying."

Kate joined their group and smiled at Kelly and her mother. She said something to her mother. Kelly wanted to know what she said, but it wasn't worth the grief of getting into a conversation with Kate to find out. She didn't want to have to defend the army, figuring it could do that on its own. And those questions about her presentation were more annoying than intrusive. Kate confounded her and no amount of thought made her any easier to understand. Their differing views of the world didn't play well together. Kelly was also sure she'd get cornered again before the day was out. At least during the ceremony, she wouldn't get bothered.

"The front row left from where we'll be coming in is where you will all be seated. Then we'll bring your husband in, Mrs. Matheson. The other side of the front row are where the pallbearers will be gathered."

Kelly was surprised by this because she had half-expected to be tapped for a pallbearer. She leaned over toward her brother. "Wasn't I gonna be one of the pallbearers?"

Tim shook his head. "Initially yes, but after seeing you the other day I went with one of Dad's friends who had volunteered."

"Why?"

Tim gave her a look that she had some trouble interpreting and turned away. The man from the funeral home said, "It's time to file in."

Kelly swallowed down her irritation with her brother and followed everyone else down a short hallway and into another room for the ceremony to begin.

CHAPTER THIRTEEN

Teresa watched Kelly head off to join the rest of her family. She shook herself slightly. When did Kelly become a hot girl? And she was thinking about going back to the army? Her head was spinning and she left the room in a daze from too many revelations in such a short time. This wasn't the Kelly she had expected to see, and the change threw her. It was like all of her expectations had been turned on their head. She followed other people down the hallway and into the other room where the services were held. The pews were filling up so she took a seat in the back. She managed to get an angle where she could see the back of Kelly's head, because she was still trying to wrap her head around all the changes.

She'd expected to see Kelly here. And she'd planned on reconnecting with him, explaining to him why they didn't work back in school. It was all to be very civil and polite. More a fixing of past mistakes than anything more, except becoming casual friends who exchanged Christmas cards. And yet, here she was feeling smitten by the fact that Kelly was the right kind of attractive to get her interested in seeing if more could happen. Kelly was fit and filled out her dress rather well. She shouldn't be having those kind of thoughts at a funeral.

But here she was thinking about the girl she now saw in place of her ex. This likely meant that in all reality she had never really dated a boy before. The revelation made her feel like an idiot, considering why she had broken up with Kelly in the first place. Though to be fair, it wasn't like she had any inkling of the truth, because maybe Kelly wasn't acquainted with the truth of things at that point. Maybe something in the army gave her the impetus to find herself.

She wanted to find more out about what Kelly had been up to in the military. Teresa remembered hearing that Kelly was going in to become something medical but wasn't sure what. And Kelly was in college now. What was she studying? Was it some other medical field, something else entirely? Was it nursing? She honestly wanted to know what Kelly had been up to over the last several years. She was also surprised to find that she was more invested in the answers than she had expected to be. Her thoughts were in a whirl, and she wasn't sure what to do now.

She looked down at her hands in her lap. Why was she so invested? Teresa sat quietly and listened to the minister talk for a moment before her mind stated, because she's cute. She looked where Kelly was sitting with her family. Sure, dating in town had been rather rough, but seriously, that was the primary reason?

Apparently, her mind was serious. Her mind was looking at Kelly like a lovely option for dating and to hell with all the other details. True, it wouldn't be bad, because if this Kelly was in any way like she had been back in high school, then the odds were she would be an excellent girlfriend. However, there were a lot of potential stumbling blocks, such as where she was going to school. Was she in a relationship already? Was Kelly even interested in her like that? All she had were questions and yet her brain was fixated on the "fact" that she was a hot girl in the right age range for dating.

She scoffed at herself. Wasn't she putting the cart before the horse, like excessively? It would be better to just sit and reconnect with her friend before going all out with trying to even think about any romantic entanglements. Maybe she needed to focus on the things happening around her rather than her mind just running wild. Sure, she'd been in a dry spell, but you didn't just run toward the first mirage of water. Besides, who picked up someone at a funeral.

She had to admit that she would in this case because Kelly looked amazing.

It helped that she knew her or more to the point, had known her. She had missed Kelly in the years since high school. She'd dated several times over the years, and had a few longish relationships, but something had always been missing. It was something that she and Kelly had before she broke things off, though she would be hard-pressed to actually define what that quality was. Maybe it was a type of chemistry or something about their conversations or the way they'd been able to be quiet together. Regardless, she had hopes that maybe, just maybe she could figure all of this out if she was able to try again with Kelly. Even if it went nowhere, maybe she could solve that riddle. That might give her the whatever it was she needed to have a true long-term relationship that went anywhere.

That conundrum solved for the moment, she started paying attention to the service. The minister had finished, and as he was moving to sit, Tim walked to the podium. She had known someone was going to speak but had half-expected it to be Kelly. "Thank you, everyone who came by today to say good-bye to my father. My mother, Kelly, Carrie, and I all thank you. I'm sure my grandparents and aunt also thank you for coming. My dad was a good father, and from what I've been told by my mother, a good husband."

There were some chuckles.

"We're all going to miss him. I know I'll miss watching games with him every weekend. We cheered for the same teams and were sad over losses. I know several of you here today could talk about him better than I could, but no one volunteered. I guess this all hit us really hard with how sudden it seemed. His COPD was far worse than any of us knew and it had weakened his heart."

He lowered his head and gathered his thoughts for a few moments. He then looked back up, eyes glistening with unshed tears. "He lived a rich life. He was union president for a few years; was involved in a number of civic organizations; was married to my mom for thirty years; coached Little League baseball, soccer, and football; and did right by the three of us. He was a good man who looked out for his family and never forgot the lessons that he credited to his father. I only hope I can be half as good a man, a husband, and a father as my dad was. Thank you."

Someone from the funeral home headed to a set of double doors set into an outside wall, and opened them. As Tim turned from the podium, the other pallbearers rose and moved toward the casket, and another employee said, "Please rise."

Everyone stood. The pallbearers lifted the casket and walked outside with it. The family followed and people began to disperse to get to their cars. Being in the back made that easy for Teresa to do. She was able to get out of her spot and pull into the growing line of cars quickly, so she would be early on in the procession because she wanted to have a little more time with Kelly before the graveside service and then time after that if she could. She had picked up a card to display in her front window, which she did now that she was in line.

She turned the radio on, to distract her and occupy her thoughts. She didn't want to think about trying to date Kelly again. With a groan, she put her face in her hands. That distraction had been very successful. And when a romantic song came on the radio, she turned it off rather than listen to the song. There were lots of other things she could think of to do rather than torment herself, like get her head screwed on right.

"Look," she said out loud. "Right now, what Kelly needs more than a date is an understanding friend. All you need to do is help her have the space to grieve and process all of this. You being a sympathetic ear is fine, just don't try to take advantage of the situation. Be her friend."

She looked at herself in the mirror. People were still getting to their cars and getting into the line, but she was sure they'd be pulling out of the parking lot and heading to the cemetery any minute now. She needed to use this time to get her thoughts in some kind of order if she was going to be able to deal with Kelly like a responsible adult rather than an impetuous teenager. Though right now the impetuousness was winning.

"Besides, if things go well, and you both get to talking, then maybe things will turn to dating. You've both done it before so it's not like the notion is all that untenable. Be a friend, and if things go well you might get to be more."

She sounded logical and it made a lot of sense. Sometimes talking to herself allowed her to work through various issues and come to some sort of rational decision. Maybe it would work this time as well? God, Alex was going to give her so much grief over this.

"Friends first. Friends first. I can do this. Friends is good. Besides, there's so much we don't know about each other that needs to be discovered before friendship can turn into more. That army comment needs to be explored because it sounded like she left the army but was thinking about going back. That would get in the way of dating for sure."

She sighed. "Friends first. Do not put the cart before the horse. She just lost her father so don't push things. How would you like it if someone took advantage of your grief to hit on you. I know she's cute and it's Kelly, but have a heart."

With a nod of finality, she inched the car forward as the one ahead of her moved. It seemed like the procession was beginning. She wasn't sure which of the city cemeteries they were headed toward so she needed to stay close in order to not get lost. They curved around the funeral home and toward the road, carefully creeping their way closer to the traffic. There was a police officer on a motorcycle blocking traffic and waving them on. She turned onto the road and headed on.

Her thoughts turned to work and she thought of some of the upcoming things she would have to write. She'd been pestering her boss to let her go to one of the upcoming events in town and do a write-up about it. There was going to be a dog show in a few weeks she might be able to cover. It was local interest, to be sure, but it was still a story that people might enjoy reading about. People liked dogs and it could be a chance to move into a spot where she would be able to cover more interesting stories. She wasn't sold on dogs as pets personally, given that Baxter might have a few things to say about the matter.

The drive wasn't all that long, but she was thankful for the police escort which made it possible to stay with the others and not get lost. They pulled onto the grounds and parked along one side of the road. Teresa scanned the people already there to pick out Kelly. She walked closer and spotted Kelly's mom and could tell that the woman next to her was Kelly, as she spotted Carrie off to the side next to Tim. Kelly looked so very different than before that it was still catching her off guard.

Kelly turned, likely feeling her gaze on her. She smiled when she spotted Teresa. Teresa neared. "How are you doing?"

"Melancholy, I think. I'm sad my dad's gone, and there's nothing I can do about it but accept it. I just wish we had had more time, you know? I miss him and want to talk to him. He always had good advice."

"Not really, but I do get it. I'm here to talk if you need someone."

"Thank you. That helps. I don't want to burden my mother with how I'm feeling and neither Tim nor Carrie cares what I think or feel in large part because they're each dealing with this in their own ways. We've all got a lot going on and having someone else to talk to will certainly help."

Teresa didn't know how to reply to that, so remained quiet, giving what she hoped came across as a supportive smile.

Kelly appeared to be dealing with something internal before she asked, "Are you doing anything after the service?"

"Not really. Why do you ask?"

"Do you want to come to the family meal the church is throwing for us? It would give me someone to talk to. My mom will have plenty of people to talk with, and I don't want to have to deal with Carrie and my aunt Kate. So if you come we can continue to catch up and I won't have to deal with them."

"Are you sure it'll be okay?" She didn't want to intrude on family time, especially at a time like this. It wasn't something she could easily agree to, though she so desperately wanted to.

"Sure. It's likely to be plenty of food so that won't be an issue. And I just want to take the time to catch up."

Teresa didn't have to think too hard before she answered, since this whole situation aligned with her own thoughts and plans nicely. "Sure, it sounds like it could fun and I want to catch up as well. Clearly, a lot has happened since we last saw each other."

"That's true."

"Besides, I want to get the whole story of you running off to the army and coming back a woman."

"That's not that interesting. You already said most of the story."

"Sure, but the details are what makes the story, and I want to learn those. It's been seven years Kelly; we have a lot to go over, I'm sure."

"That's a fair point." Kelly gave her a faint smile.

CHAPTER FOURTEEN

Kelly said, "So after the service, you can follow me over, unless you remember where St. Mary's is?"

Teresa smirked. "I still live here, so yes, I know where St. Mary's is."

Kelly chuckled. That was an excellent point. "Fair enough."

"Is there a particular time?"

"Right after the service, sort of as a late lunch."

"That should be fine. And you're sure it's going to be okay?"

"Want me to clear it with my mom first?"

Teresa blushed. "No. I just don't want to step on any toes."

The minister was stepping up to the gravesite, so Kelly smiled at Teresa and headed to her seat next to Carrie. Carrie was giving her a look, which she couldn't easily interpret. The look was chiding but she wasn't sure what was at issue. Knowing Carrie, it could be anything including the fact that she was just talking to Teresa. There wasn't time to deal with that at the moment.

Tim was sitting next to his wife and they were holding hands. Kelly thought that was sweet. Seeing how he was with Alison certainly was giving her a different view of her brother. He usually acted so aloof, as if nothing fazed him, but it was clear Alison was someone he deeply cared about. She was happy for her brother, because Tim could use someone who got through his walls. Now if only she could find someone who did the same for her.

Her attention was drawn back to things in front of her. The minister was speaking, praying over her father. She let the words roll over and through her as she sat there and looked at the casket. He was in there but he also wasn't. She sniffled as she realized he had moved on and was gone from them forever. He might check in on them from time to time, but he wasn't here. She wiped the tears from her eyes and reached out to Carrie. Carrie took her hand and squeezed it. It made her feel good knowing that deep down she and Carrie weren't completely broken, they still cared for each other in that one moment at the very least.

Once the minister finished, her mother took a rose from one of the flower arrangements and laid it on the casket. The family did the same before the others gathered about the gravesite came by and put a handful of dirt on the casket. The symbology wasn't lost on Kelly. Ashes to ashes, dust to dust was the saying. It was the way of all things. She wiped more tears from her eyes.

She needed to rein her emotions in so she could drive her mom to the church. It would be difficult to drive through tears. Her heart ached for her loss and her emotions were fighting back against her. She hugged her mom, who seemed surprised before she hugged Kelly back. Kelly managed to take hold of her emotions and get control again thanks to the hug. She asked, "Did you want to wait until they lower Dad or are you ready to go?"

Her mother dabbed her eyes with a handkerchief. "I'm ready to go. We can come back later and visit, after they've finished and put the stone up."

"Okay, Mom. Oh, Teresa will be coming to the family meal so I have someone to talk to. I haven't seen her in seven years, and I'd like to catch up with her." Kelly hoped her mom wouldn't have an issue because otherwise she would have to run over and tell Teresa the bad news.

"You don't want to talk to your brother or sister?"

"Not really. We don't have a lot in common anymore and I'm not sure what to say. And like I said, I haven't seen Teresa in years. It would be nice."

Kelly tried a plaintive look to spur her mother to accept and must have succeeded because her mother nodded, saying, "That's fine."

"Good, because I already asked her."

"Kelly!" Her mother reprimanded her with a look.

"What? I knew you were going to say yes."

"It may be mostly a formality, seeing as you are grown, but it is the polite thing to do."

"Sorry, Mom." Kelly lowered her head, abashed. Maybe she should have asked to start with.

"I have always liked that girl, but sometimes you act so foolish around her, so be careful of that."

"Yeah. I've missed her as well." Kelly smiled.

"Well, let's get going. We don't want her to beat you there now do we?"

Kelly laughed as she got into the car. Her mother buckled up then looked at her. "Well?"

Snickering, Kelly started the car and slowly pulled away from the cemetery. She drove carefully, obeying all the traffic rules so her mother wouldn't fuss at her, like she often did when Kelly drove. It didn't help. Her mother chided her about her speed twice and her driving through a yellow light. It was familiar and something she had done to Kelly when she was camouflaging her transition with a binder and a baggy shirt. Instead of being upset about it, it made Kelly think her mother was trying to do right by her, just like her father had asked. That was still something she was trying to adapt to. For so long she had only expected the bad and now that wasn't the case.

There wasn't a lot of time for introspection as the church was coming into view. She pulled into the mostly empty parking lot, then Tim pulled up, followed closely by her grandparents. They headed inside.

Several of the other seriously active church women were in the kitchen putting the finishing touches on the food. Kelly noticed that Teresa lingering in the back. She headed over to her, smiling as happily as she could manage. "Thank you for coming. Like I said, I wanted someone to talk to."

"Wouldn't a coffee shop be a better place to talk?" asked Teresa, a slight smile on her face.

"Probably. But I don't know of any good ones in town. I mean, it's not like I'm a local anymore."

"Good point. There's always a place called Blend that's been around for a few years. They're my go-to. And of course, a Starbucks."

"Maybe we can go to the coffee shop after we're done here. I figure it might take a while to catch up with everything. I mean seven years is a good length of time."

Teresa snickered. "You're probably right on that one. I have so many questions."

"Same here, though probably none as big as yours."

"I just went to college then started work. You went into the army, so there have to be stories there."

"A few." They began to load up plates with the good and basic food.

As they sat down, Aunt Kate remarked, "You really like your salad."

"Yup, always have. Well, at least since high school," replied Kelly, not bothering to look at her aunt.

Teresa jumped in and turned the conversation. "So, you joined the army? I don't remember that being something you talked about before we broke up? I heard about it afterward when you left for basic training."

"Yeah. I decided to join the army instead of heading to college. I figured I could get some of the medical training and experience I wanted without having to go to college yet. I was planning on it before the breakup, but that happened before it got to the point where I was going to tell you. Besides, you were all excited about getting into college so I didn't want to make things awkward by stating my plans."

"You didn't want to make things awkward?" There was a little heat behind Teresa's voice.

"Was I wrong?" Kelly said.

"No, you're not wrong. I would have likely made an issue out of it."

"Hey, no worries. You were excited about school. I wasn't. At least not back then. I wanted to go and do something, so I joined up."

"So, you weren't running away after we broke up?"

"Nope. It was already in the works before that happened. It helped me run away after we broke up, because that was a lot to deal with and I needed time to think things over. But no, it had been my plan for a month or so before we broke up. I just was never sure what to say to you about the whole thing, so I chickened out."

"Huh. I spent a few years sure you ran away to the army."

"I mean, I know that happens. There was one guy who had his heart broken so he joined up, but that was the exception. Most everyone else thought they knew what they were doing when they signed up. We were all wrong, but we thought we knew."

"Were you one of those?"

"Oh yeah. The army wasn't what I thought it would be and was a hell of a lot more work than I figured. That doesn't even take into consideration doing a tour in Afghanistan."

"Wait, you spent a year in Afghanistan?" Teresa seemed rather surprised by that.

"Yeah, it was...okay. Got under fire a few times, but on the whole, it wasn't that bad. Went on patrol a few times a week, and was stationed at a forward base for a month or so. Things around us were pretty quiet during that time, thank God." Kelly didn't want to go into her time in Afghanistan as it was something she was still processing years later. Nothing in her life had prepared her for the reality of a combat deployment, though the army had tried.

"Under fire a few times? Wasn't that scary?"

"Yeah, it was but they say that the bullets you can hear aren't ones meant for you. Never was in a serious concentrated attack or anything, so compared to some of the deployments I've heard about, it was pretty quiet. I think we got lucky." Kelly ate one of her deviled eggs. "Man, those are tasty."

Teresa snickered. "I remember you were always into deviled eggs. Mom still comments occasionally how much you enjoyed those when you came over for Christmas supper during senior year."

"Your mom makes really good deviled eggs. What can I say?"

They both laughed and then got back to the business of eating. After Kelly made her way back to the buffet to load up on hot food and a few more deviled eggs, Teresa asked, "So are you going to be in town long? I just thought we might be able to catch up more."

"I have to head back to school after this. I was planning on leaving tomorrow after lunch. Getting my undergrad degree is a lot of work. Like I said before, I want to eventually become a nurse practitioner, just not sure in what particular area of medicine I want to focus in. I figured that I have some time to see what specialty calls to me since I have to wait at least five years before I can become one. That gives me time to explore different specialties."

"I never thought of you doing anything medical. You seemed fairly unfocused back then."

"Me neither, until I noticed that nurses did a lot of work and were able to make a decent living without having to endure medical school. It's pretty close to being a doctor without the extra schooling, so that sounded good to me. So, I figured that being a medic would get my toes wet, to see if I even enjoyed the work. I got to try on the job in the army and found I actually enjoyed it. It's been my focus ever since."

"That sounds so fun. I've always been into journalism so it didn't seem like I did a lot to try it on as a career."

"You worked on the school paper, and I'm betting you worked on your university paper as well," countered Kelly. "That certainly would count toward trying it on."

Teresa blushed. "Okay, that's fair. I worked for those papers. I'm still working hard to try to do more at the paper, but there are staffing issues and such."

"Do you need to move somewhere where you can work at a bigger paper?"

"I don't want to, but if things continue like they have been I may need to. Mostly, we get our stories from the AP and just post them. Not a lot of local reporting is done, despite a decent amount happening in town. Just covering the city council meetings and county meetings can provide some interesting stories that people want to read."

"And so far, you've only been doing smaller stories and the scut work? So, you're the FNG?"

"The what?"

Kelly looked over at her mother and then leaned closer to Teresa before whispering, "Fucking New Guy."

Teresa started to snicker. "I think that's a term I may have heard but didn't know what it meant."

"Yeah, not the politest of terms to apply to anyone. But everyone has to deal with being the FNG for at least a little bit." Kelly marked the point with her fork. "It's basically a rite of passage more than anything personal."

"That makes sense. And if I move to a new paper, I guess I'll be the FNG there again."

"Yeah, and when I end up with a job, I'll be the FNG, at least to start."

"Glad you've come to terms with it."

Kelly was enjoying this conversation and had missed Teresa since they had broken up. They were getting along together so well that she didn't want this conversation to end. The meal was drawing to a close. If she wanted to keep talking to her, now would be a good time for a new plan. "Hey, when we're done here do you want to meet up at the coffee place you mentioned to continue talking? I've missed you and have been enjoying our chat."

Teresa smiled. "I think I like that idea. And besides, we've barely scratched the surface on your time in the army, let alone talking about what I've been up to."

Kelly grinned. This was an unlooked-for distraction from her pain and there was value in that. Besides, reconnecting had been fun so far. She would need to make sure her mom was okay with things and didn't need her for anything this evening, but she was fairly sure it would be okay to go and chat for at least a little while. The last thing she wanted to do was alienate her mother right after things were starting to get a little bit better. She figured more conversation could wait until her next trip home. "That sounds like a great plan to me."

"Maybe we can meet like in an hour after we're done here, so I have time to change and get into something more comfortable. Funeral clothes are rarely the best for relaxing and chatting in."

That sounded good to her. While her dress wasn't uncomfortable, it would be more comfortable to get back into her leggings and sweatshirt, if for no other reason than she could wear a more comfortable bra and sneakers. She grinned. "I like that idea. See you then."

CHAPTER FIFTEEN

Kelly watched Teresa head off to her own car parked farther down the line. Her mom looked at her over the car roof and said, "You didn't have to drive me home."

"I know, Mom, but she's going to go change before we meet up for coffee. The plan is so that we can chat more. It also means that I can change as well."

"That's fine. Your grandparents are coming over so we can talk a bit. It was nice chatting with them over lunch so we're going to do what you are planning to do, talk more. Make sure to be back for dinner."

Kelly started the car and pulled out of the parking spot. "You aren't going to need me, are you?"

"I'll be fine. Besides, Tim and Alison are coming over as well, so it will be alright. If I need anything I'm sure that Tim can take care of it."

"Carrie isn't coming over?"

"No, she said she needed to go see her boyfriend for a little bit. He's not feeling well or something? I'm not sure. Carrie was vague. She knows I don't approve of him so I think she uses him to get out of conversations she thinks might be coming. She's not exactly wrong there."

"Maybe. I'm just not sure she wants anyone to see her mourn. You know how she likes her privacy."

"That's a good point. Your sister has never liked people seeing her be upset. She actually hid in her room more than you did as a teenager."

"Hey," said Kelly. "I wasn't hiding. I was in my room thinking."
Her mother cut her eyes over to her. "Is that what kids are calling it these days?"

"Mom." Kelly was scandalized by what her mom was implying, especially as it wasn't the full truth.

"What? I was a teenager once. I remember going off to hide in my room so I could think about boys and process my emotions."

"Well then, maybe Carrie just needs more time to process her emotions," offered Kelly.

Her mother was quiet a moment. "That may be one of the nicest things you've said about your sister in a while."

Kelly felt her cheeks warm and focused on driving before she replied, "Well, I can't say that Carrie and I understand each other, but that does make sense for how she was as a teenager. Then again, I'm sure I wasn't much better as a teen."

"You and your sister used to be so close when you were younger. I never did understand why you two drifted apart so much."

"I don't know, Mom. Being a teenager was hell for me. So, I think I was punishing myself and everyone around me because I wasn't the girl I was supposed to be. Honestly, my relationship with Teresa helped me pull my head out of my ass and the military took care of the rest of that issue. Maybe the pressure of hiding who I was was the problem? I honestly don't know. My relationship with Carrie is just some of the fallout, I guess. Regardless, she and I no longer see eye to eye and haven't in a long while."

Kelly could see with her peripheral vision that her mother was giving her a look. She couldn't interpret it before her mom said, "Have you thought about apologizing to your sister?"

"Uhm no, I have not. It's not like I've done anything wrong in all of this. And she keeps misgendering me which is an issue."

"That's fair. I'm not sure what to do with this. I don't like seeing you and your sister at odds with each other. Maybe that's something you can start with? I know it's not ideal, but it might get through your sister's stubbornness."

"Yes, Mom. I'll take care of that before I leave or maybe when I'm down for spring break. But I'll get to that. Maybe it will work."

Kelly pulled into the driveway. Once inside, Kelly headed upstairs into her room where she started to change. She put back on the leggings and shirt she had been wearing earlier that day because for all that the dress was comfortable, there was something even more comfortable about leggings. She was happy with the fashion choice. After she slipped on her sneakers, she headed back downstairs.

Her grandparents were sitting there talking with her mother. Her grandmother came over to her, claiming a hug. Kelly enjoyed the tight embrace a few moments before she asked, "How are you doing, Grandma?"

"It's a sad day. I never thought we would be saying good-bye to your father so soon. His COPD was finally starting to get under better control and we thought things would be getting better after he got out of the rehab facility. This really came out of nowhere."

Tears gathered at the corners of her eyes. "Is there ever a good time?"

Her grandfather replied, "No, there isn't."

Kelly hugged him. "I'm so sorry, Granddad."

"It's okay. It's not like you were in charge of his health. Sometimes bad things happen to good people no matter what you do." He patted her on the back gently. His smile was a ghost of his usual beaming self.

Her grandmother looked her over and asked, "Are you taking off somewhere?"

Before Kelly had a chance to answer, her mother spoke up. "Yes, she's going to keep talking with her ex-girlfriend, the one she brought to lunch. They haven't seen each other since they broke up at the end of high school. It was quite a surprise to see her there."

With a smile Kelly could not interpret, her grandmother said, "Ex-girlfriend, huh?"

"It's not like that," said Kelly. "We just haven't seen each other in years and we're catching up. That's all that it is."

Grandfather chuckled. "You'd think that you would have gotten used to their teasing by now."

Her mother and grandmother laughed, and Kelly could feel her cheeks warm. Her grandmother then asked, "What made you decide on wearing a dress today? I half-expected you to be wearing a suit that I know you hate."

Kelly shifted awkwardly. "Well, Mom decided I was allowed to come home as I was and not as I have been. I jumped on the chance to say good-bye to Dad as myself, rather than dressed as someone else. It helped me cope with this."

Her grandfather nodded. "Like I've said before, never understood your whole gender thing, but I figure what with serving our country and all you can do whatever you want."

Her mother spoke up before Kelly could reply to her grandfather's joke. "I admit that I was never comfortable with Kelly after her…transition. I'm grateful you took my feelings into consideration when you were coming home dressed as a boy, and I'm sorry that I took advantage of that. I'm sorry that it took your father pointing out all that you were enduring for me and how that was unfair to you for me to stop treating you poorly. I hope you can forgive me."

"Arthur was concerned with things being fair," her grandfather said. "I can see where he would be concerned with how Kelly was being treated. He loved you kids so much that he would have done anything for you."

Kelly rubbed her hands nervously. "Thanks, Mom, that means a lot. I loved him too and miss him."

Her mother came over to Kelly and gave her a tight hug. Kelly hugged her mother, tears coming down her face in burning salty trails. Her mother lightly ran her hand down the back of Kelly's head as she murmured comforting sounds. Kelly pulled back and gave everyone a watery smile. "Sorry."

"For what? You're allowed to cry, Kelly." Her mother rubbed her back gently.

Kelly took a deep but shaky breath and let it out slowly. "I just… I just miss him so much."

Her grandmother said, "We all do, sweetheart."

Her mother took Kelly's hand and gave it a squeeze. "I'm glad your father helped me to see my daughter that I was neglecting. I swear I won't falter like that again."

Her grandfather shifted awkwardly in his chair, and that helped Kelly regain her composure. "I should get going. I have to pull up the map and drive to this coffee place if I'm going."

Her mother gave her an understanding smile. She squeezed Kelly's hand one more time. "That's okay, Kelly. Just don't be too late since everybody's going to be here for dinner tonight. We have a lot of casseroles to get through."

Kelly laughed, genuinely amused by what her mother said. "Thankfully, they're all good."

Her grandfather said, "Well, at least that's something."

"Maybe you should splash some cold water onto your face before you go," said her grandmother.

"Thank you, I will." Kelly headed to the bathroom where she turned the cold faucet on and let the water pool in her hands. She leaned down to splash it on to her face. The cool water soothed her and felt nice. She would need to remember this particular trick for the next time she cried, because she was sure there was going to be a next time. It wasn't the best development of her transition but one that she was still getting used to.

She headed out, waving good-bye to her mother and grandparents. Kelly was looking forward to talking with Teresa again. It had been a good conversation at lunch, but they had barely scratched the surface of their time apart. There was so much to cover, maybe sitting in a coffee shop would give them both more privacy than there had been surrounded by her family. After all, they had not even talked about any of what Teresa had been through in college or even when she had started work. Kelly had questions that she wanted answered.

CHAPTER SIXTEEN

Teresa struggled to figure out what to wear. This both was and wasn't a date in her mind, so she felt a choice paralysis keeping her from putting clothes together. She got down a pair of jeans that she thought looked good on her and put those on. That was the easy part. She needed to figure out what kind of top would work best. Did she want to wear the casual blouse or a nice T-shirt? What was she trying to accomplish with her clothes? What was the impression she was trying to make?

She had already made an impression at the funeral, so she should build on that. Look good but maybe more on the casual side of things. Not to push any agenda, just a meeting of friends? So that meant the blouse was likely out, because it had a more casual date vibe rather than a meeting of friends. She wanted to make a good second impression but not push the idea that she was into Kelly too much. Besides, was she into her? They had just re-met. What was going on in her head?

With a sigh, she grabbed a T-shirt and pulled it over her head. That would work. Socks and sneakers followed. She was essentially ready for this coffee meet-up/date/get-together of friends? Maybe it would be okay to be a touch flirty this time? No, because the same conditions applied. What was wrong with her? She didn't normally get this turned around over cute women.

Yes, Kelly was cute. Yes, it had been a year or so without a date, but that was no reason to act like a wild animal smelling meat.

She was better than that and she knew it. She could control herself. Besides, they hadn't even touched on whether Kelly was even seeing anyone. Too many unknowns to start planning on that. She had to be smart about this, because if things worked out, she didn't want to be the woman who treated Kelly callously. She had already done that once and hadn't liked herself afterward. It had taken a good bit of the summer to move past what she had done and be ready to face her future.

She headed into the bathroom and looked herself in the eyes, trying to drive that point home to herself. It was working but slower than expected. She was excited about seeing Kelly again and discovering that Kelly was a girl. It made her yearn for something more, because Kelly was the one she had loved and pushed away. Kelly had been the only boy she'd ever cared for and her feelings had grown deeper than she expected. The fact that he had been a boy had been a stumbling block for her. Now it felt like that block was gone. Maybe she needed to see if Kelly had matching feelings before she ran all the way past halfway trying to make something happen. Her thoughts were racing ahead to a possible future. She needed to calm down and get her head in the game. After taking a few deep breaths and calming herself, she felt more centered again.

This was likely merely a factor of her being pleased to see Kelly again and the surprise in her transition. That was surely more to the point than anything else could be. It was too soon for anything romantic to develop…right? And she should buy Kelly her first coffee as a sort of apology. Kelly didn't need to know the details, but she would. She was behaving like a lovesick fool, but at least she was the only witness to it and she hadn't posted anything about this on social media. It was likely that she would fess up to Alex about this but no one else. She checked her makeup and it was all still fine so she smiled and laughed at herself before heading out to the car. She really was being ridiculous.

The drive to the coffee shop was short. It was where she stopped in before going to work to get her morning coffee. She didn't know who the roasters were, but they made very good coffee and she wanted to encourage such activity. She pulled in to a spot and stopped her car. She looked at herself in the rearview mirror and said, "Be cool. Just be her friend. That's all you have to do. And it helps that you've done it before."

Teresa got into the short line. She noticed she still had some time before Kelly was likely to arrive, since it was shortly after 1:45. She ordered her usual latte, paid, and moved to the side to wait. She looked for a good out-of-the-way place to sit. She didn't want Kelly to have to be exposed to random store patrons if her grief came up. Besides, it would be nicer to talk in an out of the way corner than in the middle of the floor.

She thought about the differences in this version of Kelly, namely that she seemed more self-assured than before. Could that be a factor of her transition, or something to do with her time in the military? Regardless, it was something that she found attractive. Before Kelly was deferential in many ways. She chuckled. Seven years had passed, of course Kelly was different. Teresa had changed and was different, so of course it needed to apply to Kelly. To tell the truth she was looking forward to learning all the ways Kelly was different from the person she had known before.

The barista called her name just as Kelly walked into the shop. She waved at Kelly and retrieved her latte. She walked over and said, "Hi, want something? My treat."

Kelly smiled at her as she was taking off her coat. "That would be great, thank you."

Kelly ordered a regular coffee. Teresa said, "You sure you don't want anything else?"

"Yeah, regular coffee would be great. Not a lot of call for fancy drinks in the army. Well, not for me at any rate. I knew some people who were all about their soy milk lattes and other drinks, but I could never get into them. I'm good with just plain old-fashioned coffee. What do you have?"

"A latte."

Kelly laughed. Her drink was quickly ready, and she took it to the sideboard where she added little bit of sugar and some cream. She followed Teresa into the back of the coffee shop where they took seats around a low table. Kelly started off. "So, we know I joined the army and I know you went to college. What kind of exciting things happened to you?"

Teresa took a sip of her latte to buy herself a second. "Nothing on par with you. I took classes. I learned that I like to date girls. I joined a sorority."

"Hang on a second, you joined a sorority?"

"Yes. My mom recommended I check it out and I found I had a lot of fun. We did a lot of charity work and other social events throughout the year. It certainly got me out of my room often enough."

"They didn't have an issue with you dating women?"

"Some of them did, but on the whole most of them didn't. Besides, I didn't want to cause trouble in the house so I didn't try to date any of my sorority sisters. I was mostly in there for the friendships and the other connections that it could provide."

"I get that. There were a lot of strong friendships that I developed while in the army. Still keep up with several of them. Not too surprising that spending a lot of time with people creates friendships. Anything interesting happen while you were on the paper?"

"I got to interview a couple of famous authors who came to give talks. That was nice. I was just glad I didn't end up having to do sports the whole time."

"You covered sports?"

Teresa felt her cheeks warm. "Only for an issue or two. I wasn't very good at it. Though I ended up with a couple of dates thanks to connections made with the soccer and softball teams. So that was nice."

Kelly chuckled. "You seriously dated some athletes? I remember you being very anti-athlete back in high school."

"A few. And I was different back in high school. Besides, most of the jocks were annoying."

"I think we both were different back then. Maybe we were both wearing masks covering up who we really were. Hell, if I decide to go to our class reunion, I'm betting that I'll be most changed."

"I don't think that's much of a bet. But then again you never know, you might not be the only transgender person in our graduating class. I know I'm not the only lesbian."

"That makes sense. I know the statistics and all, so it's possible. The question remains if they would want to head back for reunion or not. I'm not even sure I want to go to a reunion because I'm not sure I want to deal with people's reactions."

"Well, you have a few years to decide before it happens, so who knows?"

"Good point. And who knows where I'll be in three years. I might be deployed or stationed far from here if I actually join back up."

"So, you're seriously thinking about going back to the military?"

"It's been something I've been playing around with the last several weeks. I know my time as enlisted would count toward retirement, and I'd get to go in as an officer this time which is a better life. Not sure about it and I still have a year to go in my classes, so I have time to figure that out. A lot can change in a year. Hell, a lot can change in a week." Kelly had some more of her coffee and set the mug back on the table. "The other thing I think with the military is that I can get a lot of experience in my job, get retirement pay, and still be young enough to get work when I get out. That's not a bad life."

Teresa sat there for a moment honestly impressed. This Kelly thought things through whereas before there was a much more lackadaisical approach to life. Granted it was all based on high school, but before today Teresa had never even heard of Kelly having a plan for her future. "It doesn't sound like a bad life at all. You seem to have thought it all out."

"I'm still trying to make up my mind because there are a lot of good hospitals out there where I can make a decent career of things, but I have to admit part of me is attracted to going back mostly to see how different it is being an officer. Granted it will still be medical and I worked with a lot of nurses and doctors in my time, but I never was one of them."

"Is being a medic that different?"

"To a degree yes, to a degree no. As a medic, my job was much more doing basic triage and treating very simple issues. When I transitioned, I got moved from the infantry to the hospital so my experiences there were different. Besides, the food is usually good with medical units. Not always, because it depends on who the cooks are. And the field time wasn't terrible."

"Your time in the military sounds so much more exciting than my time at university."

"That's a good point, because it was exciting at times but also terrifying and nerve-racking at others. How often did university get like that?"

"Things got a little scary and tense around finals but certainly nothing that would qualify as terrifying and nerve-racking. I went to classes. I read things. I thought things. Sure, I had various experiences that were very life-changing, but they were never all that unnerving."

Kelly smiled at her and then asked, "What was one of those life-changing experiences for you."

"Honestly? The first time I made out with a girl I was almost beside myself with how giddy I felt. I'd been dreaming about what that first time would be like for so long and yet it was both mundane and completely different. Her name was Valerie and she had long dark hair, that was so soft when you ran your fingers through it. I mean kissing you wasn't bad, but it never electrified me the way that her lips did. Honestly, it was magical and my whole life changed with it. I never had any regrets about kissing her, or kissing women in general after that. That relationship was life-changing for me and I'm so happy I got to experience it."

CHAPTER SEVENTEEN

K elly took a pull of her coffee trying to focus on it instead of the effect that Teresa's words had on her. Her heart raced, and she wanted to know more. In a way, that story was reminiscent of her transition, a magical and life-changing event all on its own. "You know, now that I think about it, I haven't done more than kiss anyone since my transition. I mean I never wanted to date anyone in my unit, and at school I've been mostly focused on getting my degree. I hadn't really thought about that till now. Man, is that depressing."

Teresa looked at her funny. "Wait, does that mean I'm the last person you've kissed?"

"No, I dated some people right after I got to my unit. It was mostly women I met at bars so you know that was clearly a good life choice." Kelly shrugged and laughed mirthlessly. "And I've been on a few dates at school, but they never went very far. We clicked, but things never got serious."

"Well, as long as you never caught anything I don't see anything wrong with that. Some of the people that I made out with and even dated came from meeting people at bars. I think that's just one of the ways you meet people as adults."

"Maybe you're right. I never really thought about it. I guess it was easier to meet people in high school or college." Kelly shrugged. "My focus on schoolwork has kept me from finding anyone to date in college. I was initially mostly focused on trying to get through my pre-nursing classes so I could get into the nursing program. There's a lot that goes into being an RN, and nurse practitioner is even more school. If I go back to the military, I can spend some time trying to figure out what area of medicine I want to practice. Though I did a lot of general medicine working as a medic."

"How exactly did you do that?"

"At the clinic when soldiers came in to get looked at, we had basic triage there. For most things it was your basic flu medicine or Motrin or something I was qualified to treat and prescribe. If it was anything more complex than the basics, we would send the soldier to the actual docs with our assessment. We had a big manual that would help us with triage and so we would literally start on page one and sort of choose your own adventure through their medical needs."

"Are you serious?" Teresa gaped at her.

"Yeah. It was just the basics of triage, only written for people without the basic medical training nurses and doctors get. A lot of times if there was any real complexity to the case it would simply say send to the doctor. But sometimes it was extremely basic stuff like muscle aches, a cold, something like that, and the book would tell us the recommended treatment. I liked the puzzle of it all."

"See, that sounds so cool like you actually got to do things while I just went to college." Teresa sighed and took a sip of her latte.

"Yeah, but there are downsides as well. Had to get up early every day pretty much, except on weekends. Always had to do PT no matter the weather. Limited fashion choices. Then there's that whole getting deployed and shot at portion of the event, which wasn't great. I would have appreciated going to college back then except I wasn't sure what I wanted to study nor do I think I was ready for more school."

"And yet you're thinking about getting back into the military even with all that?"

"I hear you. I'm not oblivious to all of this. There are downsides to going back into the military, but there are also some positives as well, so I'm trying to take the time to figure it all out. I want to make the best choice for me. It's my future and I want to make the most of it."

"That is so different from how you were back in high school with your whole attitude toward life being that it was just going to happen to you."

"The military took care of that attitude real quick. While being enlisted wasn't nearly as self-directed, the military did lay out some opportunities for you to excel if you chose to. I tried to take advantage of all those opportunities, partially because I thought it might give me more pay. And transition helped me find myself which helped with my depression. So there were several things that went into it."

Teresa took another sip of her latte which was nearly empty and then sighed. "I'm feeling a little peckish. Want to split a Danish or something?"

While Kelly was still full from lunch, there were corners of her stomach that were feeling hunger and maybe something small like part of a pastry would hit the spot. She didn't want to spoil her supper either. She noted that it was starting to get close to when she said she would need to head home. "Yeah, I could split a Danish."

Teresa went to place her order. Kelly smiled, watching her walk off. Meeting Teresa again was certainly unexpected, but it had been wonderful so far. Memories from their time dating kept coming back and reminding her of all the fun they used to have together back in the day. Life had been so much easier back then, certainly easier than things were now. Now she had classes and job concerns and questions about the future. And yeah, there was now some pressure from herself to date since she had not been conscious of how long it had been before this conversation. She wondered why that was.

She liked dating and enjoyed spending time with people, but life had been busy when she started her transition. Between work, therapy, and just trying to deal with all of her changes, she concentrated on the here and now, focused on the next step, and then the next one. She was doing the same thing at school. Maybe she needed to find someone to spend time with, especially since it had been pointed out. She realized that she missed dating. It took this conversation to help her pull back enough to see that she was limiting herself by not pursuing any more dates. Because no matter what the justification, she had chosen to do this to herself. Maybe this was something to talk to her therapist about. It wasn't exactly self-sabotage, more like self-neglect. She was ignoring parts of her life to focus on others. Not the healthiest of approaches.

Talking with her therapist would likely be a good idea. There was this and possibly talking about her dad's passing. Not to mention how her mother had been acting. She hoped her mother's changes would be something that continued because she wasn't a fan of how things used to be. They had been growing apart with the difficulty Kelly had in talking to her and just being around her. Growing up had been hard enough without the distance that had grown between them when she started her transition. Kelly liked this change and hoped it was a sign of future good things to come.

Teresa was heading her way with another latte and a plate. She set both things down on the low table. There was a cheese Danish on the plate cut in half. Kelly smiled. Teresa said, "I did remember right, that you like cheese Danish?"

"Yeah, I love cheese Danish. Thanks." Kelly took her half of the Danish. She bit into it and moaned happily at the taste. "Oh, fresh Danish, how I have missed thee."

She opened her eyes and Teresa was staring at her with her hand paused toward the half Danish still on the plate. Kelly felt self-conscious and felt her cheeks warm with a blush. "What?"

"I know you love pastries, but..."

"Shut up."

"Next time I'm going to get a chocolate croissant and then we'll see how things go." Teresa's grin was broad and full of mischief.

"Oh, do they have some?" asked Kelly, craning her neck as if that would allow her to see the pastry case.

"They usually sell a lot of those in the morning."

"I love chocolate now."

"You didn't used to?"

"Not really. Chocolate was okay. It's just that after transition it took on a whole different flavor."

"See, that's fascinating. What other things changed?"

"I don't like bananas anymore. I used to love them. But something about my HRT changed the flavor and now they just taste weird. I also get cold easier, which was a surprise."

Teresa laughed. "You mean you don't run around in a T-shirt and shorts during the winter anymore."

"Not for several years now." Kelly gestured to her sweatshirt. "This has become standard for me to wear except during the summer."

"That's what you get for mocking me by saying it wasn't cold all the time."

"Yeah, sorry about that. It's amazing how hormone therapy changes the way you look at a lot of things." Kelly took another pull of her coffee and looked down at the cup realizing that she was near the end. "What sort of weird things happened while you were at school?"

"Uhm...this girl and I got caught skinny-dipping at a state park. Thankfully, no charges were filed."

Kelly laughed. "Seriously?"

"Well, we weren't completely naked, so I'm sure that helped. But topless and making out with another woman certainly had to be a fun bit of paperwork for them to fill out." Teresa's cheeks were red.

Kelly grinned. "See, I knew there had to be some fun stories from college. It couldn't have been just classes and studying."

"Oh? And what have you been up to at college?"

"Classes and studying. My life is boring. The most excitement I have is going to the school's LGBT meetup, which is monthly. That has been my primary social activity since I started classes actually. I've been focused on getting into the nursing program and now that I'm in, excelling."

"That's boring. You need to liven things up." Teresa took her final bite of the Danish.

Kelly checked the time on her phone. "You're not wrong. I'll look into that. Anyway, I need to head back. Mom wanted me home for dinner, since my grandparents are here and everything."

"She's cooking after today?" Teresa seemed rather surprised by this.

"No, there's leftovers from the meal today plus casseroles that she was given. This will help her clean out the fridge, which isn't a bad thing." Kelly grinned at her.

"They let her have those leftovers as well?"

"I think it was something that Tim set up. Not sure. I don't have all those details and to be honest, I didn't need them."

"Well, before you go, let's share numbers. So, we can talk more or if you need anything."

"That would be great. I'm glad we reconnected."

"Same here. I'm glad I took the chance and came to the funeral today. I was afraid that you wouldn't want to see me considering how everything ended between us."

"It made a rough day easier. So, thank you." Kelly wiped her eyes to take care of the tears gathering.

Teresa gave her a brief hug. "I'm glad. When are you heading back to school?"

"Likely Monday, but maybe tomorrow evening, since I have classwork to catch up on. My mom wants us to all go to church tomorrow as a family. I could go back after that, but I'm not sure. I'm trying to take it easy and give myself some space to just grieve. Hey, maybe we could do something tomorrow afternoon before I head off. I want to hear more of your school stories because I'm sure there's more fun in there."

Teresa smiled. "I'd like that. I usually go for a hike on Sundays so maybe you can join me?"

"That sounds like it could be a lot of fun. It's a date."

They exchanged numbers and were both smiling at each other as they were leaving. Kelly grinned when she started her car. Today had been surprising if for no other reason than this, running into Teresa after all these years.

CHAPTER EIGHTEEN

Teresa watched Kelly go and waved when she turned back. This coffee date had been a lot of fun. She learned a few things about Kelly and wanted to know more. This Kelly seemed a lot different from the one she had known in high school. She wasn't sure why that was exactly, but it was definitely something she had noticed. This Kelly seemed more content and at home with herself, which Teresa found very alluring.

Plus, she had mentioned the word date in reference to the hike. It wasn't going to be a very long hike since the nearby state park had a one-and-a-half-mile trail that she liked to walk along, even in colder weather like they had been having. She had liked that particular trail for a while and was glad she'd be able to share it with Kelly. She'd even taken Baxter on the trail a few times but he was far more of a homebody than she was and hadn't enjoyed the experience as much as Teresa hoped. She had dreams of having an adventure cat to go on trails with her. She had started early with Baxter but he never warmed to the idea of walking on a leash. Maybe if she tried again later, he would enjoy the trip.

What was she going to do to make the hike more of a date-date and less of two people enjoying the outdoors together? Nothing came to mind. It might be best if she followed Alex's idea to just be friends, because she was sure Kelly was still grieving her father as it hadn't been that long since he'd passed. She might make it slightly more of a date-date if they had lunch either before or after the hike.

That wasn't much of an addition but could work. It was something to think about.

She drove home with her mind awhirl, trying to think of ways to turn a simple hike into something more. No idea lasted very long as she did agree with Alex's notion of being friends first before anything else. She hoped for more, because this Kelly appealed to her in several different ways, and not just in looks. However, she didn't want to chase Kelly away because she was overly impatient. Things took their own time, whether she liked it or not. And right now, some part of her was impatient and wanted things with Kelly to already be there now. Knowing it might drive her away was the only thing keeping Teresa from blurting out that she found Kelly hot and sexy. And the more they talked, the more Kelly seemed to be a better version of the person she had dated all those years ago. She wanted more.

She sighed and rubbed her eyes, focusing on the road. Why did she have to deal with this particular dilemma? She was good at her job and was a nice person. Her thoughts stalled at this, a nice person. Nice was not what she'd been going for. Nice was shallow and more about her wants and desires than the other person's. She'd been trying to become kinder. So much for her own sense of self-development.

Alex's suggestion was the kind approach. Just being Kelly's friend right now was far more important than revisiting their dating. Maybe what would be best would be to forget about the possibility of dating Kelly and concentrate on simply being a friend to someone who had lost a parent. Thinking about it that way, she felt shitty for how she'd been thinking before. If she were lucky, Kelly wouldn't have noticed anything even remotely connected to dating or flirting while they'd been talking. Maybe if they remained in contact after all of this, it would be possible, but for right now, she needed to stop fixating on dating and just be a good friend. She used to be able to be that person and hopefully she could be again. Besides, if she lost one of her parents, she would be wrecked.

She arrived at home lowered her head to her hands. "I know dating has been slow, Teresa, but for fuck's sake, be kind, not horny."

She rolled her eyes at herself. She hadn't been doing herself any favors. As contrition, she needed to feed Baxter, then maybe call Alex and let her best friend berate her for a little bit. Well, maybe not that because she didn't want to be berated. It had been a long and exciting day and what she really needed was a bath and then maybe to talk to Alex about the big surprise of the day. It sounded like a much better use of her time and wouldn't get her yelled at.

Baxter was lying on the couch and looked up at her as she came in. She smiled when she saw him. "Hey there, big man, how was your day?"

He responded with a big yawn and stretch.

"You didn't throw any wild cat parties, did you?"

Baxter purred at her and then began grooming. She headed into the kitchen to refill Baxter's food bowl. He came over, nuzzled her leg, and then got to crunching. She petted him some and scratched behind an ear before heading off to take a bath.

As she ran the water, she added bath salts to the mix, enjoying the change in the scent of the bathroom as the lavender essential oils in the salts filled the air and colored the water. They would help her relax from the stresses of the day. She lay back in her tub and let the hot water seep into her muscles, helping them to relax further. Her thoughts drifted and she kept herself from getting too sleepy thinking about what she wanted to do for supper.

As they had been all day, her thoughts returned to Kelly. She had never gotten any inkling that Kelly was trans. What she gathered from Kelly's stories was that she hadn't been aware either until after her deployment to Afghanistan. That seemed hard to believe, but then again, she hadn't figured out that she wanted to kiss girls until her senior year so clearly it was possible. She'd been dating Kelly when the idea surfaced and she followed it, leading to her decision to break up. The workings of the mind were not something she had studied or even thought a lot about. People were just the way they were. But maybe she needed to reassess that since it seemed likely she made that assertion through faulty logic.

Teresa shifted in the tub, bringing warm water up her back. That felt much better. She hated when her body started cooling off before the water did, but all that meant was that she had to move and re-expose those body parts to the water. She yawned and settled back down in the water, using her hands to direct water to parts not covered.

Maybe her infatuation with this new Kelly would fade in the morning. Maybe they would be just friends or maybe become no more than acquaintances. It was possible that her surprise at seeing Kelly made her react outside of her norm. Sure, it was possible, but was it likely? She had no idea since she'd never acted this way before. It felt like she'd been driven to distraction by Kelly and there were other things she would have preferred to be driven to distraction by. Okay, to be fair, nothing came to mind as her dating life was dry at the moment. There had to be other women who loved women here in town, but she hadn't been able to find them, at least none she hadn't gone to school with. Maybe she could take out a personal ad.

She scoffed and shook her head. Yeah, she needed to get her head on straight. Talking with Alex would be sure to help. She got out of the tub and changed into her pj's. She sent Alex a quick text to see if she was available for a chat since this was not the usual day. She hated to interrupt people unless there was a good reason for it, though to be fair some of the revelations of today seemed like a good reason to interrupt.

Alex texted back several minutes later, letting Teresa know she would be available for a chat. Teresa pulled up her chat program. The video connection clicked open quickly, since Alex was expecting it. "Hey there, how was the funeral? Clearly, something happened."

Teresa rolled her eyes and shook her head. "The funeral was fine, like most funerals. What was different was that Kelly was there."

"You kind of figured that Kelly would be there. So how is that any different?"

"That's true, I did. I just didn't expect that Kelly had transitioned in the time since I had last seen her."

"Come again?" Alex blinked a few times as her thoughts tried to catch up.

"Kelly is now a she."

"Wouldn't it be fairer to say she was always a she, just she wasn't always aware of it? That's what I've heard from a number of my trans friends out here."

"I suppose that makes more sense."

"I'm so glad I could help." She grinned mischievously at Teresa. "So, what seems to be the issue? You wouldn't have mentioned this if there wasn't some sort of issue going on."

"She's also really cute." Teresa could feel herself blush when she admitted that.

Alex just stared at her for a long moment. "I see."

"I've been good. I'm just being her friend right now because I figured she needs that more than anything else. Though I have to admit that I'm interested."

"Well, interested is good. So, this means you're reconnecting that friendship?"

"I'm certainly trying to do that. Honestly, that part seems to be going all right. It's just that I keep wanting to push things to be more, but I know this isn't a good time for it."

"Didn't you tell me years ago that your relationship with Kelly was the touchstone you had for new relationships? That everybody you went out with ended up being compared to Kelly in one way or another? If that's true, then of course you would probably want to reconnect in that particular way."

"How is it that I can think of a thing that comes across as tawdry, but you say it and it sounds perfectly reasonable?"

Alex just gave her a big grin and said, "I assure you it's pure skill."

Teresa snorted so hard it actually hurt her nose a little and she rubbed it. "Like that's believable."

"So, what do you need from me if all of this is going well? I assume you wanted something because of the extra call this week."

"I guess I wanted some reassurance that I was going about things the right way? We're going for a hike tomorrow and I'm just nervous that I'm going to screw things up somehow by chasing after Kelly too hard."

Alex chuckled, shaking her head in disbelief. "You know, you're always this way when you're at the start of something. I remember when you started dating Debbie Myers. You were so concerned that you were going to screw up her studying for finals that you almost talked yourself out of dating her. If I recall, you two were quite the item into the spring semester. Just stick to what you're doing and be her friend. If something more is going to happen, why don't you let her make the decision?"

Now it was Teresa's time to be quiet a moment as she thought about what Alex had said. "You think that'll work?"

"I think it's better than you overthinking yourself into inaction as you often do. Besides, you literally just met her again after something like six or seven years? You need to give yourself time to get to know her before you jump into anything. If you really want something to come of this, take your time."

"Thanks, Alex. That helps."

"That's what friends are for, to listen to you and give you what advice they have. You've done the same for me."

Teresa's stomach gurgled. Her cheeks heated and she laughed. "I need to get going because my stomach is now providing commentary. I should get something for dinner."

Alex laughed. "You and that stomach of yours. I swear it's better than any clock."

Teresa stuck her tongue out at her and grinned. "Talk to you later, Alex. Love you."

"Love you as well, Teresa. I hope things go well between you and Kelly. You could use some success in love right now and this almost seems like your best chance."

"What do you mean by that?"

"You haven't had a lot of luck with dating since you left school. I'm hoping you can find a more stable relationship than anything you've had. If it's with Kelly, then it's with Kelly. Just don't rush into things headlong and not think things through. I don't want to see you get your heart broken again."

"I'll try. I mean I have no idea if Kelly is even thinking along those lines. I just want to be happy. I've been happy over the years, but it never lasts. Kelly and I were good together and I would like to try that again."

"I know. You've told me. But it's been seven years, and she may be different than what you remember. Try to get to know this new her before you jump in with both feet, or is it already too late for that?"

Teresa felt herself blush hard enough that it was sure to be visible on the video call. Alex tutted and said, "I see. Well, hopefully, your heart won't get too broken if this falls apart."

"You think it will fall apart?"

"I don't know, and right now it seems as if you're so enamored by her that you aren't thinking clearly."

"That's why I called you, to try to think this through clearly."

"Right. Hopefully, you remember that the next time you're hanging out with her and are more focused on jumping her bones than looking out for any red flags."

"What sort of red flags?"

"Any red flags. You just re-met her, Teresa, you don't really know anything about her."

"She's just the same as she once was."

"Are you sure?"

Teresa paused and thought. She'd been thinking to herself earlier about how Kelly was different, so maybe that assertion was wrong. "No, I'm not. She is different and in some pretty attractive ways. I'll try to just focus on being friends, but it's so hard to think about it when she's near me."

"Trust me. Let her come to you in this rather than the other way around. You are so focused on making this work that you might miss things. I worry about you sometimes, Teresa."

"Thanks. I'll heed your advice and try to let her come to me. I'm interested in seeing where this goes, but I also see your point. That's why I love talking with you, you help me keep the perspective I need, especially in dating."

"Not that I am a dating guru because I'm still in the same relationship I was in college."

"That's an accomplishment. Tell Greg I said hi."

"I will. I hope it all works out. Now go get some food before your stomach takes further action."

The video screen clicked off. Teresa headed into the kitchen to try to figure out something to have for dinner. This call certainly gave her plenty of things to think about.

CHAPTER NINETEEN

K elly drove back to the house smiling. Catching up with Teresa had helped her day become more positive. She still felt melancholy but had managed to get a little bit of space between the emotions of the day and herself. She'd been worried the day would be all about her grief, so it had been a pleasant surprise. Who would've thought that Teresa had gone on to become a journalist? This was a terrible reason to be able to reconnect, but it was better than not reconnecting at all.

She missed her dad. He would have been pleased Teresa showed up to his funeral. He also would have been tickled to know she'd been the one to write his obituary. In one of their last conversations months ago, he had asked her if she knew what had become of Teresa and now, she knew. She didn't know what to do with this, but she felt like her father had a hand in bringing Teresa back into her life. That made her thank her father for doing such a wonderful thing. Now all she had to do was make sure not to lose touch with Teresa again.

It helped that she had Teresa's phone number and would be able to get a hold of her fairly easily. She didn't want to lose track of her again. That brought her up a little short and she sat up straighter in the driver seat. Why did it matter that she not lose touch with Teresa again? Why was it good that she had her phone number? They were just old friends reconnecting, right? Surely there was nothing more to it.

She realized she might still have some feelings for Teresa. She blinked a few times trying to process that particular bit of information. Did she want to try to get back together with Teresa? No, there was no way that would be true. She'd moved on and Teresa had moved on, so there was nothing there, right?

She was still dealing with that realization when she pulled up to the house and noticed her grandparents were still there, as was Tim and his wife. Carrie's car wasn't visible so she had likely gone back to her apartment, if she had even come over at all. That was good as Kelly didn't want to push the truce that their mother had established yesterday. She hoped it would last. Was that really only yesterday? So much had happened today that it was hard to keep things in the proper time perspective.

As she stepped in the house, all eyes focused on her, and she smiled at everyone. Tim said, "Back from your date already?"

Kelly bristled. There had been nothing date-like about it. "It wasn't a date. She and I were merely talking. There was a lot to catch up on. I mean I haven't seen her in seven years, Tim. A few things have happened since then."

"And yet you're the one who took off after the funeral to go hang out with someone else, rather than your family."

"Tim, stop teasing your sister. How is Teresa doing?" asked her mother.

"Well, she's working for the local paper right now and has been here for think it was almost two years. She mostly does smaller stories and obituaries, as the other reporters had been here a while and have seniority. But yeah, she came back after she graduated college where she had worked on the paper there." Kelly shrugged. "We didn't talk for a long time because I knew you had a dinner plan and I didn't want to miss that."

"Kelly, it's just going to be more heated up casserole. You could have talked longer and it would've been fine." Her mother smiled at her.

"I know, Mom, but she and I are going to go for a hike tomorrow after church. That'll be fine. I can wait until then."

"Oh, so that's the date. Today was just talking. Tomorrow you two are going on a date to go 'hiking'?" He chuckled.

Kelly groaned. Why did Tim have to be like this? Was being an annoying older brother an important part of his personality? "It's not a date, Tim. It's just two friends getting together and hanging out. What's wrong with just hanging out?"

"You can hang out with someone while you hike?" asked Alison, who seemed sincere with her question.

"Of course I can. I was in the army. We hiked a lot of places, sorry, road-marched is the more technical term. After a while, it got so that you could chat casually as you covered the distance."

Everyone chuckled.

"Anyway, I was thinking that after the hike I might head home, well, back to school at any rate. I don't want to fall too far behind in my classes. I'm already at least a week behind and I want to stay near the top of my class. I've got a lot of work to catch up on."

"You're really buckling down on your classes, aren't you?" asked her grandmother.

"Absolutely. I want to do well enough that I have no trouble staying at the top of the nursing program. It took a couple of semesters but now that I'm in there I want to graduate with honors."

"Is the program you're in very competitive?" Alison asked.

Kelly nodded. "The program has a number of excellent students. My training as a medic has helped me be able to stay ahead of some of them, but it's a lot of work. I'm constantly studying so I can keep up with them. After I graduate, I can get a job anywhere, but I'm thinking about maybe going back into the military. Both of them are options and I'll have more choices if I am near the top of my class."

Tim shifted forward his chair and looked at Kelly. "Didn't you get enough of the military when you were in?"

"I did, but I'd be going in as an officer and not back as an enlisted. That makes a big difference. I mean, I'm not sure about it, but I have some time to think about it before classes are over." Kelly smiled. "Regardless, I'm looking forward to working as a nurse. It seems like the natural follow-up to me having been a medic. I thought about becoming an EMT, but I think I want the stability more. EMT would be too much like being a medic."

Dinner was easy to put together for everyone and the meal was pleasant as they all shared stories about her father. They were mostly funny stories about shenanigans he had gotten up to in his youth told by both her grandmother and grandfather. Her mother shared a story about something cute he had done when they were dating. Kelly appreciated all these different views of her father. It made her feel closer to him and miss him more. Sometimes the laughter turned into tears, and she wiped her face with her napkin.

After dinner, Kelly went upstairs to do some of the reading she had planned for today. Her initial plan hadn't included hanging out with Teresa. The semester break was approaching and that meant midterm tests. She wanted to do well on those. Once the reading was done, she found herself yawning rather wide with some tears leaking from her eyes more from the motion than any emotion. It wasn't much of a surprise to realize she was exhausted. It had been a long day with a lot of emotional ups and downs. Maybe sleep was what she needed.

She put a bookmark in her book and headed to the bathroom to get ready for bed. She headed downstairs to say good night to her mom. Her mom paused the show she was watching and looked at Kelly. "Night, Mom."

Her mother checked her phone for the time, raised an eyebrow, and then said, "You're going to bed early."

"Yeah, I'm really tired and I just want to crash. Today has been a lot."

"Today would have been a lot even without you reconnecting with Teresa."

"Yeah, that was a big surprise, seeing her there."

"It certainly was. It's nice to see her. And I am glad you brought her to the family dinner after the service. It's been a long time since we last talked and I always liked her. She was one of your better friends in high school."

"You're right. She was a pretty great friend." Kelly gave her mom a hug. Her mom patted her on the back. She went back upstairs and was asleep fairly soon.

CHAPTER TWENTY

Teresa woke up later than she usually did. All she had planned today was going on a hike that afternoon with Kelly and maybe having lunch with her. This particular development was a surprise, and she was excited about what it might mean because she hadn't gone hiking with someone else in a long while. Yesterday had been a long but fulfilling day. Part of her wanted to just lie around the house and relax, but she found hiking relaxing and it got her out of the house. Her job and life kept her indoors more than she wanted.

Before she could lie there too long, Baxter jumped onto her and nuzzled her face. The cat certainly knew what he wanted, and what he wanted now was breakfast. She got up, then Baxter jumped off the bed and wove between her legs. "Let me get up, Bax. Then I can feed you."

The cat was fed in short order and she got started on her coffee. When her breakfast was ready, she sat down to eat. Baxter was still by his food chowing down when she started eating, she would be able to eat in peace. Did Kelly like cats?

With a sigh and a roll of her eyes, she dropped the question. Kelly was going to school and was unlikely to move here to move in with her. That was of course if they even clicked enough for them to become a them. The possible of Kelly re-upping in the military also confused her. Why would she want to do that to herself? Did she like taking orders all that much? Then again, she took orders from her boss all the time, so maybe she needed to be in the military as well.

After a quick shudder, Teresa took a drink of her coffee to wash that foul taste out of her mouth. Did the military even have journalism? She had no idea. And why the hell was she thinking such profane thoughts so early after getting up? It was clearly all Kelly's fault. She would have to make sure to point out that fault when they met later for the hike. Her good sense was being overwhelmed by the sheer ludicrousness of Kelly. She smiled, as she had had that thought before, back when they were last together. So much had changed and yet so much was the same. Kelly was still kind of sweet though she did have this different focus about her that had partially developed when they had been dating. And this time, rather than using that change to spur her toward breaking it off with Kelly, this time she wanted to lean into this change, this focus, and just enjoy the ride that she was going on.

Sleep made her thoughts clearer, and she was fairly certain she wanted to get together with Kelly again if it was possible. But what if Kelly didn't want to get together with her? Maybe she needed to look extra nice for this hike and help draw Kelly to that conclusion, that this was something she very much wanted and thus would be the one to ask. That was an approach, just be available and interested and let Kelly do all the work. If Kelly was too dense, then maybe it was for the best to let the whole thing lie. She would definitely need to think on this approach more as she got ready. Some of her early morning ideas were not the best.

This plan of hers had a lot of points going for it. One, she wasn't being the pushy one trying to start something, which was a point that Alex had made. Two, Kelly just lost her father, and maybe overt flirting wasn't exactly the best plan at this time. Three, if Kelly was interested, then she was sure to do or say something that would indicate it. Kelly had never been one to go for subtlety when being forthright would work, and hopefully, that hadn't changed. And four, it might be fun to make Kelly's eyes pop out of her head when she showed up. Yes, this idea had merit and was certainly something she wanted to try. She had a pair of leggings that were comfortable and hugged her curves which should do nicely. Kelly had always commented on what a nice ass she had when they'd been dating, though it wasn't exactly phrased that way. It had been framed more delicately than that.

Fashion ideas aside, Teresa was just looking forward to spending time with Kelly. She enjoyed it back in high school, and this Kelly was even more interesting and quite possibly easier to talk to. She still wasn't sure what to make of the whole military thing, but there would hopefully be time to hear funny stories about her time in service, or any stories really. She was sure there would be some stories that were not even remotely funny and far more action-packed. Kelly had spent time deployed after all. She was thinking about some of the funny stories of her time in college since those would be good ways to draw Kelly in.

Teresa hadn't thought about a lot of those stories in a while, and some of them had slipped her mind. Very few of them had anything to do with school and were more about things she'd done with her friends, but they were still school stories. There were a number of times the group she hung out with in college went down to a stretch of river that was good for swimming. It even had a rope swing you could swing out on and drop into the water. There were a couple of campouts as well that had been quite memorable. Those things had very little to do with school and explained why she didn't think of them immediately. They'd been things she'd done with her friends.

Her phone buzzed and she went picked it up. She had a text message from Kelly. *Where do you want me to meet you?*

She texted back: *at the trailhead for Lirkey Trail.*

When?

How does noon sound?

Want to do lunch afterward?

Teresa grinned when she read that. Maybe this ridiculous plan of hers was going to work. She thought about places to eat and then realized getting feedback would be helpful. This would need to be discussed. *Sounds good. We can talk about it on the trail.*

I'll see you there.

Teresa smiled down at her phone, rather pleased with how things were coming together. She would have to think through places to eat to try to come up with some options to present to Kelly when they met. There were a few good ones, like the diner, or one of the Italian places, or even the Chinese buffet, but that place was usually crowded with the after-church crowd so might not be as good an option as another. There would be fewer people when they went to eat, which would be nice. They wouldn't feel rushed and the restaurant wouldn't have to chase them off.

Now all Teresa had to do was keep herself occupied for a few hours before it was time to go. That shouldn't be too difficult as her plan from before seeing Kelly was to read a little before going for her hike. There certainly was no reason to change her plan now. The book would be a nice distraction. She set an alarm on her phone and then grabbed her book. It wouldn't do to be late when she was the one who chose the place and time. And she was sure Kelly would be on time, maybe even a little early thanks to her service with the military.

It didn't take long for her to get enmeshed with the story, a sapphic romance she had bought. She read until her alarm went off.

In short order, she put on comfortable and snug hiking clothes, making sure she had on the leggings that would make her rear look its best. The trail was easy enough that she wouldn't need either the support or traction of her hiking boots. This hike was just a fun relaxing trail through the woods near the river. Most of the trail was paved and the unpaved sections were generally level and right by the river.

If things went well, then she and Kelly might even hook up today, or at least get the ball rolling in that general direction. That was something she really hoped would happen.

As she was pulling into the parking lot, she spotted Kelly, already there bent over and doing some basic stretches. It took some effort to not keep watching. Once her car was parked and she was getting out, she fully noticed that they were similarly dressed. Great minds thought alike or at least dressed alike. Come to think of it, leggings and a sweatshirt were what Kelly was wearing last night. It was an attractive look on her then and now.

She waved and Kelly waved back, and that was when Teresa noticed the red eyes and tear marks. Damn. She knew Kelly was grieving but had hoped that it wouldn't be too bad today. Maybe she should tone down her plans for flirting. Right now, Kelly needed a friend.

She reached out a hand and rested it on her arm. "Are you okay? Do you need a hug?"

CHAPTER TWENTY-ONE

K elly knew church was going to be rough. Her parents had
been very involved with the church. That was why there
were so many people at the funeral. Her father was well known and
well liked. Well, had been. Her breath caught and her eyes grew
wet. She closed her eyes and took deep breaths, until the feelings
receded. She so didn't want to cry this early in the day.

There were of course words of condolence from everyone
they encountered, even from people who had been to the service
yesterday. It was just another day of every conversation revolving
around how her father wasn't there anymore. At some point she
would be grateful for all these kind words, but that time was not
now and she resented people shoving this in her face all the time. It
wasn't likely she would have forgotten about it by now, so why the
constant reminders. Part of her just wanted to grieve in peace. But
that wasn't the agreed upon social model.

She tuned out the service, spending the time thinking about
her father and how she missed him, but also distracting herself with
thoughts about the hike and then the drive back to campus. A lot was
going on and she didn't want to get too caught up anything to the
point she began to monofocus on any one thing to the abandonment
of others. Kelly's thoughts were a whirl all throughout service. She
was still distracted by her thoughts on the drive back to the house.

When they got home, her mother asked, "Are you doing okay,
sweetie?"

"I'm not sure. I mostly just caught up in my thoughts right now."

"Do you need a nap or an early lunch?"

"I don't think so. Mostly thinking about Dad and everything else that's going on. I miss him."

"I know. I miss your father as well. He was my best friend for years and now I'm not sure what to do."

Kelly embraced her mother. Her mother hugged back and they stood like that for a little while. Her mother let go first and Kelly took a step back. They both had wet eyes close to tears. "Well, you still have me, and Tim, and Carrie."

"That's true. I don't know what I'd do without all of you. As it is this house is going to feel empty soon enough."

"I'll be back for spring break in a couple of weeks. That is if you want me to stay here?"

"Of course I want you, sweetie. I'll be grateful for the company, but wouldn't you rather go off on a trip somewhere?"

"Not really. And besides, I'm sure I'll still be dealing with my grief and it seems like a better choice to spend time with you. That way we can make up for lost time."

Her mother got a pensive look on her face. "I'm sorry for how I treated you, especially after your gender transition. I am grateful to your father for pointing out how I had been treating you. I just wasn't sure if you were making the right choice or even if there was a choice. I didn't mean to alienate you over this. I love you."

"I understand, Mom. I know you've said this before, and I get it. Just never understood why my gender seemed to be more important to you than you just loving me. I've always tried to make you proud of me and love me."

Her mother gave her another quick hug. "I always loved you, Kelly. It was more that I just didn't understand you, didn't understand how you could take the downgrade of being a woman. Men have such freedom to do and be whatever they want that I couldn't understand why you would make such a choice."

Kelly gave a mirthless laugh. "Then there I was feeling like I didn't have a choice either because I was facing and dealing with who I was. It turned out to be someone very different than I expected."

Her mother gave her a very sympathetic smile. "Maybe our problem is that we're too much alike."

"I can think of worse things than being like you." They smiled at each other.

"You go get ready for your date. You don't want to be late."

"Mom," whined Kelly. "It's not a date."

"Go. We can always talk later. Go have some fun before you head back to school and your classes."

Kelly headed upstairs to get changed. She hadn't brought her boots with her so she was just going to do the hike in her sneakers, which should be fine so long as the trail wasn't too rugged. Once she changed, she packed her bags so she could head back to school after lunch. It wasn't necessarily what she wanted to do, but it was the responsible thing to do. She gave the room one last pass to make sure she had all of her stuff, then grabbed her bags and headed downstairs. She called out, "Okay, Mom, I'm going."

"Call me when you get back to the school."

"I will, Mom. It'll probably be later this afternoon. I'm not sure how long this hike is going to take, but I'll be leaving right afterward. Well, probably after I grab some lunch."

"Tell Teresa hi for me."

Kelly rolled her eyes a little but smiled. The changes in how her mother was treating her were profound. She was grateful. She didn't feel like the black sheep of the family, whose existence was generally denied. It was a wonderful feeling she hoped would stick but as sure it was going to take work. She would talk more with her mother over spring break.

She used her phone to pull up directions to the trailhead because she didn't know where Lirkey Trail was or how to get there. It didn't take long to get to the trailhead which was in the back of one of the city parks. She'd been to this park before with her father but hadn't known about the hiking trails. She got out and started to stretch. The military had made the importance of stretching very clear and she had been sedentary for a while now and wanted to ensure she didn't injure herself. As she stretched, she could see one of the park shelters where she recalled sitting and talking with her father over a year ago.

That memory and pain of missing him brought her to tears. Her father had been so understanding even though he barely understood the gender issue. He tried but he just didn't get it. Sometimes she barely understood it either, despite it being a part of her life. Gender was so strange and so varied that it was hard to nail down sometimes. Why did her life have to be so confusing? She wiped her eyes and noticed that Teresa was there, asking, "Are you okay? Do you need a hug?"

Teresa hugged her and it helped Kelly regain her equilibrium. "Thank you."

"You're welcome. After all, what are friends for?"

Kelly wiped her eyes with the back of her hands. "Right, so we were going to go for a hike?"

"We can if you're still feeling like it. Grief takes its own time, from what I've heard."

"That's true," replied Kelly, feeling the grief recede and a touch of embarrassment rise. The last thing she wanted right now was to be scrutinized by anyone for her display of emotion. "Let's go. I've been looking forward to this."

Teresa nodded and stepped past Kelly and uphill toward the wooden sign at the boundary of the woods, reading Lirkey Trail. Kelly followed and her eyes were drawn to Teresa's outfit. The leggings she was wearing cupped her legs and rear rather enticingly, holding her focus. Maybe following Teresa as they hiked would be a good plan after all since Teresa was the one familiar with the trail. She would get to enjoy this particular view throughout the walk. Just because she wasn't dating anyone didn't mean she wasn't interested in dating anyone. And the view was rather attractive.

Teresa turned and caught Kelly's glances. She smiled at Kelly, seemingly okay with being looked at. Kelly's cheeks warmed and she averted her eyes. Teresa chuckled and continued into the woods. Kelly picked up her pace to walk alongside her. Maybe she could look later. "Do you often walk this trail?"

Teresa turned to face her without breaking stride. "At least once or twice a month. It's a nice hike and is still in town so I don't have to go very far for it."

"Well so far it's been nice," said Kelly.

"The view down by the river is actually lovely, especially in the spring when the trees are just budding. You can climb down and get access to the river which is nice in the summer. There is usually a cleanup effort every spring to make sure the river in this section is clear of debris. No one wants to get injured swimming," Teresa said while picking up the pace a little bit more, especially as the trail was leveling off.

Kelly had no trouble matching the pace set by Teresa. It was casual, far less than what she was used to from her time working with the infantry. The pace that was standard then was quick, especially with the thirty-five-pound ruck and full battle rattle, trying to do twelve miles in three hours. She had hated that pace because it was rough and she always ached afterward. This pace was much more pleasant. Instead of rushing to get to a place they were moving toward, this pace helped them be able to enjoy the forest about them, the fallen logs, the bits of rock outcroppings, and the tall but barren trees. She sighed as they walked on. "This is nice. Thanks for the offer to come with you."

"You're welcome. I wasn't sure you'd be interested in a hike to tell the truth."

"This is far more pleasant than when the army goes for a road march. At that point you're simply trying to cover a certain distance at a certain speed, which sucks. I was never a fan of jogging with a rucksack full of gear."

"You're serious?"

"Oh yeah. It wears out your knees and back something fierce. A lot of people came in complaining of those things after we did road marches. Not a fan. This is something I prefer, just going through the woods at a light pace enjoying the trees. I keep forgetting that I like this and forget to hike on my own because the army turned hiking into an endurance sport."

"Have you heard about the Japanese practice of forest bathing? It's basically a form of health care where you walk through the woods and it helps your blood pressure, stress levels, and other things. It's fascinating and one of the reasons I try to go on a hike once a week if I can manage it."

"I've never heard of that. Sounds interesting. I'll see if I remember it enough to look into it when I get back to class. Forest bathing. Almost makes it sound like you show up at the woods with a towel, strip down, and bathe in the leaves." They both laughed.

"That would be more bathing in the forest. I think one is for your spirit and the other is for your body. How would that even work?"

"It probably doesn't work, at least not the whole 'bathing in the forest' bit. But even on marches with the military, it was always nicer to go through the woods whenever possible. Well, except when it rained, then everything just sucked."

"And yet you want to go back?"

"I told you about the fact that I need to wait before I can get the job I want, so I figured why not. My previous time in service counts toward my retirement, which means that I can get in my twenty for a pension, and still be fairly young when I'm done. It's not that bad of a deal."

"It sounds like you have your future all planned out."

"More sketched out than anything else. For all that my time in the military was good, it was also all-consuming. I'm not sure I want that with my life anymore. But I haven't done any job searching otherwise, so I don't really know what sort of work is available once I graduate. And my personal life is pretty much nonexistent given that I have been focused on schoolwork more than anything else. The military is more of a safe bet than a sure thing."

"Things I never expected to hear, that the military is a safe bet."

Kelly chuckled. "Well, not safe safe, but an easy choice. I mean, the GI Bill is paying for my degree, and I was wondering if I should rejoin and sort of pay them back."

"But isn't that more of a paying you for time you already spent in?"

Kelly took a few steps as she pondered that. "True. I put in the time to earn it."

"Then maybe you need to look at places you want to live and jobs that are available in those areas rather than simply go for the easy fix."

"Is that how you ended up back here?"

"Kind of. I wanted to be close to my folks, especially when my mom had a health scare a few years ago. I'm getting some experience in the job I want and I get to spend time with my parents. Not a bad thing all in all."

"Not a bad thing at all. You want to move?"

"Probably at some point. I'm not really sure yet. It feels like I'm still trying to get my feet under me here." They moved to the side of the trail when a woman came by pushing a baby carriage from the direction they were heading. "I'm kind of in limbo about all this to be honest."

"How so?"

"Well, part of me is content to be here, doing my job, while another part wants me to go off and try to get hired at a larger paper where I might have a chance to cover far more interesting stories. It's not like the stories around here aren't interesting, but I'm not one of the ones covering them. I'm just doing basic stuff, filler work mostly. I want to write interesting and important articles, not just obituaries and summaries of other stories."

"I'm sure you can get to that. Have you tried anything online? Like working for one of the online writing gigs I've heard about?"

"I haven't looked. I probably should, so I can get some extra money. Anything would be a nice bonus to my current salary."

The background sound was changing and as they walked on, they could start to see the river off to the right. The trail ended in a circle with a couple of dirt paths headed off, one continuing the way they had been headed and the other down the slope and to the water's edge. The trees and rocks had created almost a series of steps down about ten feet to where the river flowed over the rocks in small falls. There were some people down there looking out across the water. She wondered what they were doing considering it was too cold to dangle your feet in the river. Maybe they were just enjoying the sound of the water as it flowed over the rocks. It was a soothing sound. "My dad would have liked this little hike."

"You think so?"

"Yeah. Not too strenuous, lots of nature. What's not to like? Thank you for letting me join you. This has been wonderful."

CHAPTER TWENTY-TWO

You're welcome. Shall we head back and get some lunch?" said Teresa smiling broadly. This approach was going rather well so far. She was just being Kelly's friend and could already tell they were starting to fall back into familiar patterns. There were differences of course, but those differences were all to the good. Kelly was far more confident and open now and that was powerfully attractive to her.

"Lunch sounds good to me. What options do we have?" asked Kelly as they turned and headed back up the trail.

"Well, there's always the diner. We've both been there before and I recall you liked their patty melt."

"Anything else new?"

"There's a newish Italian place that has good pizza, and someone said their pasta is tasty. There's a place that has Thai food that's also newish. Otherwise, not a lot of new food in the area. What of that sounds good?"

"The diner is good, but some pasta could be lovely. Let's check out the Italian place, because I'm in a noodley mood."

"You get noodley moods?"

"Don't you? Sometimes noodles of all types are just what sounds good. Need to see what they have to properly decide which noodle dish wins."

"When did you get this into noodles?"

"I watched an Anthony Bourdain video when deployed where he talked about how common noodles were and how good they are and it got me thinking. When I next approached noodles, I realized they are a great goodness and I needed more of them in my life. I've rarely been sad while eating noodles. I'm sure it's possible, but the noodles do help."

"A quote by Bourdain got you into noodles? Maybe I need to watch more Bourdain videos."

"They're fun to watch. He was a good show host and writer. He had a couple of different travel shows over the course of his career so just pick any of them and check them out."

"Can I find them on YouTube?"

"I think you can find some of them on there. Searching for them should get you some results. It shouldn't be that difficult to find Bourdain shows."

"And that will help me discover noodley moods?"

Kelly rolled her eyes. "It couldn't hurt."

They chuckled as they kept walking, and Kelley said, "I just like noodles. It's not that big a deal."

"True," replied Teresa with a grin. "But it is funny."

"That's fair." Kelly didn't seem like she wanted to concede the point, but was gracious in that. The singing of birds filled the space between them, and they continued down the trail.

Kelly started to look rather pensive so Teresa jumped in and said, "So how much time do you have left toward your degree?"

"A year after this semester at this point. I've mostly been doing hands-on training, which has been nice. I feel better knowing that the interning at least ensures I'm comfortable with the work. I'm looking forward to actually starting the work for real though. Some of the busywork is annoying, but helping the patients is nice."

"So, do you have to make the decision about the army quickly?"

"Yeah, making it sooner would be better than later, but I still have time. I guess a lot of the decision-making time will be while I'm working as an intern. I'm going to be working at a regular hospital and that'll give me a feel for working in the civilian world. I already know what working at an army hospital is like."

"It still messes with me that you joined the army," Teresa admitted. "I mean I know I've said that, but it still gets me."

"I get that. At the time I was considering it myself and talking to my dad about it. That was it. My mom was also surprised when I told her what I was planning. It was just something I felt I needed to do." Kelly shrugged. "It wasn't commentary on anyone or anything. Well, maybe commentary about trying to be a man, but likely no more than that."

Teresa nodded. "And to think, if I hadn't written your dad's obituary and decided to come to the ceremony, I would still think that you were in the army."

"Well, the breakup seemed very final at the time, like you were making sure nothing was tying you down to this town. I was certain I would never see you again, which I thought was sad. We parted not knowing the really important stuff about each other."

"It wasn't personal, Kelly. I just needed to start my new life unfettered by high school expectations. I wanted to move on with my life, though now I feel like an ass for doing it that way. I should have talked to you about it."

"Don't. You weren't an ass. We were both in different places but wanting the same thing, something new, something that wasn't here. I feel we can forgive ourselves for being teenagers and not going about it the best way. Deal?" Kelly stuck out her hand.

Teresa turned sideways and shook her hand. "Deal. And now we get a new start at friendship with new opportunities. I think we can both feel good about that."

Kelly cocked her head to the side and looked at Teresa intently for a moment. "New opportunities are good."

The admission made Teresa feel good, like this whole thing was moving toward something different with potential to move toward something great. They'd been very happy together before the breakup, and she'd had nothing but praise for what sort of boyfriend Kelly had been, so there was little concern over what kind of girlfriend Kelly would be. She was sure to be an excellent one if prior experiences held true. "Good. To new opportunities."

Kelly chuckled. "If only we had something to toast with."

"Well, we can toast with water when we get back to our cars or we can wait until we're at the restaurant," said Teresa.

"If you're eager to get to the restaurant we could jog the last little bit of the trail and get there double-time."

"You want to run?" Teresa gaped at Kelly for a moment, then shook her head. "The whole point of a hike is to, you know, hike."

Kelly grinned at her. "What's the matter? Scared of a little run?"

"I'm not scared of a little run; I just don't want to get so sweaty that we make people we're seated near uncomfortable. That's not a good look."

"If you're not sweaty, are you even having fun?"

Teresa quirked an eyebrow. Was Kelly flirting right now? "The point of my hike today was relaxing, not exercising. My exercise routine is already set. I don't need to add to it."

"Fine. I see how you are. Going to do more of your forest bathing."

"That's right. And you're bathing right alongside me."

Kelly raised her eyebrows. "We are bathing together? So soon?"

Teresa sputtered and felt her cheeks heat. Kelly was flirting. This was a great development. "That's not what I meant."

"But it is what you said," said Kelly before she started laughing.

Teresa joined in on the laughter and they continued toward the cars. Kelly would occasionally mime washing herself which would set them off again. Teresa just couldn't stop grinning the rest of the way down the trail.

Once they reached the end of the trail, they did some cool down stretches before they headed for their cars. Teresa called out, "You want to follow me to the restaurant?"

"That'll work. I should be able to stay behind you."

"See you there." Teresa got into her car and had a drink of water, toasting a successful start. Her stomach grumbled at her and she shook her head. The flirting seemed to have worked a little toward the end. Maybe this plan was working even with all the challenges she was facing. Most of the challenges were on her side of things, wanting to be more open and obvious, but this subtle game was opening up things where it almost felt like the old days when they'd been friends back before she broke things off. Things were looking up.

CHAPTER TWENTY-THREE

K elly had some water and watched in the mirror to see what
Teresa was going to do. Mostly she was sitting there not
moving, which was fine. She was surprised to be smiling again soon
after her father's death. That made her feel both glum and happy.
There would have been little cause for smiling if she hadn't run into
Teresa again, that was for sure. That had turned yesterday around
and had improved it.

There were so many memories tied to Teresa, so many thoughts
from back before everything changed with joining the army. But
Teresa was being very accepting of her, and she wasn't positive, but
it felt like there was some flirting in and amongst their banter. If so,
that was another change from the past and one she was pleased to
see. It was nice being flirted with and so different from how she'd
expected things to go. She even flirted back a little, which was fun.
Maybe giving their relationship another chance was worth it, seeing
as they had both grown up and were now living more authentically
as themselves. They had been kids before, but now they were adults
with adult life plans.

Maybe she needed to flirt back even more? That should be
doable and enjoyable.

Her dad liked Teresa and her mom did as well. Even Carrie
liked Teresa, so maybe that would help with her sister. Carrie seemed
to have something against Teresa. But did she want to get into a
relationship when she was so unsure about her own future? She had

a lot of plans in flux and was trying to consider different versions of her future. That was a big question and one she wasn't sure of the answers. She wanted to make the best choice and wasn't sure what that would be. But the possibility of being in a relationship was enticing and would give her someone to talk to as she completed her nursing degree. That wouldn't be bad. Plus, it was a lot of fun hanging out with Teresa and just talking. She missed that.

Sure, she had friends in the program, but friends were not the same as...as what? A girlfriend? Was she seriously considering that? They had just reconnected, but things just felt right to her. She wanted to hang out more with Teresa but she needed to get back to school, as there were tests and papers and other things demanding her time. And if she decided to date her it would be a long-distance relationship, because a four-hour round trip wasn't the easiest thing on anybody. But with chatting options, and phones, and weekends it should work.

The running lights on Terea's car turned on, so Kelly started her car and waited for Teresa to pull out of her parking spot and drive past. Kelly backed and followed her out of the park.

Things felt sudden. Sure, she was lonely, but she was busy with classes and studying, and making time for a relationship would eat into her available time. She already felt stretched thin with schoolwork and life, so would it be a good plan to add another distraction? That quieted her thoughts until they reached the exit of the park.

To be fair, she wasn't all that worried about her classes at this point. She had her studying down well, and with practical work being a large part of her last year, she wasn't stressed about that either. It would be similar to the work she had done in the army, when she worked at the hospital. Some of her duties would be different, but that was all. Procedures would different then her prior workload. That would open up time for dating. It wouldn't be an impossibility.

Kelly wanted to roll her eyes, but refrained. There was just enough traffic on the roads she didn't want to risk it. It would be bad form to get into an accident on the way to lunch, and she didn't want to be inattentive while she drove. Maybe she should broach the topic during lunch. That might be good, and if Teresa wasn't interested in getting back together with her, then it would still be all good. There was no reason they couldn't hang out together when she came home over spring break and reestablish their friendship. So long as asking about dating didn't immediately ruin everything, it should be fine.

Great, now she was conflicted. Ask about dating and hope for the best, while fearing the worst, or keep her mouth shut and not take the chance. She missed Teresa and had for years. Their relationship felt special and strong before the rug was pulled out from under her. Now there was a chance to see if that feeling from before was accurate and true. She wanted it to be true, but there was no way of knowing if what she was feeling was real or something brought about because their reconnecting brought a respite to her grief. It was annoying.

She took a deep breath and let it out slowly. "Take a chance and possibly win or not take the chance because of the possible negative consequences. What the hell am I going to do?"

While they were stopped by a light, Teresa waved at her. Kelly grinned at the silliness. Maybe she was too serious most of the time and failed to play as much as she needed to. Dating could bring that out of her, the playful person she used to be before the army. She remembered being goofy and silly a number of times before the military and she missed that. She had gotten more serious and focused, especially after her time deployed. Lightening up even more would be nice because she was far too serious far too often for her taste. She waved back with a grin. It was fun.

The light changed and they drove on. Kelly followed safely behind by a few lengths, giving herself plenty of time to react to turn signals and such. That reminded her of following behind Teresa on the hike and the nice view the leggings had given her. It had been a while since she had made out with anyone, and she had to admit she was indeed interested in what Teresa was showing her. Maybe thinking about that wasn't a good plan while she was driving. The last thing anyone needed was her getting horny and crashing. Explaining that to anyone would be a nightmare.

Thankfully, she was distracted by the sign for the restaurant. Several types of hunger were making themselves known and she wanted something to eat sooner rather than later. She parked near the front door and waited for Teresa who had parked farther back. Teresa said, "Ready to get your noodley on?"

Kelly rolled her eyes. Two could play at that game. "Bring on the noods."

Teresa giggled. "Noods...nice."

"You're welcome."

Teresa held up two fingers to the hostess, who nodded, checked her seating chart, and smiled as she grabbed menus. "Right this way."

They walked past the Tuscan-style art that adorned the walls and were seated in a booth with a print of a lovely landscape of Tuscany showing a house surrounded by a vineyard. The waitress got drink orders, while they looked over the menus. Teresa smiled. "I'm going to get a pizza. They have a brick oven and that makes for great crust."

Kelly nodded. "Tempting as that sounds, I think I'm going to go with the Carbonara. I love it and I want to see how theirs is."

"I've never tried that before."

"Well, maybe I can let you have a bite, if I can have a bite of your pizza. Would that be a fair trade?"

"That could be arranged." Teresa was clearly happy, and Kelly thought that broaching the topic of dating might not be as ridiculous as she had feared in the car. She had missed that smile and it was warming her heart to see.

The waitress returned and took their order. As she walked off Kelly said, "Thank you for inviting me to the hike. It was nice."

"I'm glad you enjoyed it. It's a lovely hiking area and one of my favorites. I hike there at least once a month."

"Also thank you for coming to my father's funeral. It's been enjoyable to reconnect with you. I hadn't realized how much I missed you as a friend until yesterday when we started talking. Thank you for being there."

"You're welcome. I liked your father and I was saddened by his loss. I was glad I got to write his obituary and be there."

"He would have been happy we reconnected. He always thought we could make a great couple."

"I think we were pretty great until I broke us up. Again, I'm sorry about that."

Kelly waved that off with one hand. "You were doing what you felt like you had to do to be you. I would never judge you for that because I also did what I had to do to be me. How could I judge you for something I also did?"

"Fair point. And I have to admit, you're more attractive than expected."

Kelly blushed, her cheeks warming. "You look better as well. I guess growing up into ourselves was a good thing for both of us."

"I'll drink to that."

They took up their water glasses and clinked them together. Teresa said, "Wasn't there something we were going to drink to while we were on the trail?"

"Yes. To new opportunities."

"To new opportunities." They again clinked glasses before drinking down some more water.

"Are there any particular new opportunities you're looking for?" Kelly was trying to test the waters and see if Teresa was thinking similar thoughts. She didn't want to put the idea of them dating out there only to be shot down. But if she didn't take the chance, how would she ever know?

Teresa blushed. "Nothing in particular."

"So, I remember you saying you weren't dating anyone at the moment. Do you want to fix that?" Kelly looked Teresa in the eyes before nervously looking away.

"You want to go out with me?" Teresa looked surprised and pleased at the same time which Kelly had trouble making sense of.

"I'm here, aren't I? After all, I did say today was a date."

"I thought you were talking about this in general, not specifically."

"Well, maybe my subconscious knew something my brain didn't last night. But I would love to give us another go if that's alright with you."

Teresa smiled. "I'm willing to give it a go as well. But it is going to be tough with you going to school a few hours away?"

"I'll be coming back for spring break in a couple of weeks, and I would love to spend a lot of that time with you catching up and moving forward. Plus, we can chat over video calls whenever we want, I mean outside of classes and your job. It can work."

"But what about the army?"

That threw Kelly for a loop. She had no idea why Teresa even brought that up. "The army?"

"You told me you were seriously considering going back once you got your degree."

"That's true. And we can talk about it. I can share more of my thoughts and we can see where that conversation goes. This won't be like last time where I just take off. If we're doing this, then I'll want to do things right. Besides, I still have at least a year until I graduate so there will be plenty of time to discuss that before I need to make a decision."

Teresa nodded and looked at Kelly. She smiled and then said, "Okay."

"Okay?" Kelly looked at her questioningly.

"Yeah, okay. Let's do this. It sounds crazy with all the details and such, but I can deal with that."

"So, it's Kelly and Teresa Two: Electric Boogaloo?"

"Ugh... I forgot that you grew up with a lot of eighties movies thanks to your dad."

"As a reference, it doesn't happen to be in the right place a lot of the time, but when it is, score." Kelly chuckled. "But we're seriously doing this again?"

"Yes," replied Teresa. "I'm interested in dating you."

Kelly's happinessfaded while melancholy rose up in her. She looked down at her plate, gathering her thoughts and said, "It feels weird that I lost my dad and because of that it resulted in me dating you again."

"Is it a bad thing?"

"No, I just wish he were still here because he really was a fan of us. He thought we might be able to make it past high school. I guess, in a way, I can thank him for bringing us back together."

"I can as well. Your dad was wonderful and I could see this being some sort of scheme, if he had known that I was in the area."

"Who knows? He read the paper a lot, so he might have noticed your name in there. He was sick for a long time, but this came out of nowhere. I'm sure it wasn't intentional, but it worked, because we found each other again."

The arrival of their food broke the chain of conversation briefly and they began eating.

"You know this means that I need to get all your contact information, besides your phone number."

"Same here." She twirled some of the noodles onto a spoon, before taking a bite. The flavor was wonderful. "This feels surreal. I haven't dated in a while, so I'll probably mess things up a time or two."

"We're in the same boat, Kelly. I think we'll do okay."

"Good," Kelly said that with finality. She hoped this went better than her last several dates where things were over shortly after they had begun.

"Good?" Teresa looked confused.

"Yeah. I think this situation is good. It's certainly taking advantage of a new opportunity and making use of an old one. We were kids and it didn't work out because we both had to do some growing and learning about ourselves. There's no reason to think that we might not work out this time."

"Because we've grown and changed?"

Kelly nodded. "We're not the same people who broke up, or were even together. So much has changed, not the least of which has been me and all my changes. And I'm still learning about the ways you're different. I'm excited by this new opportunity."

"Me too. I've been thinking about it since yesterday, but I didn't want to push anything because of your grief."

Kelly cocked an eyebrow. "So, you hoped I would come to the realization on my own?"

Teresa's cheeks reddened and she looked away. "I was hoping for that."

"That' a big risk. But then again, if it hadn't happened now, I'm sure I would've had this realization over spring break as we hung out. I wanted to spend the time with you and that would surely make me realize something."

"What brought you to the realization?"

"I was playing around with the idea last night, but today, seeing you in those leggings brought it home. And our conversation was like before only perhaps a bit more playful. I've missed that."

Teresa looked smug and took a victory bite of her pizza. Kelly was confused before having an ah-ha moment. "You mean you wore those on purpose?"

"What can I say." Teresa grinned mischievously. "I remembered that when we were dating in high school that you liked my ass, as you certainly played with it enough. I was betting that the old information was still relevant."

Kelly's face burned, prompting her to take a drink of water. She knew she had a type and apparently Teresa understood that well. "I don't know what you're talking about."

"Right...that's very believable."

Kelly shook her head before taking another bite of pasta. She realized she was nearly done with her lunch. "Would you like some?"

Teresa smiled warmly. "I would love some."

CHAPTER TWENTY-FOUR

So how are we going to do this?" Teresa said after she had her bite of pasta. She wiped her mouth with her napkin.

"What do you mean?" replied Kelly.

"This whole distance dating thing you propose. I'm not sure how you do long-distance relationships as I've never been in one before."

"I thought you agreed to it?" Kelly stared at Teresa.

"I did. I do. It's just that you're going to school two hours away and we're supposed to be dating. I'm so used to being in the same space with whoever I'm dating that I'm not exactly sure how this is going to work. How did you want to do this?" Teresa held her hands open in question.

"I figured we can talk on the phone daily or as close to that as we can manage. That and alternate who comes to see who on weekends, so neither of us is the primary one driving. And in a couple of weeks is spring break, and I'll be back here for a week where I can see you daily after your work. That should help."

Teresa nodded her acceptance. "So that's the short-term. How are we going to make this work long-term, especially with you going back to the army."

"I haven't exactly made that decision yet so there's no reason to get hung up on that. I'm still looking at different factors. Hell, if I go back, I might go to another service altogether. I hear the air force is rather nice and it would be quite different from the army."

"That doesn't really build confidence. It's still the military."

"It's still a discussion for later. I have more classwork to go through before I'm even close enough to graduation to worry about it. I also need to talk to recruiters before I even try to make a decision like that, as who knows, there might not even be a spot for me. There's plenty of time before I make that choice."

"I just don't want to start something if it's going to fail."

Kelly looked pensive for a moment and then shrugged. "If it fails, it'll be because we didn't want it enough, not because of anything else. I'm willing to try to make distance work, because I know people who face even greater challenges with their distance relationships who are happy, so there isn't a reason that we can't work this out. It's a question of logistics and communication."

Teresa nodded. "That's a fair point."

"Thank you." Kelly grinned. "I get being nervous about it, but nothing ventured, nothing gained."

With a quirk of her eyebrow, Teresa asked, "And you think we can gain from this?"

"We toasted to new possibilities. This is a new possibility, a second chance for us to see if things work out. Regardless of how it works out, I have enjoyed reconnecting with you. I was worried about coming back to the community after I transitioned. But nothing happened. My mom might have heard something from the church, but I haven't, which is nice. Besides my mom changing her mind about me thanks to my dad, this has been the best part of my father dying, if there could be a best part." Kelly seemed to be turning pensive again.

"I know that I'm glad we reconnected. And I want to give this a try. I've had a lot of relationships where things have just petered out for one reason or another. And they were relationships where we were neighbors or something, able to see each other every day. This seems like it might be a challenge."

Kelly smirked at her. "I like challenges. That's why I have my Expert Medic Badge and my Air Assault wings. I wanted to challenge myself to do the most I could once I transitioned. And making this work, with my schoolwork and your work at the paper, is going to take effort and desire on both our parts to make a go of it. Success is ours if we want it."

"You sound like a recruitment poster."

"I was aiming for a motivational poster personally." Kelly beamed at her.

"I guess that would work out as well."

They both grinned at each other. She thought about it, and despite having a few relationships fail on her when even temporary distance was involved, she was willing to give this a chance. It was true that perhaps this time would be different and maybe something was missing from those other relationships that would hopefully be found in this one.

Teresa looked at what was left of their meal and realized something was missing. "Do you want to split a tiramisu?"

"Sure. Sounds good."

They ordered dessert and Kelly ordered an espresso as well. "Gotta have the caffeine to help me make the drive home."

"I don't recall you needing this much caffeine back in high school."

"I became a coffee drinker in the army since it was everywhere. But in high school it was a lot of Cokes instead. Surely you remember how often I had sodas. Coffee seems healthier overall."

"So, the army got you hooked on coffee?"

"Oh yeah. And then college just cemented that shut. Now I'm a woman who needs her bean juice every morning and sometimes during the day just so I can operate at anything close to full capacity."

Teresa chuckled and shook her head. "You do know there is espresso powder on top of a tiramisu."

"I do, but I'd get stared at if I snorted it."

"Ewww..."

Kelly laughed. "Oh, the look on your face."

"You just had to put that image out there, didn't you? Ick."

"I like espresso but have no interest in doing lines of it. And yes, I had to put the image out there, it was funny."

"Your sense of humor leaves a lot to be desired."

"As long as it's not a hard limit I'm sure we can work something out." Kelly batted her eyes.

Teresa glared a little at Kelly. "I guess it was too much to hope that time in the army fixed your sense of humor."

"Are you kidding? The army only made my sense of humor worse because it was filled with people who make jokes like this all the time. My sense of humor was basically standard issue."

Teresa didn't appreciate that and frowned as she stumbled over the same issue again. "You're seriously considering going back with them?"

Kelly sighed and shook her head. "Technically, the term is re-upping. But we don't need to focus on that right now. There is little chance of me heading off to the military any time soon. While there are a number of benefits that I could get from re-upping, such as if I decided to work at a VA hospital, then my time in the army would count toward retirement, it's not something we need to focus on right now. You just need to accept that it's not a bad situation but also one that's not close."

"Your time in the army would count toward retirement if you worked for the VA? That's a decent benefit. Here I thought you were just going back for no particular reason." There were things Teresa didn't know about the military or working for the government. She would have to learn a lot if they were in a relationship, especially because Kelly was serious about re-upping. She didn't understand it, but it wasn't her life. Besides, Kelly was trying to change the subject away from that.

"Well, I really like the work. Being able to help other soldiers with their healthcare is important. It also puts me in an environment where I can aim to improve constantly. I can learn a lot in a military setting that I might not learn in a civilian one. I just don't know if I can become a nurse practitioner in the military as I had never met one while in. That's something I can talk with a recruiter about."

"If you re-up, there's no telling where you might be stationed. It might be far away from here, like more than a comfortable drive."

"Seeing as that would be at least a year from now we might be well practiced at long-distance by then, or who knows what else might happen with us. A year isn't a tremendously long time, and a great deal can happen in that period. I'm more concerned with the short-term than I am with those longer-term plans."

Teresa conceded the point with a shrug and a nod. "I guess things feel more real now that were deciding to give this a shot, and I just want to make sure I haven't forgotten anything. I would hate for us to start this and drift apart because of the distance."

"Right now I think we need to focus on the next few weeks rather than a year out. No need to put the cart before the horse. So that's video calls, talking on the phone, and then I'm coming back here for break. That can be the real test as we'll be in the same place for about ten days. We can go on several dates and just see how we work."

"How do you know so much about long-distance relationships anyway?"

"One of my friends is in a long-distance relationship with someone in Canada. They go on video dates where they both watch the same movie or TV show and talk about it. They chat a lot over the phone as well. So, I've mostly seen it from the outside, but it's been very informative. I have no idea how easy it is practically, but I'm willing to give it a shot. We were good in high school so there's no reason to believe we won't be good now." Kelly cocked her head quizzically at Teresa. "Why do you ask?"

Teresa felt her face warm. "For some reason, I thought you were in a long-distance relationship before. I mean you sounded so confident and sure as you were talking about this, like you had actual experience with it."

"That's the army for you. You learn to say all sorts of things as if you know what you're talking about." Teresa laughed and Kelly just beamed at her.

They finished the tiramisu, and Kelly was lingering over her espresso. "When to you need to get going?"

"I should've been on the road already because I still have some schoolwork to catch up on when I get back to campus. However,

I haven't wanted to leave yet because this has been nice. I enjoy talking with you and reconnecting. It's helped me deal with my dad and everything a lot easier than I had expected."

"We should say our good-byes then so you can get on the road and head back to school."

"I should but I've missed just sitting and chatting with someone. I mean I sit and chat with people, but there's something different when it's someone you're starting to feel something for. That's what I miss. That lovely feeling of growing intimacy."

Teresa smiled and felt her cheeks warm a little. "I like that too. And maybe I can come up next weekend to see you."

Kelly sat up straighter as she smiled. "That would be excellent. It would be great to see you."

"Same here." Teresa grabbed the check and stood. "Let's get you out on the road while you're filled with espresso."

Kelly laughed and stood as well. Once Teresa paid for both of them, they headed outside to Kelly's car. Teresa smiled at her and said, "Call me when you get home."

"Will do. Right after I talk to my mother. She currently has dibs on the first call. I figure we might talk a while and she doesn't need the grief of waiting until we're done talking. You will definitely be the next call after that one though. I promise."

"Fair enough." Teresa was at a loss for what to do now but felt like it was time to do something active that would certainly make her views on their getting back together more solid. She closed the distance between them and slid one hand alongside Kelly's face before she leaned in to kiss her. Kelly seemed surprised for a moment and then closed her eyes. Their lips touched softly and it felt good, comfortable, right. Kelly opened her mouth to deepen the kiss and Teresa leaned in more to oblige. Kelly gave a short moan into her mouth. Teresa moaned back in response and the kiss deepened even more as her body was responding to how good everything felt. Kelly's arms wound around Teresa's waist, pulling her in tighter. The kiss broke and they stood there, looking into each other's eyes. "I'll see you Friday night."

Kelly nodded, her lips still open after the kiss. "Friday."

"Have a safe drive." Teresa stepped away with some extra sway to her hips. She could practically feel Kelly's eyes on her as she walked away. When she reached her car, she turned and noticed Kelly was still standing there, watching her leave. She gave a slight wave.

"Talk to you soon."

CHAPTER TWENTY-FIVE

The week was slow going for Kelly. She'd managed to keep pace with the classwork and only needed to make up a few assignments she'd missed. She had to cut short a few calls from Teresa since schoolwork came before the wonderfulness of having what passed for a social life. She was looking forward to being able to relax over the weekend, as she should be caught up by then. Just letting her brain shut off thanks to being ahead on papers and studying for midterms was more of a next-week task than a this-week chore. She'd worked hard this last week to be in a place where she could take the weekend off and enjoy Teresa's visit.

There was still some time before Teresa was supposed to arrive and she was impatient. She wanted to see her again, despite the fact she'd gone seven years without thinking about her except in passing. Things were different now. They were trying to make a go of long-distance dating and it was going…well, she wasn't sure it was great, but it was improving. She was cutting calls short, and Teresa had forgotten a call because she got caught up at work. They were struggling to find the time to keep the connection going due to their busy schedules. Maybe being together in the same place would help.

That was her hope for this weekend. There was a second bed in her room that she had made up so that Teresa would have someplace to sleep. Trying to get two bodies onto one of those mattresses comfortably would be a trick, but she was hoping they would give it a try. It had been a long, dry spell for her, and based off Teresa's comments it had been one for her as well. But honestly, she just wanted to spend more time with Teresa.

Knowing Teresa from before helped them get past some of the early stages of dating since they had been friends before they had started dating in high school. True, it felt like a different life somewhere far in the past, but it wasn't like she'd forgotten Teresa's history. For all the similarities, this Teresa was different and Kelly was okay with that. They had both changed since high school and Kelly thought that was far healthier than being stuck in that time.

Her phone buzzed with an incoming text. She grinned as she picked up her phone. *At the parking lot.*

She quickly typed: *I'll be right down.*

Kelly grabbed her keys and ID and was soon downstairs and headed out the door toward the parking lot. She spotted Teresa and waited for her to reach her on the sidewalk. They hugged, which was a bit awkward given that Teresa was toting luggage. Kelly grabbed one of the bags to lighten her load. "Come on. I need to sign you in and then we can head off for dinner whenever you're ready."

The signing in process was quick and they were soon on the way upstairs, standing together in the elevator. Teresa chuckled, "This is giving me flashbacks."

"Oh?" Kelly turned to face her.

"Yeah, I went to school here and I dated at least one girl from this dorm back then. This elevator hasn't changed in all that time."

"Talking about another woman when coming to see me... rude," Kelly teased Teresa.

"You're the one living somewhere that takes me down memory lane. And that was at least three years ago. There's no way she's still here."

"What if she was a freshman?"

"She wasn't, but I get what you mean. Anyway, if she was still here, she might have moved off campus by now. Speaking of which, why are you still in the dorms?"

"I thought about it but decided that the dorms were convenient enough for me. I'm close to my classes, the dining hall isn't that bad, and I have a single, so that helps. Besides, it's cheaper than renting a place, since I don't need to get furniture, pay utilities, and such."

"That makes more sense then. I wanted to get off campus as soon as possible so I could have my own space. You said you had a bed for me?"

"Yes. The room came with two beds and so I just left them separate, in case I had a guest. And surprisingly, I have a guest."

"Why surprisingly?" Teresa asked.

"Well, I wasn't looking for anyone to date, given that I was more focused on school than dating. Sure, I've had some lonely nights because of that choice and on the whole no regrets. Running into you again was definitely a surprise and that changed things."

"I hope it's a goodchange."

"It has been so far." The elevator came to a stop and they got off on her floor. Kelly unlocked the door to her room and opened it wide, allowing Teresa to go first. "Your bed is on the left."

Teresa put her bags on the bed. She took a seat in one of the desk chairs. "This is bringing back so many memories. It's only been a little over two years, but it feels like it was yesterday."

"Dorm rooms have a similar feel everywhere. The furniture is nicer than it was on base, but it's familiar with the whole bed, dresser, and desk. I get to save money by not trying to live off campus and having to deal with those extra expenses. That nest egg will be nice once I have to make a decision."

"You mean about the military?"

"Yeah, or if I am going to stay in the area or go somewhere else to look for a job. I still have time before I graduate so I'm not in a rush to discuss it. When do you want to go have dinner?"

Teresa gave Kelly a look that made her blush. Teresa said, "We can go whenever you want. But first things first, I have something I've wanted to do all week."

Kelly was confused. Teresa held her arms out. "I've been thinking about hugging you and kissing you. It's been distracting me."

"I think I can be persuaded to take care of that need."

They hugged and kissed. Teresa deepened the kiss and Kelly pulled her closer. It made her lightheaded and breathless. She'd been replaying their first kiss for days now, and now she got to have a second, even longer kiss. They broke apart and stayed close, gazing into each other's eyes. Kelly gave Teresa a gentle peck on the lips. "As enticing as further prospects are, I didn't have lunch, so I'm ready for dinner if you're okay with that?"

Teresa laughed. "Certainly. And it's been a while since lunch for me as well. I left right after work. Thankfully, I got someone to look after Baxter, so he's sorted. Now, let's get going. Where do you want to go?"

Kelly grabbed her purse and smiled; things were going well. She had hoped things wouldn't be awkward when they got together, and it felt natural and familiar. The easy companionship they developed after her father's funeral was still there. "I'm craving pizza, and there's a place that has good New York style pizza. Will that work?"

"Great. Let's go."

They headed out. Kelly was humming some Taylor Swift song softly along the way, occasionally singing the lyrics. She stopped and blushed when she noticed Teresa was watching her. "Sorry"

"What for? It was cute. I hadn't expected you to be a Swifty."

"Yeah, well, some of my musical interests changed when I transitioned and I was trying to be all girl. Some of the music I tried was suboptimal, but a lot of the stuff I finally allowed myself to listen to was good, better than expected. Transition is kind of weird as a lot of it is just getting out of your way and allowing yourself the things you said no to years ago. It's mostly about opening up rather than anything else. That's what makes it so freeing."

Teresa nodded. "I guess that makes sense. I never really thought about anything trans-related until seeing you last week."

"If it's not something you're going through why would you ever consider it?"

"That's a fair point, but I'm learning about it now because I want to try to better understand you. You're one of the first trans people I've ever known."

Kelly felt her face warm. "Thank you. Right now, it's mostly just taking me as I am rather than who I was before. Other than that, I'm pretty much the same."

They reached the car and Kelly drove toward the pizza place. The restaurant wasn't far off campus and so they made the trip in a few minutes. As they walked inside, Kelly paused at the door and took a big sniff. She turned back to Teresa and said, "Doesn't that smell great?"

"Almost all pizza places smell great, so that's not saying much of anything. The proof is in the slice."

"That's fair. I think you'll be pleasantly surprised. I've had it before, several times, and it's really tasty."

The waitress took them to a table where they sat and placed their order. After Teresa got settled, she looked at Kelly and asked, "When did you ever have New York style pizza?"

"A friend of mine and I took our leave at the same time and went to New York. We saw the sights, met his family, I caught a Broadway show, you know tourist things. It was a lot of fun."

"Was this before or after your transition?"

"This is right after we got back from Afghanistan, but before I actually started transition. We had the leave accrued after being deployed so I thought I'd go meet his family. They live in Brooklyn so it was close to Manhattan and all the tourist sites. It was a great visit; he showed me so many things."

Teresa smiled and looked down at the menu. "So, this compares favorably to actual New York style?"

"Yeah. I mean it's not the same because there's something about the water in New York. However, it still feels and sort of tastes like New York pizza. It's the best that could be done outside of the city."

It didn't take long for their pizza to arrive. Kelly chose a slice that had a nice bit of cheese pull and bit into it. It was hotter than she expected, and she tried cooling it in her mouth. Teresa took a slice and put it on her plate to allow it to cool. Once Kelly managed to finish the hot piece, she took a drink of her water and let the cool liquid sit in her mouth. Teresa asked, "Are you okay?"

"I think I burned the roof of my mouth. I should have waited. But it smelled and looked so good."

"Well, you did say back at the dorm that you were hungry. It makes sense you would attack the piece before it had a chance to cool."

"Well, I guess it wouldn't be fresh hot pizza without someone burning the roof of their mouth." Kelly took another sip of her water and let the cool liquid in her mouth soothe the burn. It felt good, and her stomach was starting to let her know that she shouldn't keep waiting. She hoped that the few moments' respite would be enough to cool the rest of the slice.

Teresa picked up her piece, blew on it, then took a bite. She moaned in pleasure and took a second bite. When she swallowed, she said, "This really is good pizza."

Kelly just smiled and went back to her own slice. They focused on finishing their pie before they gave in. They waved down the waitress and got the last three pieces in a to-go box. They walked back to the car to drive back to the dorm. Teresa laid her hand on Kelly's thigh, squeezing it gently.

"That was great pizza. That place must be new. I don't think it was here when I was in school or I would have totally gone there."

"It opened last year sometime. They're doing plenty of business, so that's good. They should be here until I graduate."

Back in the room, Kelly put the box with the pizza into her little fridge. She turned and kissed Teresa. The kiss turned deeper and they both moaned into it. Kelly brought one hand up and cupped Teresa's face before sliding her hand to the back of her neck. They broke the kiss and Teresa said, "I've been wanting that since last week."

"Same. I missed you." Kelly looked into her eyes.

"I missed you too. This being apart is not very fun."

"Next week is spring break and I'll be home then, so we can see lots of each other."

"I'd like that. Though that first Saturday I have to cover a dog show. You want to come with me?"

"I like that idea. But that's for next week. Future us can talk about that. I think right now I have something else in mind. That is if you don't mind?"

"Oh?" Teresa raised an eyebrow questioningly.

Kelly began to kiss and nibble lightly on Teresa's neck. "Oh! Oh yes. I'm good with this."

They began to kiss again, and it was much deeper this time while their passion for each other began to build. Teresa's hands went about Kelly's waist pulling her closer. They stood there kissing for several minutes before Kelly started moving them toward the bed. They stopped kissing when Kelly's knees buckled as she backed into the mattress.

Teresa pulled her shirt off and tossed it over to the other bed. Kelly moved more onto the mattress allowing room for Teresa to join her. As Teresa was lowering herself onto the bed, Kelly pulled off her shirt and sports bra and tossed them to the side. Teresa paused and took in the sight of Kelly's breasts. One of Teresa's hands reached up and cupped a breast before she ran her thumb over the nipple that was already hardening. Kelly moaned with pleasure.

Kelly was lost to sensation before she sat up and began kissing Teresa. She undid the back of Teresa's bra and let the cups fall forward onto her as she slid the straps down. Teresa took her bra tossed it to the side before leaning down to kiss Kelly much more thoroughly. They continued for a while before Kelly slid a hand down Teresa's back to her pants and fondled her ass. Teresa leaned back from kissing her and smirked at Kelly.

"You just can't help yourself, can you?"

"Nope, you have a great ass and there's no two ways about it. I've always thought so."

Teresa looked at her with eyes partially closed and said, "We should get the rest of these clothes out of the way."

Kelly grinned. "I can be convinced to do that."

Teresa took off her pants and underwear. Kelly arched her back and pulled down her leggings. They got under the covers and began to kiss again. Soon Kelly's hands drifted downward over the smooth skin of Teresa's back. Kelly moaned into Teresa's mouth again, as the kissing warmed her core.

Teresa sucked on her nipples, and the sensation drove her crazy, making her shiver from a wave of pleasure rolling up her back. Kelly luxuriated in the feeling as she ran her fingers through Teresa's hair. Teresa kissed her way lower and Kelly spread her legs, letting Teresa's hair slide out of her fingers as she moved down Kelly's body. Teresa looked up at Kelly questioningly. Kelly gave a slight nod and then Teresa leaned down to kiss her folds before she let her tongue explore Kelly.

Kelly gasped in pleasure and gripped the headboard tightly. She moaned under Teresa's ministrations, feeling the wave of pleasure build and build. When they reached a peak, she muffled her yell into her pillow to avoid advertising what they were doing to the rest of the floor. Teresa kissed her way back up, and Kelly pulled her up faster. Once they were again face to face, she kissed her deeply. She then turned Teresa's body, so that she was now the one on the bottom. Now that Teresa was in the orientation she wanted, Kelly began to kiss her way lower. They took turns pleasuring the other until they were too shaky to keep going.

They lay next to each other, trembling from post-orgasmic aftershocks. They both smiled. Teresa muttered, "Wow."

"Wow indeed," said Kelly, as she turned on her side to look at Teresa. "I remember us being all enthusiasm and no technique back in the day. This was a lot different than what I had expected and far more wonderful."

"One of many things that have changed for the better. Thank you for that."

"You're welcome. It was my distinct pleasure." They cuddled together and fell asleep.

CHAPTER TWENTY-SIX

Teresa woke with the comforting warmth of another body next to her. She just lay there for a few minutes luxuriating in the sensation before her bladder woke up, reminding her that things needed to be taken care of. She slid out of the bed and looked around for her clothes. They were still scattered about from last night's activities. The memory of them made her smile as she took a few moments to find her clothes and got dressed for her walk to the bathroom. Before she left, she grabbed a change of clothes and her shower stuff.

It didn't take long for her to come back to the room where she was greeted by the smell of coffee when she opened the door. It looked like Kelly had simply pulled on her underwear and thrown on a T-shirt before making coffee. She looked cute and sleepy as she stood there. Kelly looked up at Teresa and smiled. "Good morning."

"Good morning. I hope you have a mug for me because I could really use some coffee right now."

Kelly gestured to the coffee pot, and there sat another mug. "I'm sorry I don't have any milk of any kind or creamer, since I don't use it. But I do have sugar."

"Thank you. This will certainly help me wake up even more than the shower did." Teresa busied herself with making her morning cup of coffee, putting a good bit of sugar into the bottom of the cup before she added the coffee. She then took a sip of the coffee and sighed. "It would be better with some creamer, but it still works. Thank you."

"I was thinking that going out for breakfast would be better than DFAC food. Interested?"

"DFAC?"

"Dining facility. Sorry, military acronym. It's still peppered in some of my speech, especially in cases like that where it's essentially the same thing as civilian speech. Lunch and dinner we can decide on later. I just want to hang out and talk more today. We're somewhat caught up with the past, now we need to get to the now and the future."

"Sounds good to me. Alternately, we can just hang out, go to a movie, go for a hike, something like that and just chat as we do that?"

"That could work as well. I just want to spend time with you. It doesn't matter to me how we make that happen."

"So, movie or hike or what?"

"Why don't we get breakfast first and then decide."

Teresa just smiled and nodded. "That does sound like a better plan."

Kelly smiled at her with the slightly lopsided way she used to have. "Let me get some pants on before we go."

Teresa leered playfully and said, "But the view is so lovely."

Kelly's cheeks reddened and she lowered her head slightly, allowing her hair to fall into her face. "Thank you. But it's also cold out there."

"You're welcome." Teresa watched as Kelly dressed, enjoying the sight of her. It made her remember last night and her cheeks warmed in memory. That had been rather pleasurable, and she hoped they could have a reprise of it later.

Kelly led the way toward her car and they got to the breakfast place relatively quickly. There was a brief wait where they just stood next to each other, but they were soon seated.

"So, what's good here?" asked Teresa.

"They make great waffles and French toast. Both are very tasty. Most everything here is good. The frittatas are usually excellent as well. I may go for a slice of that."

"I like a good French Toast. I think I'll go with that. Does it look like the picture on the front cover?"

"Sometimes. The food usually looks appealing as well is delicious."

Soon their orders were in and their plates served. As Teresa was eating, she noticed Kelly wasn't eating and looked rather somber. "You okay?"

"The last time my parents came up to see me, I brought them here for breakfast before they headed back home. My dad also got the French Toast. He said it looked better than the picture before he ate the whole thing." She drank some coffee. "I miss him."

Teresa took Kelly's hand, running her thumb over the back. "I'm sorry. Should I send this back and get something else?"

"No, that's silly. I just miss him and wish things had turned out different. I mean, his COPD was really bad, and we were all looking toward his breathing issues as a problem that might end his life. He was taking steps to better deal with it, and it seemed like things were improving a little. So, him going because of a heart attack almost felt like a bait and switch. It just came out of the blue."

"I didn't know he had COPD. They never covered that on the information for the obit, otherwise I might have added that in there."

"Yeah. He used to get bronchitis a lot and it severely damaged his lungs. He had the pneumonia shot to help him out because that had worn him out a few times as well. He was dealing with treatment for it, and from what my mom said was doing everything his doctors had told him to do. He had gone inpatient to a rehab facility for more concentrated treatment on his lungs and it was helping. He had literally just gotten out when the heart attack hit him. It fucking sucks."

Teresa squeezed Kelly's hand. "Sorry for inadvertently bringing this up. I didn't know."

"It's not your fault. Grief hits people differently at different times. I've been trying to work through it since the funeral, so I'm not surprised it hit. I just never expected French toast to be at fault." Kelly took a bite of her frittata.

Teresa was at a loss for what to say to help, as there was no one to teach you about how to deal with grief. She had never dealt with this in her own life and had no personal experience with death, at least not death that hit close to home. But her heart reached out to Kelly, and she wanted to hug her until she felt better. She did the next best thing she could, tightened her hold on Kelly's hand until she looked up at her. Kelly smiled faintly and asked, "So movie or hike or museum or something?"

"What sounds good to you?"

"Well, there is a movie I was wanting to see."

"We can go do that. We can share a popcorn and a soda and it will be just like high school."

"At least I don't have to pretend I don't like whatever we're watching, for fear of seeming less manly."

"Oh, which movies in particular that we watched did you like but grumbled over?"

"You know how I often deferred to your choice to go see girly movies. I secretly wanted to see those. Even when you made me sit through *Pride and Prejudice*, I was secretly enjoying it."

"I told you it was a good movie."

"I believed you then, which is why I sat through it. I would often go with Tim to go see action films because that seemed like the thing to do as a guy. I did a lot of stuff for stupid reasons. I got better with both the army and my transition. It helped me be me, instead of pretending to be someone I'm not."

"Well, I thought you were convincing, but then again, I was into you. Given that you were the only male-presenting person I've been involved with, maybe my ability to tell is not that great."

Kelly chuckled and had another bite of her frittata. "That is a fair point. So, you were secretly dating another woman at the time."

"So secret that neither of us knew?"

"Yep. That was super top secret until it wasn't. I didn't even have the clearance for it until later. And then things changed." Kelly laughed at her joke. "I missed you."

"I missed you too. You know I kept judging the women I dated off of you because you really got me. It hurt to have to stop things like I did. I just couldn't in all fairness accept a proposal from you if I was wanting to date other women."

"And here we are."

"And here we are. I'm happy I went to your dad's funeral. I wanted to explain myself and let you know why I broke things off. It may not have been bothering you, but it was certainly bugging me."

"I get that. I can kind of see it at least now, with the distance. Neither of us were the people we wanted to be and stuff was getting in the way. We were both looking for a change and were ready to try anything to make that work. I know I'm better and happier now than I was back in high school. I'm fairly certain that I wouldn't have figured out I was trans for a while without going into combat. That made me take a good look at myself. And you know, I wouldn't go back to who I was in high school for anything."

"Not even for the reunion?"

Kelly took a sip of her coffee as she considered her answer. "Maybe. That's another reason to join back up. The dress uniform does look impressive, especially the officer's uniform. So, if I do show up, I'll look pretty impressive."

Teresa scoffed a little and stared at Kelly. "Is that decent a reason to join back up?"

"Not really, no. I keep thinking about the fact that the army paid for my transition and that was a decent amount of change. I want to give something back. I'm going to be a nurse and that keeps me mostly out of the line of fire, depending on if my unit deploys or not. I can happily focus on learning as much as I can about my job until I retire. Retirement pay plus another income would be a pretty penny. And I would only need fifteen years instead of twenty because of the time I already served. It does seem like a winning plan. I'm just not sure yet."

"Wow...the person I knew didn't seem like the military type and yet you joined. I may not grasp this because I would never make that choice. It's not something I would do but if this is what you want, I would support you. It's clear how serious you are."

"Yeah, I'm serious. I've even started talking with the ROTC program this last week to get some ideas. I could do officer's basic this summer and then go in when I graduate next summer. That's at least an option. I can also wait until I graduate to go in. Joining also saves me from having to think about finding a job somewhere when I'm still trying to figure things out. I don't even know where I want to live after I graduate. At least the military moves you around. I might get to go somewhere fun."

"While I would be stuck here in the middle of nowhere?"

"I wouldn't abandon you because of this. This is just the job, not everything else."

"But the military is more of a lifestyle than anything else. I'm not sure how I would play into it."

"You would be my girlfriend, that's all. And who knows, maybe by then you'll be something more. It's all up in the air. We just got together after all."

"But long distance is hard enough right now. I mean the calls are nice, but it honestly doesn't compensate for you actually being where I am. I would rather have you there with me than just sticking with this."

"Yeah, long distance sucks, but we have over a year before it comes to that, which is greater than what we have now. If we make it through my schooling that would be quite a while, and longer than we were together in high school. Isn't that enough?"

Teresa sat back and pondered. Was that enough? Did she want more, when things had just started again? She wasn't sure so she said, "That's enough. So, you'll be gone over the summer?"

"Only part of it. Then I come back and get ready for the next semester. That is, if I decide to do that."

"I guess that I just don't understand the wanting to go back to the military, especially if you're unsure. From where I am it seems to dehumanize you. Didn't you get enough of that?"

"I did get enough of that. The military is a lot, but it's also more than that. There is the feeling of comradery with the people you are with, of doing something good for the country. I also feel like I owe it to them and myself to do this. They stood by me while I was trying to figure myself out, and that means a lot. Besides, it will irritate Aunt Kate if I go back and I'm okay with that."

"That is a terrible reason to join back up and you know it."

Kelly grinned. "It's more of a bonus than anything else. I would be happy to get a job, but I don't know where I would want to go. The travel aspect appeals to me because I can make a better choice with inforation. And I'm considering other services besides the army. It adds to the work I have to do to figure it out so I might not be leaving for training over the summer after all. This is a big decision and I understand that. I don't want to make a poor decision because I didn't properly think it through. Besides, so long as we are together, you also are a part of that calculation."

Teresa said nothing since she couldn't think of anything to say about that. She returned to her French toast. It was delicious and served to buy her time to figure out what she could say. She didn't want to argue just to argue with Kelly over what was ultimately her choice but it was nice that she was being considered in the decision.

Things were becoming special with Kelly, and if things kept going, she might want to do something to show how special Kelly made her feel. Maybe she needed to figure out better ways to deal with the distance issue. That was the biggest impediment to their relationship right now. She wished they could be in the same spot for more than stolen moments. Spring break was coming up and that might be time to spend together. They would be in the same spot for a decent number of days. Maybe she could invite her over to stay with her? Or deal with the fact that they would be in separate places. Waking up with her was nice this morning, and she could easily want more.

That had been one thing she had missed, not being physically close to someone. Usually when dating she would be able to see the person, often several times a week, but this enforced separation was tough to deal with. She wanted to be close to Kelly to enjoy more of what they had last night, but needing to travel two hours each way just the be with her seemed daunting. She was positive she could deal with the travel the whole time, but she wouldn't enjoy it. It felt like wasted time and she hated that.

She looked up from her plate and asked, "So you said before that you were thinking about other services?"

"Yeah. I am not sure if I want to go navy or air force because I know nothing about them. The air force has a reputation for being smart and the navy has a reputation for having good hospitals, even a few that sail about. That's kind of neat and might be fun, at least for a little while. But at least with the army I know what I'm getting into. That is at least some consolation."

"The air force wouldn't be bad. That reputation might help you when you're trying to get a job afterward."

"True, but any military medical job would have about the same look, I think. It just ensures that I have enough experience to do the job and do it well. Some of the people I've been in classes with wouldn't do well in the military, because they're not as organized as would be expected. There is an ethos you need to develop to do well in both the military and nursing."

"Same ethos?" Teresa stopped eating and looked at Kelly questioningly.

"Similar. It's about being well prepared for most anything and having a good work ethic, of trying to do the best you can at all times. There's nothing wrong with relaxing and hanging with friends, but you need to be focused on the job whenever you're working because the patient's life may be on the line."

"That sounds more like just a regular good work ethos than anything else. I try to have the same approach when I work. It doesn't have to be a purely nursing or army thing."

"Okay, I'll give you that. I've just seen it more in the military than anywhere else."

"Well, yeah, they probably train that into you. And it's not like you've been in the civilian work force long enough to learn otherwise."

Kelly snickered. "I can give you that one. They train you so long and so hard that you forget how to relax and have fun once you leave advanced training."

"That doesn't sound like a lot of fun to me." Teresa scrunched her face up.

"Well, the job isn't focused on fun. They want you to do a job plus be a soldier, which is an all the time sort of thing. It can be rather a lot."

"And you seriously want to go back into that?"

"I'm seriously considering it."

"I just don't get it. Wouldn't you rather have the freedom to do or say whatever you want?"

"Can you?" countered Kelly.

"Sure I…" Then she paused and thought a moment. "I guess I can't, not really. At least not at work. I have to toe the party line if I want to do well. My private time is not monitored, and that's something."

"Some companies do monitor you though. At least that's what I've heard from several people."

"Yeah, but I know that my social media is safe because otherwise I'd likely be the one going through people's Facebook or Insta or whatnot to try and find dirt on them. It would be a huge part of my job. Thankfully, that isn't the case."

"You get to cover a dog show."

"That's something that I'm looking forward to actually. It's at least a larger story than what I usually get and possibly a step up for me."

"I'm excited for you. Do you still want me to come along? I should be back in town Friday night, so I would be free on Saturday morning."

Teresa knew that she'd asked her to come along that morning before breakfast, but as she pictured going around the dog show with Kelly something else occurred to her and that image made her mind up for her. "Probably not now that I really think about it. I think you'll distract me."

"I distract you?" Kelly looked surprised.

Teresa smiled. "Yes, because I'm sure that I would rather talk to you than dwell on dogs."

"Don't you like dogs?"

"I'm more of a cat person and there isn't a cat show I can cover. But I do like dogs enough. I just need to interview the organizers and maybe a few of the people who are there to ensure I have a well-rounded story. Then it's writing it, submitting it, and seeing what my editor thinks. If I'm lucky, then it will get in the paper and I will have a bigger byline. I might even keep the article for my portfolio if it's good enough. So yeah, there's a lot riding on the success of this dog show article."

Kelly looked at her, eyes wide. "Clearly, there's a lot to your job that I know nothing about."

"And the same here with both of yours."

"Well, then here's to spending enough time together that we can start to understand each other's life."

CHAPTER TWENTY-SEVEN

K elly was having a good time. She was glad she and Teresa had reconnected, which hadn't even been something she had ever considered. She still felt odd about the fact they used to date years ago and things had certainly changed since then. She'd been planning to propose, but Teresa broke up with her before she could ask. That just sat strangely now that they were dating again. Did things go back to then or was the fact that they were both different people now enough for this to be classified as new? Teresa had certainly been passionate in bed last night and that still surprised her.

Back in the day, passion wasn't a word that applied to the few times they had slept together. It had been awkward and neither of them had any idea what they were doing, since they were each other's first experiences. They both consented to sleep with each other, but it just wasn't the best. Maybe the fact they were both hiding things from the other had something to do with it. They were not hiding things now.

Now it was the things they were not hiding that seemed to be bones of contention. Her desire to return to the military was one of those things. Teresa's hesitation in dealing with their long-distance relationship was another. She got how the whole situation was awkward and took a lot more effort than a regular relationship. There'd been times when she hadn't felt like calling Teresa but did so anyway, to try to keep their conversations going, to keep communication open between them. It seemed to be working so far, and Kelly had little doubt it would keep working if they applied themselves. But it sucked. Long distance was hard. Being able to only see each other on weekends was hard. And the drive was annoying. The distance was just enough to take extra effort but small enough that there was a feeling they should be exerting the effort to see each other. Maybe things would improve as they got more used to it. Practice helped most things. It was early days.

Right now, they were standing in line at the theater to watch a movie. There was one she wanted to see and Teresa was good with it. She said, "I can buy the tickets."

"Sure, then I can pick up a late lunch for us. Or maybe make it an early dinner?"

"I'm not sure which idea I like better. Both sound like they could work out."

"Play it by ear then?"

"Sure."

Kelly paid for the tickets and Teresa made a beeline for the concessions. Kelly then remembered Teresa had a popcorn problem. She always wanted popcorn and occasionally shared some with her when they were dating. Since Kelly wasn't a huge fan of popcorn it worked out. She stood in line and said, "So, you still need your popcorn fix."

"Well, it's hardly a movie without it." Teresa grinned at her. "We can share. And I'm only getting a small size, since we're likely to eat after this."

Kelly shook her head and waited off to the side while Teresa got her fix. "Ready now?"

"Yes, thank you." Teresa was already munching on some of the kernels, and they moved to the ticket taker. They went into the theater and Kelly found some seats a little way up the aisle. Teresa looked toward the back of the theater and kept moving upward toward the projection room. Kelly sighed and headed up there with her. "Why sit back here?"

"Well, we can kiss and stuff back here without distracting anyone. I mean, that's what we did back in high school."

"Yeah, but this time I actually want to see the movie."

"We can still watch the movie from up here."

"But the seats I initially stopped at were a perfect sight line and between the speakers and everything."

"I'm sorry. We can go back down there."

"No, we're here. It'll be fine. Maybe next movie you warn me about your making out plans before we hit the theater?"

"I think I can do that. Popcorn?"

Kelly sighed and took some of the popcorn. It left a little sheen of butter on her fingertips. As she sucked it off, she realized that Teresa was staring at her. "What?"

"That was rather distracting."

Kelly laughed and then realized that Teresa wasn't laughing. "I'm serious. That was kind of hot."

Blushing hotly, Kelly turned away and sat. Teresa sat next to her and leaned over to kiss Kelly on the cheek. "Thank you for humoring me."

"You're welcome."

Teresa worked her way through the popcorn as the previews started. She set it to the side and slid her hand into Kelly's. Teresa's palm felt good in her hand and Kelly squeezed gently. They turned toward each other and grinned.

Kelly was only partially focused on the movie, and she was distracted by the warmth of Teresa's hand in hers. Things were moving fast between them and she wasn't sure if that was a good sign or bad. Good because there were still some residual feelings from when they dated before. Bad because it could be a sign that Teresa wasn't all that serious about them and was just using her as a hook-up despite all her talk of the future. Kelly tried to avoid short flings if she could help it. She dated seriously and always had. This made her nervous since she wasn't entirely sure which was true.

The movie was cute and the romantic pairing had chemistry. Kelly would have preferred it if the female lead and the best friend got together, as she thought they had better chemistry, but it was unlikely that Hollywood would do that without it being directly marketed that way. There were some cute scenes and, on the whole, it was a nice way to spend a few hours.

They spent a fair bit of time kissing during the film and so some of the nuances of the film's plot were lost to her. But she liked the movie and making out during it like a couple of teenagers. They had done this several times when they had dated and it had been fun then as well. Being at the very back kept them from being spotted by others except a few other couples who had also taken to the back rows with similar thoughts on their minds. The kisses tasted a little of butter and salt. That wasn't a bad thing.

Teresa, whose lips were a touch swollen, beamed at her as the lights came up and said, "That was fun. We'll have to watch the film again to catch all the things we missed, but I rather enjoyed that. You're a lot of fun to kiss."

"You're fun to kiss as well. I enjoyed that. Thank you for thinking of that. And yes, I will want to watch it again to see scenes we missed out on entirely."

"I try to have good ideas when I'm on dates. Honestly, I haven't done this, making out in the theater, since I was with you. Lots of making out watching videos and such but never at a movie. I think I missed that."

"I missed doing that as well. Usually, I avoid doing that because I don't want to cause a scene when out at the movies. I guess you really don't care about that do you."

"Nope, and given how much you were getting into it I can say you didn't care all that much either when you were in the moment. So, what do we want to do now?"

"Well, there's a lake on campus that we can walk around, unless you're ready for lunch or early supper."

"I could do a short walk around a lake."

When they got there, Teresa snickered to herself. "I forgot how big the lake is. I think this will be a nice walk, like our hike last week."

Kelly's cheeks warmed as she remembered how much of that hike she spent watching Teresa's rear rather than the surrounding scenery. It had been a rather compelling view. The weather was a touch colder today but not uncomfortable. The coats they had would be enough for the walk, so long as they kept to a good pace. Kelly got out of the car first and started to head over to the other side of the car. Teresa got out and grinned at her. "Ready to go?"

"You bet."

They walked side by side as they moved about the lake trail, hand in hand. It made Kelly alter her stride as she had done on their hike to make sure they kept apace of each other. The ground-eating stride the army taught her wasn't suited to a casual stroll. She supposed she should get used to that pace again if she were serious about joining back up, but now was certainly not the time for it. She caught the sight of Teresa's face and it made her smile. This felt right.

The memory of getting the phone call when she broke up with her back in high school came back up. That breakup really hurt back then, making her think she had done something wrong, and she had had no idea what it could have been. The explanation about why it happened helped some, but it was still a spot that was raw even after all this time. She trusted this new Teresa but there was hesitancy in giving too much of her heart away at this point. Maybe if they spent more time together and got to know each other, Kelly would grow more comfortable with the idea. But still she smiled and asked, "So you went to school here?"

"Yeah. I think I said I dated someone who was in your dorm. And I've walked this lake before. Not on a date mind you, but I'm familiar with the loop."

"I rather like it. I've jogged this path before and it's nice in the morning before too many people are up and moving. Though I'm glad I slept in today. Can't do it all the time, but it was a nice change of pace."

"Why can't you sleep in? I would have thought you would have gotten used to sleeping in after getting out of the army?"

"I still jog for exercise, and I guess I got used to it in the mornings. It's kind of nice."

"I'm not sure I could be down with jogging outdoors. No real reason to run."

"You'd prefer that someone chase you?"

"No. I just prefer running on a treadmill in the climate control of inside. That or use any of the other machines they have in the gym. Besides, I don't like getting rained on while jogging."

"I'll give you that. Exercise in the rain is not very fun. Hair gets in your eyes and such. Not a fan. But it does keep you cool on a run, so that's something."

"Looking for bright points?"

"As often as I can. That helped me through a lot. Like Afghanistan. The deployment was rough, but the scenery had this rugged beauty. It was something that I had never seen before." Kelly closed down a little as other thoughts from that deployment ran through her mind. She accepted the reminders and breathed her way through them. "Yeah, bright points and good thoughts are helpful."

"Are you okay?"

"Yeah, just bad memories."

"You don't talk about your deployment."

"No, not really. It was a lot. Thankfully, nobody on my team died, but a number did get injured, some rather severely. We were under fire a few times, which was rather scary. I try not to think about it too much. It's just that coming back from there made me realize I needed to be myself, whatever that meant. That's when I started my transition. It wasn't easy." Kelly looked out over the dark water of the lake as she spoke, her memories playing in the background of her thoughts.

"Thank you for sharing that with me."

"No problem. It's the clean and edited version of the story. The real thing is a lot grimmer."

"Maybe you can tell me later?"

"Maybe. It's not all that pretty."

"From what I've heard, combat deployments never are."

Kelly ran a hand through her hair and sighed. "That's true. I don't like to think about it much. There were a lot of bad things that happened, a lot of times when I was worried that one of my guys would die before I could get them stabilized."

"That had to have been scary."

"They were counting on me to keep them patched up, and I did the best I could with the training I had. We made it through with no permanent losses, but it was close. It's one of the reasons I wanted to stay in the medical field, the need to help as many people as possible. But also, because of how tough the mission is I wanted to go back in to help more guys who might not have a chance without the best care that could be managed."

"And you're that care?" Teresa looked over at Kelly.

"I can certainly try to be that care. I can do a lot as a former medic and a nurse. I'm not sure I have the patience to be a doctor, but I want to do more than simple nursing, hence my desire to be a nurse practitioner."

"I know I haven't said anything about this yet, but I think you would be a good one. You certainly have a lot of experience that other nurses don't have."

Kelly chuckled. "That's what I heard. I mean, in some of the exercises, I knew the answers not from studying but from practical training. It's made several of the exercises extremely simple. I lean on that training a lot."

"I can imagine."

"Having given IVs in the field made that particular class a simple one. I mean, it's actually not that difficult if you follow the directions you're given, but it helps to have a steady hand. Though some of the classes on other things were not like the army so that was fun, trying to relearn skills. That made some things tricky, because I would fall back onto my military training."

"Do you think you'll need to relearn a lot if you go back in?"

"Probably. I don't know all the SOPs and such, so training and working will take care of that. I'm not overly worried about it to be honest. I think it'll probably be a lot of fun."

"Fun?"

"Yeah. Learning more about your job, doing it even, sounds good to me. I can't wait to graduate and get out there."

"I felt like that when I graduated, but the daily grind of the work has worn me down. I'm not as excited by it as I used to be, which I miss."

"I'm sorry to hear that. Is there anything that can be done?"

"Doing well on the dog show piece is what can be done at the moment. If I do good on that I might be able to do more small stories that are similar and start getting some of the more real and serious stories as I build experience. I like my job, but I want to do more than what I'm doing right now."

"I guess it's a good thing I'm not going to go with you when you go to the dog show. Can't have you be all distracted and do shoddy work."

Teresa bumped her with her hip, making her move a little. Kelly laughed. "I just want to do a good job. It's my first real break since I've been at the paper."

"Then I hope you do really well."

"Thank you. Maybe we can go out for dinner afterward to celebrate."

"That could be a lot of fun. When were you going to write the story?"

"Probably on Sunday. I was going to take plenty of notes and use my recorder to capture quotes. I'm ready for this. I'm even going to have a digital camera to take any interesting pictures I can find so that they'll be available for the article."

"Great. Here's hoping you get the promotion hopefully coming your way."

"Thank you." They walked on a little bit before Teresa said, "I've missed this, just casually talking with someone."

"Yeah, I'm enjoying it as well. It's odd the things you miss when you're not in a relationship."

"Friends are good for this as well, but there's something different about talking with a girlfriend," Teresa said. "My best friend Alex is always telling me that I need to get back out there. They were surprised when I told them about you."

"What'd you tell them?"

"Well, I had talked to them about you and how I wanted to apologize to you. They thought that was a great idea by the way. So, when we next talked, I told them about your transition and my attraction to you."

"And?"

"They said they hope everything works out for you."

Kelly turned to face Teresa looking confused. "That's it?"

"Yeah. I'm much more used to her saying more in such situations. That it was that brief made me think they might be against my seeing you or maybe it's an issue with the speed with which we got together. Which isn't like them. It was odd, but I can ask more about that later when we next talk."

"And yet, here you are," quipped Kelly.

"Here I am. And I'm glad to be here. I think things are going well for the two of us so far, which is good. We might not be great at the long-distance aspects of things yet, but I'm sure we'll get there."

"Same here. Things are going far better than I had honestly expected them to go. I'm so glad you're here."

"Ditto."

CHAPTER TWENTY-EIGHT

Teresa just couldn't stop smiling. The weekend had been a lot of fun, and getting laid a few times had been a wonderful way to celebrate their time together and grow closer. While she still had some worries about the long-distance dating thing, this weekend set a number of concerns she had aside. They were still getting to know each other again, but everything had a familiar comfort and that made her feel good. In some ways, the relationship with Kelly felt like coming home.

The radio was on, giving her some nice classic rock to listen to as she drove. They had parted right after lunch considering Kelly had to get back to some of her schoolwork, especially since midterms were coming up. She was going through the information from her classes over and over again, to make sure it was in her memory solidly. Back in high school, Kelly hadn't been that great of a student, but she had apparently found her groove either in the military or university just agreed with her. She took this extremely seriously.

Teresa looked forward to next week, when Kelly would be in town for a week. They made plans to see each other as much as possible, but Teresa wasn't sure how much that would happen given that she was often too tired after work to do much. It took brain power to do the research and write what she did, and that could be exhausting. And she hoped she would get another good story during the week to cover, that is if the dog show story went over well.

Hopefully, she wouldn't have to choose between Kelly and her job because she was fairly certain that right now, even with how thrilled she was with Kelly and their burgeoning relationship, she would choose work.

She took a deep breath and let it out slowly. This train of thought was ruining her good mood, and she would rather sit with the happiness for a few miles longer before she started worrying about work. Saturday night was fun because they went to a bar and hung out with a few of Kelly's friends from the LGBTQIA+ group on campus. They did this every weekend and insisted on dragging Kelly along so she would do something besides study. That had been a very different view of Kelly. She chatted with the others and didn't drink nearly as much as she had expected.

It was fun meeting some of Kelly's friends. They were all nice for the most part and on the whole several years younger than Kelly and Teresa. It was weird thinking of these people as kids, but they were younger and seemed to not have the world-weariness both Kelly and she had picked up. When had they gotten old?

They stayed up late talking about some of their dreams. Teresa still had dreams of getting a job at a larger paper and maybe writing something that won a Pulitzer. She had no idea when or if she would ever do that, but it was a dream, something to strive toward. Kelly mostly talked about wanting to help other people and getting to see more of the world. Honestly, it made her feel that Kelly was going to choose the military, so she could have more adventures. It was just a hunch, but her degree taught her that hunches could often be real.

Her high was starting to fade, and she frowned, moving past a slower car on the road. If Kelly was going to join the army or some other branch of the military again, then they had a definite timeline. Things would likely end because she couldn't imagine a long-distance relationship where she was more than a few hours away. This short distance was hard enough. Kelly being stationed somewhere across the country would certainly put a damper on things. And what if Kelly got stationed somewhere else in the world?

But was that a reason not to enjoy what they had while it was still there? She was very attracted to Kelly and wanted to be with her despite all these other worries. It made her feel better about things, to be with Kelly. She was in a much-improved headspace overall since they had formalized the relationship and it wasn't just the sex, which was lovely, it was the companionship. It would be easier to feel that if they were in the same place for a while. Were they even getting a fair shot at a relationship if they weren't even living in the same place?

This wasn't where she wanted her thoughts to go, trying to see the negatives in the relationship, but there went her brain. This had been a problem with all her relationships so far. When things were going well, she overanalyzed everything and that made her more cognizant of faults and flaws in the relationship. She was her own worst enemy when it came to being with someone. Over time, she got to the point where she looked for the ways they would fail and that would inevitably bring those imagined flaws out into the open. She was aware that this sort of thinking led to her self-sabotaging her relationships but wasn't sure what to do about it.

To be perfectly fair, things were going great with Kelly. They both seemed happy with how things were turning out, they talked a lot and approached the relationship maturely, thinking through things instead of just rushing ahead. They had had a conversation that weekend about what sorts of things might make the relationship work better. It came down to more communication and never taking the other for granted, ways that all relationships survived. Nothing they came to consensus on was earth-shattering, but it was nice to see that Kelly understood some of the challenges associated with the way they were dating. It wasn't as easy as being there together and they both acknowledged it.

She sighed and shook her head. She needed to talk to Alex about all of this, to share with her some of the things Kelly had brought up and to voice some of her concerns. It certainly seemed like it was impossible for her to be in a relationship without some concerns rising up. That wasn't a trait that she liked about herself and figured it was anxiety. It hadn't gotten in the way of much else in her life except for her relationships and trying to get promotions. Her worries and concerns always made her almost too nervous to apply for them in the first place.

Trying to get her mind off such thoughts and back to the earlier happiness, she started singing along with the radio. That kept her occupied for several songs before her thoughts turned back to the negative. Were these things even actual negatives or were they just issues blown out of proportion by her overthinking? She had to give herself that one. It was probably the most on point, though it did nothing to provide an answer. She was making herself miserable inventing issues when they were still in the early stages of their relationship. It was still new and different despite the familiarity she felt.

She wondered if that was one of the issues she was facing, that it was familiar? Groaning, she started singing again and focused on the road. The last thing she wanted was to dwell on all of this and make herself crazy. This wasn't how she wanted to be. She had had a good weekend and had a lot of fun with Kelly. Things were good, so she needed to accept that it was okay for things to go well.

That thought carried her the rest of the way home. She headed to her apartment with a little bit of a spring in her step. Baxter was waiting for her to come into the apartment as she cracked open the front door. She pushed him back with one foot and set her luggage to the side. "Yes, Baxter, I see you. Who's a good kitty?"

Baxter meowed and rubbed against her legs. She petted him for a little bit before she took her bag to the bedroom to unpack. She'd made good time. She would be rested before her call with Alex. She wanted to talk with her and get her input. Maybe she could also help her quiet some of the negative thoughts she was having. Alex had been able to do that before.

After she sent off a text message to Kelly to let her know that she got home alright, Teresa turned to the fridge and got herself a drink.

Part of her was unsure if she could do this on alternating weeks. The drive was long and boring even though anticipation helped on the way there. Maybe she needed to look into books on tape to help make the drive more bearable. That didn't change the grind that the drive would be, but spending time with Kelly would make up for a lot of things. All the negatives she discovered were things Kelly had no control over, like the length of the drive from her apartment to the school.

Her phone buzzed. It was just Kelly saying she was glad that Teresa had gotten home in one piece. Teresa smiled down at her phone.

Yeah, talking with Alex sounded like a good idea. Her thoughts were in several different places and that was never a very comfortable place to be. The long drive took it out of her and she hadn't considered how much that was going to affect her. She still wanted to rest more before work tomorrow and part of her mind said that what was left of the evening wasn't enough time to truly refill her batterie before the week ahead. She grabbed a book to read until it was time to talk with Alex. Maybe it would be enough rest if she could manage to stop fretting.

Her phone alarm went off and she sat up, yawning a little. She had almost dozed off on her couch, but the alarm woke her just in time. Teresa got the laptop plugged in and ready. Her message program chimed and she sat down to answer it. "Hey there, Alex."

"Hey there, Teresa. How was your weekend?"

"It was good. Spending time with Kelly was great."

Alex raised an eyebrow at Teresa's tone and said, "I sense a but in there."

"You know me too well. I'm having some doubts, but they're mostly around the drive and the whole long-distance issue rather than anything to do with Kelly."

"No one ever said that long distance was easy. You told me Kelly had talked to you about that."

"That's the truth."

"But other than your relationship worries starting early, how was the trip?"

"My relationship worries?" Teresa sat up a little straighter. Was this something that was easy to see from the outside rather than simply an artifact of her own thinking?

"Oh yeah. After a while it's like you expect things to go poorly and that starts to become all that you see. It's been like this since I've known you. This is the fastest that the negatives have cropped up for you. You usually take at least a month or more for it to really kick in and start to become a problem."

"Yeah well, a two-hour drive one-way is a pretty serious stumbling block for anything."

Alex sighed and gave her a look. "You knew this going in."

"True, but the reality of the drive was different from just thinking about it."

"Maybe instead of the negatives, which I am sure you can rattle out, you can tell me about the positives. I assume there are still positives?"

Teresa paused and looked at her. "I was worried you didn't like Kelly."

"I don't even know Kelly so I have no reason to dislike her. I'm just worried about you. You dove into this rather fast and now the negatives are bouncing around in you pretty badly if they're coming up this quickly. That has me concerned. This isn't normal behavior for you at this stage of a relationship."

"I think part of it is that I've never been in a long-distance relationship before so I was ill-prepared for how tough it is. If I want to see her it's not a simple thing of driving to her house or apartment that's maybe fifteen minutes away, but instead it's a two-hour trip by car. That's a lot."

"Yes, it is a lot, but that's not necessarily a bad thing. You're busy with work, and she's busy with school, both of you need your own time and space to take care of these things. That will probably be a helpful thing over time if you just let it. I think you're so focused on needing to be near the other person that you're forgetting other good things."

"How did you get so knowledgeable about distance relationships?"

"I was in one for a while. The separation wasn't long, say three months, but it was a lot. We had phone dates and tried to talk to each other daily. We also sent emails to each other regularly. It did the job, but it was a lot of work to make it work. More work than a regular relationship takes that's for sure, because you don't have physical presence to take some of the load. Being with someone is easier because you can fall back on the physical instead of dealing with the intimacy that all this talking brings."

With a sigh, Teresa picked up her water bottle and took a sip. "We talked about this over the weekend, and it's been hard being apart, but the time I spent with Kelly was wonderful and so worth the drive."

"Some part of you doesn't think it's worth it, hence the negative thoughts. That or you're busy sabotaging yourself."

Teresa was quiet for a moment as she pondered this issue. Was this relationship worth it? Worth the travel and stress of upkeep? Worth the long spans of time without actually being close to her? "Some part of me may think that, but I don't think it's all of me. I know I'm not a fan of that two-hour drive. I'm going to try an audiobook on the next trip to see if that makes a difference. If I fill the time with something, I might enjoy myself and the miles may pass faster. I really care for Kelly and want to give this the best chance I can."

"That's good. Usually when these thoughts arise, it's like you're already on your way out so this is a positive development. And yeah, it sounds like it's just the inconveniences that are giving you pause, not anything about the relationship itself."

"That's what it feels like to me. I just wish she were in town and we could hang out whenever we wanted." Teresa frowned.

"Didn't you say that she was planning to come down for spring break?"

"Yeah. And I'm looking forward to that. She'll be down on Friday night, but I have a story to cover that Saturday so we probably won't see each other then. Hopefully, we can see each other Saturday night or at the very latest Sunday."

"Email her with your idea for plans so you both can have something to look forward to. It's all about the anticipation for more that really helps with long-distance things," added Alex with a smile.

"Thank you, oh wise one." Teresa bowed her head to Alex.

"Oh hush. I'm just worried about you and want this new relationship to have the best chance it can. You've had too many bad relationships for me to be happy for you. I just want you to have the kind of happiness that I've found."

"I'm trying, and if I can deal with the distance issue better than I think this could have a decent chance. The only other thing that has me concerned is that she's thinking about rejoining the army."

Alex looked confused for a moment and asked, "Why would she do that?"

"She said she can work as a nurse, retire from the military, and still be young enough to have a good career in the civilian sector afterward. She thinks it might be the right choice for her and it very well might be. I'm just worried it will keep us as a long-distance couple and I don't want that."

"When does she plan on going in?"

"Not until after she graduates next year. She still has one more year of the nursing program to go through."

"And you're worried about this now why?"

"Like I said, I'm not a fan of this long-distance thing and I would like to know when it's going to end."

"You said that her joining the military is over a year out?"

"Yeah."

"Then what are you worried about? You don't even know if you'll be able to make it a year, and you're worried about this now. Your priorities need to be more focused on the here and now, not a year or more out. It's almost like you're borrowing trouble."

Teresa felt her face warm and she looked away from the screen. "That's a fair point. I just don't want to spend all that time together only for it to fall apart at the end."

"It almost sounds like you want this to be something permanent?"

"I wouldn't mind. When I'm with Kelly we have a great time and it reminds me of how good we were back in high school. You know how Kelly was the standard I held everyone else to."

"I think you're again putting the cart before the horse. How about you see if you can make it at least a month before you start planning out your wedding."

Teresa laughed and said, "I get your point. I'll try to just take it as it comes and not jump to the ending before too much has happened. And maybe you're right and I'm inventing things to be worried over."

"Good. Taking your time is not a bad idea. You always were big on rushing into things, especially relationships, just like you did with this one."

"Hey, I'll have you know that I waited until Kelly asked me." Teresa crossed her arms and glared at the screen.

"And I bet that was incredibly difficult for you as well."

"Shut up."

Alex laughed and Teresa stuck her tongue at her. It was good to have friends that you could talk issues through with. Now if she could only follow through on the advice and stop jumping toward the end.

CHAPTER TWENTY-NINE

Kelly yawned as she drove through the darkness on her way home. She was almost there and looked forward to getting something for dinner and then sleeping. It had taken her longer than she wanted to finish one of her papers and turn it in. Once she had, she was able to gather her things and start the drive home. She had hoped she could have left earlier so she might have the time to see Teresa tonight, but that wasn't happening. She grumbled to herself about that.

This hadn't been a good week for communication. They'd only had one call and the rest of the messages were either by text or email. That was fine because she'd been working so hard on studying for her midterms and writing that damn paper, which didn't get as much focus as she wanted considering that she'd been busy studying for other tests. She certainly paid for it today as she struggled to get everything typed up.

She turned into her parents' neighborhood and let out a sigh as she made her way to the house. As she rounded the corner of the cul-de-sac, she was glad to see there was room for her to park her car next to her mother's. She grabbed her suitcase and backpack before she headed inside. Her mother was still awake and sitting in her usual spot in the living room reading. "Hi, Mom."

Her mother looked up from her book and then glanced at the clock. "Kelly. You're later than I thought you would be."

"It took me longer to finish a paper than I expected. Formatting all the sources I had took a long time as it has to be done just so. But I got it in on time, so that was good."

"Have you had dinner?"

"No, I haven't. I hit the road rather quickly after getting done. I just wanted to get here. I had plans to meet up with Teresa if I got here early enough, but my paper ate up all that free time. Now I just want something to eat and then sleep."

"How have things been with Teresa?"

"They've been going good so far. She came up last weekend and we got to spend the whole time together, which was nice. I'll be able to see her tomorrow evening. I'd see her earlier but she has to cover a story tomorrow morning."

"What story?"

"There's a dog show here in town and she gets to cover it."

"Not the most riveting of stories," commented her mother.

"True, but she's going to do her best because it might lead to more work on the paper than just covering obits and other small blurbs. She certainly has her hopes up that it will lead to better things."

"Really? That would be good for her then."

"I thought so. We're not meeting until the evening so she has the time to go to the dog show and work on her story. She's taking the whole thing very seriously, even asking me not to be there so I don't distract her."

"So, what are you going to do?"

"I'm going to try to sleep in. I don't have to get up early for classes, so I can just catch up on my sleep, because I wasn't getting as much as usual with all the studying and research I was doing. Then I'll start my day. Thankfully, there are no assignments to work on while I'm here. I just get to spend the time relaxing and hanging out with you and with Teresa."

"Well, go grab something to eat. We can talk more after you're done."

"Thanks, Mom." Kelly put together some dinner. There were leftovers in the fridge from something her mom likely cooked that looked good. She ate quickly at the table, then put the plate in the sink and headed back out to the living room where her mom was waiting.

"All better?"

"Yes, Mom. Thank you. It was tasty."

"Good. Now how have you been doing?"

"I'm doing alright. I think about Dad off and on and it often makes me cry. Thankfully, my grief isn't so bad that it gets in the way of my studies, but it's still there like a cloud I'm always under."

"Grief takes time to sort through. It's more like something that scabs over only to open back up if something picks at it, and there are a lot of things that can pick at it. I miss your father so much and the house seems empty without him here." Her mother teared up.

Kelly gave her a hug. Her mom tightened her grip on Kelly for a moment before letting go. "Thank you."

"No problem, Mom. You've hugged me through tough times before and it's only fair to return the favor."

Her mother looked down and sighed. "But I didn't hug you through your transition and for that I'm sorry. I just kept thinking of you before and how much I was going to miss my son. I was grieving for you even though you were right there. I couldn't see the young woman you became. I was just blind to the truth until your father set me straight."

"You got there and that's what matters. I was disappointed for a while because I hadn't really become someone different, just the packaging had changed more than anything else."

"No, that's not exactly right, you did change. You became more open, more expressive, and more you. You never used to be this driven and goal-oriented before, you were more aimless and just took things as they happened."

"Other people have said the same thing. I've tried to make the most of my time now. I just wanted to make you and Dad proud of me."

"Of course we're proud of you. Your dad was so impressed that you wanted to become a nurse and wanted to have a career helping people. I think it's a great career for you, though I was surprised when you enlisted to become a medic. I had half-expected you to join as a regular soldier or something."

"I had no interest in becoming infantry or anything like that. You know I'm thinking of going back, right? I can't remember if I told you or not."

"Well, as long as you put some thought into this that'll be fine. Before you hadn't thought about a career at least you had never mentioned one to me. One of the things I was concerned with was that you never had any plans for the future."

"I know. I'm sorry if I worried you."

"I just want you to be happy and successful in whatever job you decide to get into."

"Thanks, Mom." Kelly yawned. "Oh, I think the lack of sleep is catching up to me."

"You head on up to bed then. Sleep well, Kelly."

"Night, Mom." Kelly headed upstairs and to her bedroom. She quickly changed for bed and then turned the lights out. Her sleep was dreamless and deep.

The morning arrived and Kelly stretched and got ready for the day. Her body was stiff when she woke up and she needed to do something about that. After breakfast, she wanted to get a little bit of exercise and do some thinking. A walk around the neighborhood sounded like just the ticket to her. She put on her shoes and headed out. Her mother was back at work because they had only given her a little bit of time off to grieve, which Kelly thought was horseshit.

After a brief warmup where she stretched her legs and back, she took off down the hill. The walk was nice and loosened her up some, getting rid of the stiffness she felt after waking. It was a nice day for walking considering the weather had warmed and there were clear skies. She was able to turn her thoughts to what she was pondering rather than focusing on putting one foot in front of the other. Her thoughts turned to Teresa as they often did lately.

It was clear to her some of her thoughts and feelings were carry-overs from when they dated before. For all that Teresa was different from back then, she was also very much the same. Kelly's feelings for her reflected that, as she was rather more invested in the relationship than she normally would be this far into one. She wanted to spend as much time with Teresa as possible and see where things took them. Considering that in the past she'd been planning on proposing to Teresa, she had a ring and everything, her feelings were stronger than what she would expect this far in. While part of her loved Teresa and was glad to be back together, another part wanted to be more cautious because she had been hurt before. That internal tug-of-war was hard on her.

Maybe she was being overly sensitive, but she wasn't sure where Teresa stood in terms of their relationship. At first, she seemed all gung-ho for it, but over last weekend Kelly got a few notions that she wasn't pleased with something and was worried if it was her. Maybe they needed to talk some more about them and the long-distance relationship thing. She didn't know, and that was anxiety inducing. It was tough being apart from her and the two-hour drive sucked, but it was nice to be with her whenever they could manage it. She was looking forward to seeing her that evening. Maybe just being together would settle those obvious nerves. After all, it had only been a little over two weeks since they had gotten together, so maybe she was just being overly touchy about all of this.

The drive was a lot but it didn't bother her all that much as she liked the drive time. It gave her time to think or just listen to music. She worked so hard with classes that it was nice to just enjoy a relaxing drive and listen to music. That made a big difference to her. There were times at school where she had just driven around the town for a few hours, to let her thoughts drift as the rest of her was focused on the here and now. Walking also did a similar thing, and she enjoyed that time as well.

There were some concerns on her part because it seemed to her some of Teresa's interest came across as rather shallow, like she had gotten used to just being surface interested in someone rather than go for depth. That wasn't good and she would keep an eye out to see if that was true as all she had now was a feeling. Kelly was interested in taking things as far as they could go, as she was tired of trying to date. She still had the ring she had planned to use to propose to Teresa back in the day, and if things went well, might just use again. But it was way too early to entertain such thoughts. They had just literally gotten back together and she didn't want her past emotions to cloud things. This was a different time around and she wanted to make sure things were going well before she found herself too invested. She wasn't sure that her heart could take being broken again by Teresa.

Honestly, she didn't even know what she was looking for to prove that it was good to get reinvested. Maybe if they made it to the summer. She knew driving back and forth to see each other would wear on them both, but it was the best plan she could think of right now. The other option was to just communicate through phone and email and see if that was enough to sustain their relationship. She was glad they were close enough to even do this. In her mind, it was helping to make them even closer.

The sex was quite lovely and certainly far better than when they had slept together back in high school. They had both fumbled their way through it, which had been embarrassing to both of them. They had rough ideas of what went where thanks to self-study on the topic, but it had been brief and she was fairly certain Teresa had not fully enjoyed herself. Over last weekend, they'd made love until they'd both been too sensitive to continue. It was a great improvement in her mind considering they were able to physically express how they felt about each other and were sure that each of them had fully enjoyed the activity. And based on that, they were doing just fine.

Kelly finished the lap she made of her neighborhood and headed inside. She had thought enough about her and Teresa, and it was getting close to lunchtime. The plan was to contact Teresa around lunch and see how things were going since she should be finished with the dog show by then. She was excited to get to see her this evening and wanted time to hurry up. There wasn't much she could do about that except get a hold of Teresa and see if there was a plan. She would then be able to follow the plan to its logical conclusion and all would be well.

CHAPTER THIRTY

Teresa was exhausted. The dog show started early and ran late. Thankfully she didn't need to be there the whole time but she had stayed long enough to watch some of the agility course runs. Those dogs had been seriously impressive with how fast they moved through the obstacles. She had a number of pictures from that and was sure they would be good enough for the paper. There had been a lot of information available from the people putting on the show and it led to what she thought would be a good story. It surprised her to learn this was the second annual show, and she would certainly mention that. She knew that it hadn't gotten covered last year because she would have remembered that. She had gotten a promise to have the winners of the various categories texted to her so she could include them in the story because she thought people might like that detail.

Part of her just wanted to stay home and rest after the early morning, but Kelly was here and she wanted to spend time with her. She still had her concerns and was looking forward to seeing if being together with Kelly quieted them. The fact that she would be in town for the week was nice and she hoped they could hang out for the majority of it, of course barring work. Work was enough to keep her busy for most of the day, but maybe she could make the most of her evenings.

As it was, she needed to get cleaned up and ready to go out with Kelly tonight. Since she was tired maybe they needed to go out to eat and then just hang out afterward. It would be nice just spending time with each other. She had missed Kelly over the week and the emails and calls helped but didn't take care of that sense of longing for her. All she wanted to do was have Kelly be here with her, was that really too much to ask? Maybe she would be in town over the summer, which would be great. Then they would have over two months to just hang out with each other and see where the relationship took them. It was an appealing thought.

She peeled off her clothes and got into the shower. Her hands smelled a bit like dog as she had petted so many dogs at the event that it was ridiculous. Almost everyone had been okay with her meeting their dogs. There had been nearly a hundred dogs there competing in the various categories, more than she had expected, and it felt like she had petted most of them. This little dog event was more of a big deal than she had expected as it had been well attended. But she didn't want to meet Kelly smelling of dog, so shower time it was.

Baxter didn't appreciate the scent either and stayed away from her, looking confused by the various dog smells she was covered in. That reminded her that she might want to get some treats so Kelly could get onto Baxter's good side when she came over, which might happen tonight. It mattered a great deal if Baxter approved of Kelly, since Baxter had been here longer and she would hate to upset her cat.

It was hard to conceive of Baxter not liking Kelly. If she remembered correctly, Kelly had gotten along great with Tommy, her old cat when she was in high school. She smiled at the memory. Tommy had been an excellent cat and she still missed him. The grief of his loss still touched her and might give her a better handle on dealing with Kelly's grief. She would see what there was to see soon enough. That is if Kelly wanted to come home with her tonight, at least for a little while. Then she could get Baxter's approval or not.

Once she got out of the shower, she got dressed in something comfortable. There was no reason to dress up if they were going to any place in town, which was likely considering they would be going to the diner, or maybe the Italian place again, given how much Kelly had enjoyed it. There was no dress code there so she might as well be comfortable. She felt like having some diner food so would push for that, if Kelly asked for an opinion. Hopefully, Kelly would agree to eating there tonight as it would be just like their date nights back when they were in high school, and taking a comfortable trip down memory lane might be nice.

She looked at the time and realized she needed to get dressed if she was going to be ready before Kelly got there. She already had an idea for what to wear, now she just needed to get dressed. Once she pulled her clothes on, she headed back out to the living room, where she sat at her table and went over her notes from the day's event. The dog show had been interesting and something she never expected to go to let alone enjoy. She was going to make sure it was a great story despite starting the day with no idea what went into a dog show.

There was a knock at the door, and Baxter ran out of the kitchen and stared at the door. "It's okay, Bax. People do come over here."

She opened the door. There was Kelly, smiling at her, waving her phone. "Oh good, I entered your address correctly."

"You were worried about that?"

"I didn't want to get lost in your complex driving around trying to find you. That would have been embarrassing."

"But you found it just fine."

Baxter meowed and Kelly crouched down to get closer and extended her hand toward him. "Who's this?"

"This is Baxter."

Baxter sniffed the fingers before he nuzzled into them. Kelly scratched the top of his head and made appreciative sounds. Baxter turned and headed off to the window to stare outside. Kelly stood back up and said, "He's really cute."

Teresa smiled, pleased that her cat liked Kelly, as that was one less worry to have. She didn't want to deal with her cat disliking her girlfriend. "So, are you ready to head out?"

"Sure. Where do you want to go?"

"I was thinking the diner, as I've been craving their chicken fried chicken all day."

"I may have to get something besides the patty melt."

Teresa looked at Kelly skeptically. "Right. I believe that one. You always got the patty melt."

"Because it's good, but I do like other food as well."

"That's true. You do get noodley moods, as we have already established." Kelly laughed. Teresa grabbed her purse off the kitchen counter and said, "Shall we?"

"Sure."

"Baxter, be good. No wild cat parties." Baxter was still looking outside and ignored her.

Once the door was locked, Kelly asked, "Does he often throw wild cat parties?"

"He did when I left out the catnip bag one time. There was nip everywhere and Baxter was just rolling around in it without a care. It took me a while to clean it all up."

Kelly laughed again, shaking her head. Teresa huffed and said, "It really was a lot of cleanup."

"I can well imagine. That's a great cat you have there."

"He's a good cat. Thanks for noticing."

"I like cats. I also like dogs. I'm generally good with most animals. Well, I don't really like guinea pigs, but that's probably because I've never been around them. They just seem like a big rodent."

"That's good because Baxter and I are a package deal."

"That's perfectly alright."

They got into Kelly's car and headed for the diner. Once she was out of the apartment complex she asked, "So, how was the dog show?"

"It was interesting. I got a lot of good quotes I can use, and I saw a lot of dogs doing agility tests and other things. It was pretty interesting. I was there for several hours getting more information than I can ever write about, so I have my pick of quotes. That's going to make writing it a lot easier."

"What's an agility test?"

"It's basically a doggy obstacle course where the best time wins. Some of those dogs were superfast at it. That was fun to watch. It should be a good article."

"That's nice. Part of me wanted to drop by, but you were clear with the desire to not have me distract you. So I listened to you and hung out with my mom instead."

"Thank you for that." Teresa rested her hand gently on Kelly's thigh. "I get really focused on work and I would have either spent all my time talking to you or all my time ignoring you. Not sure which it would be, but neither would be a good plan."

"That's fair. If you had shown up where I worked, I would also be unsure what to do, at least now. Maybe as things continue, I'll get a better idea of what to do if you visit me at work."

"But you aren't working."

"I meant if you showed up where I'm going to be interning. That would be awkward. How would I explain that to whoever was supervising me?"

"So, you understand then?"

"Yes. I'm glad the story went well. I know you were very concerned with that. So, you're going to write it up tomorrow?" Kelly looked over at her and smiled.

Teresa smiled back. "That's my plan. I have a lot of resources at my desktop at work that would help me process the pictures I took and find a way to tie them to the file. I might be able to get the story done in a few hours and then I can get to work on my usual pieces. I have a few more obits to get to for this coming issue."

"I really hope they decide to use your story."

"I do to. It would mean a lot to me."

The diner was an old restaurant that had been in the town for at least fifty years and had steady business because the food was so good. They were shown to their seats after a very short wait. They took the menus and scanned them. Teresa already knew what she wanted, as it was her usual, and was ready quickly. Kelly was going through the menu looking at most everything. The waitress came and took the drink orders while Kelly was still scanning the menu. Teresa was amused with this. "Having trouble finding something to eat?"

"Yes. Nothing is jumping out at me right now. I still kind of want a patty melt and fries, even though I wanted to try something else."

"There's nothing wrong with getting that, though I will tease you over it."

"Figures. Okay. I'll go with what I know works."

The waitress returned and Teresa just shook her head when Kelly ordered. She smirked at her and said, "I knew you wouldn't try anything else."

"I like a good patty melt, what can I say?" Kelly shrugged helplessly.

"Not much, in all honesty. In some ways you're a creature of habit, but then again so am I. So how were your midterms?"

"Not bad. I think I aced a few of them and did well in a couple of others. The paper I had to turn in took longer than I thought, but I also got it in on time, just closer to the wire than I wanted to be."

"That's good to hear. I wouldn't want you to have class issues just before midterm break."

"Yeah, neither did I. I'm still on track toward graduating with honors if I can keep up my grades. It's a lot of work, but I think it'll be worth it."

"Does that make a difference in the army?"

"No, they won't care what my grades are. They'll make sure I know how to do things the army way."

"The army way?" Teresa looked at Kelly questioningly.

Kelly grinned and said, "Yeah, there is the right way, the wrong way, and the army way."

Teresa giggled. "That sounds ridiculous."

"But very, very true. The army takes its way of doing things very seriously and they drill it all into you until it becomes second nature. I may need to retrain when I get out to learn whatever system the hospital or clinic I work at uses as there are sure to be some differences."

"Well, every place you work has its own way of doing things so I'm not too surprised that the army has its own quirks."

"Too true. I just want to graduate and help as many people as I can. I'm actually looking forward to that."

Teresa smiled at Kelly. "I like this caring part of you."

Kelly's cheeks reddened. "Thank you. I'm just trying to learn and excel at a job that I'm interested in."

"Well, from here it looks like you're doing a good job."

"Thanks." There was a lull in the conversation, that Kelly filled by taking a drink of her water and Teresa just sat there looking at Kelly trying to think of something to say. While the silence was comfortable, Teresa didn't want to just sit there and stare at Kelly, no matter how pretty the view was. Conversation was important.

"So, how's your mom doing?" she finally asked.

"She's fine or at least that's what she said when we talked. She says hi by the way."

Teresa smiled. She had such good memories of the Matheson family. "Your mom is great. I missed both your parents after we broke up because they treated me so well."

"Well, you are pretty nice so I am sure it wasn't a hardship for them." Kelly chuckled.

Teresa scowled at Kelly. "Hey."

"Just teasing you. Yeah, my dad even asked about you before he passed, wondering if I knew what had happened to you. You were a favorite of theirs. None of my other girlfriends ever met them so it's not like there was lot of competition for the position."

"I wasn't aware that it was a competition?"

"It wasn't. Not really. You were one of the best people I ever dated and I'm glad we're giving it another try. Thank you for that."

"You're welcome. And I am also glad we're giving dating another shot. This has been interesting so far."

"Interesting?"

"Yeah, it's been a challenge compared to some of my old relationships."

Kelly furrowed her brows and looked at Teresa with concern. "What's been the challenge?"

Teresa wasn't sure where the concern was coming from and that put her on guard. What was Kelly thinking? "Well, I've never done the distance thing, always had the person be closer and there nearly every day. That's what I've been used to relationship-wise as I've told you. It feels strange to be building that sort of connection through emails or text, and I'm still trying to get the hang of it."

"Has it been too hard?"

Teresa paused and looked at Kelly, noting how focused she had become. She felt a chill go down her back and thought about how she wanted to answer that. Was Kelly having second thoughts? "I'm not sure hard is the right word. It's been tough because we're at the beginning of things and have to deal with this separation. That's certainly not been very easy. It would be much better if we were able to be near each other most of the time as it would make building a relationship easier."

"True. But has it been too hard?" Kelly's eyes were boring into hers. She glanced down at the table and asked softly, "Do you want to back out?"

Teresa sat back in her chair, staring at Kelly in surprise. "Back out? Why would I want to back out? Where is this coming from?"

"I just know that you aren't comfortable with the distance issue, since you've mentioned it several times, and I know you aren't comfortable with my thinking about going back into the army. I would understand if you wanted to stop dating me because of these issues."

Teresa gaped at her. "Where is this coming from? I mean it's not easy, sure, but I'm still interested in being with you. Have I said or done anything that would indicate I wasn't interested?"

A look of relief crossed Kelly's face, and Teresa felt something unclench within her. "That's good. I was afraid that you would take the easy out if it was offered to you. That drive is not a lot of fun, and I could understand not wanting to have to do it multiple times a month."

"It's also not the hardest drive one could do. The roads are good there and back. I was also thinking of getting books on tape to listen to as I drive, so it's not going to be that much of an imposition on my time. Hell, it might even make it enjoyable."

The waitress brought their food. Once she walked away, Kelly said, "I know, but if we're serious about us, we're both going to put a lot of miles on our cars and that's just when we're free to come visit each other. That's a good amount of effort."

"Well, you'll be here over the summer, yes?"

"I'm not sure. I'll check with my mom. I could get an apartment at school, but that's money I don't want to spend. I'm also not sure if I'm going to be taking summer classes or not."

Teresa gave Kelly a look that she hoped conveyed the annoyance she felt at that moment. "You can't make this easy, can you?"

"Sorry. I'm not trying to be too difficult; I just have my school plans mostly mapped out. I'm trying to be honest with you."

"Well, at least you take school seriously."

"I've done really well in my classes so far, making it onto the dean's list for the last several semesters. That certainly has been different compared to high school."

"You really are focused on your classes."

"I don't want to be wasting my time while I'm there. I want to spend my time learning. That's one of the reasons I haven't dated much since I've been up there. I may be a bit too focused on my classes if anything, and failing to have a good time."

"Well, you're dating someone now, and you still seem to be focused. I don't think you're in any danger of that."

Kelly laughed, and Teresa cold see tension drain out of her. "We'll see. It's still early days."

CHAPTER THIRTY-ONE

K elly was sitting in her bedroom looking at a picture on her phone of her and her father. It was still too early to go see Teresa, and she was tired of just doing a lot of nothing. Between the military and school, she was far more used to keeping busy. This actual break was awkward. Staring at her father's picture was the best thing she could come up with, because her thoughts had been turning that way. She was feeling nostalgic and wanted to be reminded of him. The smile on his face made her smile as well.

The picture wasn't making her tear up, which was nice. She missed her father, but her feelings of grief were lightening as time continued and her relationship with Teresa kept developing. She was able to go most of the day without crying, which was an improvement. That wasn't something she enjoyed doing and it threw off her schedule but at least she wasn't fighting the grief. It was taking a lot of time for her to sit with her feelings and not try to bury them like she used to back before transition. She was grieving and had no real idea when that would end, if it ever did. She'd never had to deal with the loss of a parent before and it was all new to her. She certainly didn't like it.

She remembered his smile, just like in the picture. It was a smile that she shared. Looking in the mirror, she could see reminders of her father and her mother, but mostly she had gotten her looks from her father. Kelly lowered her phone and looked at the posters on the wall of her old bedroom. They reminded her of high school, when she would just sit in her room and brood, since she'd always felt a little out of place in her life, but she had never known why that was. Dating Teresa helped her get over the brooding, until after they had graduated and she broke up with her. Then she returned to brooding at least until basic training started and she no longer had the luxury of time for a good brood.

Feeling like this was when she would usually call her father to chat. He usually had plenty of time for her. Now what was she going to do without him? Sighing, she knew she needed to do something before her mood grew worse. She headed downstairs. Maybe talking to her mother would help with her melancholy. It was something she had never really tried.

She found her mother in the family room watching TV. "Hey. Mom."

"What's up, Kelly?"

"I'm just feeling down. I was thinking about Dad again."

"That makes sense. It's not even been a month since he passed. Everything is still fresh. I know that's how it feels with me. I miss him all the time."

"Sorry, Mom. I just miss him. I used to talk to him when I was feeling down and he always managed to cheer me up by the end of the call. I wish he was here so I could do that."

"I miss him as well. The bed is awfully lonely without him there, without his CPAP running. I got used to the sound and now, without it, I don't sleep as well. I feel like something is wrong when I don't hear it. I figure I'll get used to it after a while, but I'm not there yet. It's kind of funny the things you miss."

"Has Carrie come by lately?"

"She was here last weekend. Tim checks on me fairly regularly, which is nice, but I'm not yet old enough that I need to be minded. He's trying to step up and take charge, but he needs to remember I'm not an invalid."

"Never thought that, Mom. On a different subject, what do you think of my idea to re-up with the army? I figured I can serve there until retirement and then get hired at one of the VA hospitals."

"That's not a bad idea. There would be good job security with a nice government job. But you already know these things. Why are you asking me?"

"I wanted more feedback because Teresa isn't thrilled with the idea and it's making her wary of a relationship, or at least that's what it seems like to me. She implied that she doesn't want to invest the time in the relationship if it's just going to stay long-distance when I join up. I don't think it will end up like that so it's hard to understand her point of view."

"I can see her point of view on that. I think it's a valid concern."

"What?" Kelly's eyes went wide.

"She's thinking long term and is feeling unsure with that one bit of information. That's not a good place to be. If you're serious about the military then you need to make sure she doesn't feel unsure about you. If she's dithering over things, you haven't done that. So maybe you need to work on that."

"I keep telling her the decision is at least a year away and that I still have people to talk to before I decide. I want to keep my options open and I'm not sure of the job market in the area. At least I know that the military almost always needs nurses. I've been telling her the truth about what I've been thinking and not trying to hide any of my plans going forward."

"At least a year away is not as comforting as you think. If she has hopes for the two of you, she may already be thinking that far out, at least subconsciously. That ambiguity would make me nervous about where things stood."

Kelly was at a loss, thinking she had been doing the right thing with telling Teresa her thoughts and not hiding the things she'd been thinking about. "Well, how do you think I can help calm her nerves?"

"You need to talk more about where you see each other in this. Like what are your plans for the summer?"

"I was thinking about talking to you to see if I could stay in my room over the summer. I don't have any classes I need to take over the summer and this way I can be here to spend time with Teresa."

"Tell her that. If too much is left nebulous then there's little to keep a person focused. You two are trying to make a long-distance relationship work so maybe you should talk to her about times when you will be close together. That would give her something to look forward to."

"You think that will do it?"

"It couldn't hurt." Her mother shrugged, then took a drink of her water.

Kelly nodded and looked at her phone. Teresa would be getting off work soon and there was a plan to eat at her place tonight and maybe they could talk. She had hoped they would just be able to relax and not have to deal with all sorts of issues surrounding their dating while over spring break. They'd just dodged one issue and now the military was another concern Teresa had. Honestly, if they were still together into the next year, she might seriously consider marrying her, which should take care of the whole issue. Or maybe it wouldn't. She wasn't sure but at last they would be together at that point and could face anything that came that way.

With a shake of her head, she chided herself. She had told Teresa to focus on the now instead of the future, and it was apparently something she needed to pay attention to as well. She was thinking too much of tomorrow rather than today. There was no guarantee they would stay together for anywhere near that long, just a hope. Long distance relationships were hard and took constant work, but the successful ones were strong. It would not do for her to make the same mistake Teresa made. She needed to make her own mistakes.

However, she could try and get something right. Talking to Teresa would be good and she could clarify her thinking, so that they would be on the same page. There was just so much they needed to talk about, and she would rather spend her time kissing or just catching up with the day compared to dwelling on issues. She never found such conversations to be fun, as they always felt like the other shoe or boot was going to drop during them. It might be necessary but never fun.

She shook her head to clear her thoughts. This wasn't something she needed to ruminate over. There were other things she should be doing. She realized it was time to head over to Teresa's apartment. Teresa was planning on cooking dinner for them, which Kelly was looking forward to. She had no idea what the meal was going to be and just hoped it wasn't going to be too much work for Teresa, especially since she would be cooking right after work. She wanted to talk with her and didn't want the cooking to get in the way.

"Mom, I'm going to take off to see Teresa."

"Alright, have fun."

Kelly grabbed her purse and coat and headed out to the car. The drive over to Teresa's apartment was easy and not too terribly far, but then again, nothing in this town was all that far from anything. Everything was pretty much within fifteen or twenty minutes from her parents' house, and that included Teresa's apartment complex. Once she got there, she searched for a parking spot close to Teresa's apartment. It took a bit but she found one.

She knocked on the door and waited. She heard a faint voice call out from within, "Coming."

Teresa opened the door and smiled once she saw who it was. "Great, you're here. Dinner is nearly done."

"What is it?"

"It's just some baked chicken and roasted vegetables. I have it a lot. I'm a bit better than just a basic cook, but simple and basic food is what I'm best at. I've never been good at anything too fancy."

"Sounds good to me. I'm more of a subsistence level cook myself, so this is better than I could do. I excel at reheating and cooking things that have directions on the box."

Baxter was sitting next to a window looking out and turned to look at Kelly before dismissing her and turning back to scan the outside. Kelly sat on the couch. She must have looked pensive because Teresa asked, "Are you okay?"

"I've just been thinking."

Teresa turned from the kitchen and looked over at her, eyes narrowed in concern. "About what?"

"Us. I want you to feel that I'm committed to us. I know I talk about joining the military a lot and that you don't really get it. I don't want that to make you miss how I feel about you."

"I don't get it, but it's your life." Teresa shrugged.

"Thank you, but I also don't want you to be out of the loop like you were when we were in high school. I never talked to you about my plan to join up then, and given that I was planning on proposing to you, it wasn't fair to you."

"I'm aware you're thinking about this. I may not understand your reasoning, but you do, and it's your career. I have no intentions of getting in your way."

"You were talking about not wanting to waste your time if circumstances are going to break us apart. That concerned me, and I've been mulling it over ever since. I want you to know that I'll do my best to keep that from happening. I think we're doing okay so far. We're getting better at the distance dating, and I plan on being in town all summer, which should give us a lot of time together."

"You've said as much before. Why are you telling me this again?" Teresa narrowed her eyes in concentration, clearly trying to follow her point. "And did you just say you're going to be here all summer?"

"Uh… Yes, that's my plan right now. I want you to know I'm committed to us, to making us work. And that means taking more time to think about my military plans rather than rush off over the summer."

"I didn't think you weren't committed. You're the one who knows more about distance relationships than I do, and that has helped me be okay with the whole situation. I'm not sure what you're saying or why."

Kelly took a moment to make her point clear in her own head. She thought she'd been doing well but apparently wasn't being as clear as possible. Maybe she needed to slow things down and explain things in smaller chunks and not broad swaths. "My mom made it clear to me that my talking about my plans might be taken as not being serious about us. I am serious about us. I wouldn't have asked you out if I weren't. Just know that I will consult with you on any plans I make in the future so you won't be blindsided by any choice I make about my future."

"Okay. Thank you. That does help. Now come help me set the table."

Kelly joined Teresa in putting the plates and utensils out. Teresa's phone alarm went off signaling the food was ready. Once they were served and seated at the dining room table, Teresa said, "I do feel better with you explaining that, but I'd already come to terms about you and the military. I feel like you've been worried about this over nothing. I took to heart that I should focus on us now rather than worry about next year."

"I caught myself with that as well. I guess we're both looking for something more out of our relationships."

"I do want us to succeed and I'm not sure what else we can do right now except just keep going."

"That's true. I just want us to be happy, so I fret over things." Kelly shrugged.

"I do the same. I guess we both want things to work out."

"That should count for something. Right?"

"I think it does. It makes me feel better about us. And I think that with all this conversation things down the line might just go well. At least that's my thinking."

Kelly filled the silence with some of her dinner. "Well then, maybe we need to stop fretting over challenges and focus on other things."

Teresa set down her fork and smiled at Kelly, her eyes bright. "What did you have in mind?"

"Just having fun together this week and see if that leads to us doing a better job keeping in touch with each other for the rest of the semester."

"That makes sense. I'm concerned about coming up to see you because they liked my story and I might get tasked with covering more weekend events. That would certainly eat into my time with you and mean that you would need to drive down more."

"If that happens, we'll work it out. That's not exactly a deal breaker."

"I just don't want you to think I don't want to do my share of the driving."

"Work is work. It's not like you can just say no to them. Besides, it might not be every weekend so that would free you up."

"So, I drive up to see you on the weekends I can?"

"That works for me. I don't mind the drive that much because it allows me time to just think and relax. I don't get that a lot on campus."

"Do you want to stay with me when you come down? I have that nice queen-sized bed." Teresa waggled her eyebrows suggestively.

Thinking about the other night when they used said bed, Kelly felt her cheeks warm. That had been lovely and she felt tempted to say yes. But she was still holding back. "Maybe not at first, as I'm happy spending time with my mom. I just want to make sure she isn't too lonely."

"That's probably fair. But know that you're welcome to stay with me whenever you want. I'm happy to share my space with you."

"Thanks. That means a lot to me."

"You mean a lot to me and the thought of waking up next to you does have a great appeal."

Kelly thought about that, just being able to spend all their time together. It was a wonderful idea, but she was going to stick to staying with her mother for now. "Maybe over the summer I could stay with you for some of the time. That could be good."

Teresa beamed at her, clearly pleased with the idea. "I'll hold you to that."

"Good. It would be nice, and at that point I won't be as worried about my mom. It will have been months since my dad's passing and she'll probably be doing about as well as she can be."

"How is she doing? How are you doing?" Kelly could hear the concern in Teresa's voice and it warmed her heart.

"She says she's doing fine. She misses my dad and is trying to adapt to a quieter house. I'm doing mostly okay. I've been missing him, as I talked to him about all of the plans I had. He helped me figure out what I wanted to do with my life. Now I have to figure out who to talk to about those things. Today was with my mom and that wasn't bad."

"That has to be rough on both of you. Are you talking to your mother more?"

"Yes. She allowed me to come to the funeral dressed as myself and that was nice. For a while there she didn't want me to show up to the house as myself, but rather playing that I was still a boy. Some issues with my sister and aunt over my being me, but you were there for some of that and got to enjoy. It's still a work in progress, but things are getting better."

"Well, you can always talk to me about things. I'm willing to listen and give feedback." Teresa took a drink of her water and then smiled at Kelly.

"Thanks. I just want to have some time where I'm not grieving. With you it's easier to focus on the here and now, but when I'm alone I deal with a lot of issues." Kelly frowned, thinking of all the things she had been brooding over recently. Sure, not all of it was her father, but thoughts of him seemed omnipresent.

"That's to be expected. Your dad just died a little while ago. I figure you're going to be grieving at least until the summer. Maybe longer."

Kelly nodded. "That's probably right. The military taught me a little about how to deal with grief so I could help troubled soldiers but not all that much, and my nursing classes haven't touched on that topic either. Learning this firsthand rather than having more of a clue is not fun."

"Yeah, but it's not like anyone teaches you this stuff. It just sort of happens." Teresa smiled gently at her.

"Yeah… I just wish I knew things that could make the pain and loss less, you know? I was doing fine in school and now I'm concerned I might not be doing as well as I was. Since so much of my focus is on my classes, this distresses me."

Teresa quirked an eyebrow. "You think you might be doing badly in class?"

"Yes, no, I don't know. I just know that it isn't as easy to focus on class work as it used to be."

"You need to give yourself some grace. You're dealing with some pretty serious stuff and that can shake anyone's focus."

Kelly sighed. "I guess you're right. I should try to be nicer to myself."

Teresa put down her fork and sat there looking at Kelly with a soft smile. "I think you've been doing fine so far in that area. You've told me about all the classwork you've been doing so you're probably not doing as bad as you fear. I mean how do you think you did over the midterms?"

"I think I did okay. I at least knew all the answers on the tests or so I believe," replied Kelly, thinking back over the tests. "I'm more worried about the paper which took me longer to get done than I thought it would. Some of that was formatting issues, but some of it was just getting my ideas down in an orderly manner."

"Well, you'll find out when you go back to classes next week how you did, so I wouldn't stress over it now. It's not like you can do anything to change the results at this moment."

"That's true. I would much rather focus on us here and now over my classes. This is supposed to be a break so I can enjoy spending time with you and let my brain rest."

"So, what do you want to do to rest your brain tonight?"

Kelly thought about it before she took another bite of her chicken. "We can watch something and see what happens."

"You have to go home tonight, right?" asked Teresa, looking at Kelly speculatively.

"Right, but that's not for hours now. Right now, I just want to spend time with you and enjoy myself. That is at least the plan I was thinking of. Are you good with that?"

"I'm sure we can find something to watch. And there are other ideas we can try to get your brain turned off if necessary."

Kelly blushed a little at the insinuation. It was something she wanted to do as well but was always pleased when it was also on Teresa's mind. Being on the same page regarding their sex life was a good thing as far as she was concerned. She grinned at Teresa and almost purred out, "That could be a lovely diversion."

"Well, once we clean up from dinner, perhaps we can get to that."

CHAPTER THIRTY-TWO

It had been a week since Kelly returned to school, and Teresa was busy with work. She missed Kelly dearly and found it easier to text with her than it was to call, as she was usually tired in the evenings and just wanted to veg in front of the TV. Typing was just so much less effort and she could have enough time to think of something. She now knew she would have her weekend free to go up and see Kelly, and that was something to celebrate. Also, her story about the dog show was well received and she had gotten some new responsibilities at work. It came with an official pay raise and everything. There was a lot of positive news to share.

She finished her dinner, fed Baxter, and then got out her laptop so she could video chat with Kelly. First, she grabbed her phone and texted her to make sure she had free time to chat. It wouldn't do if she interrupted a lot of studying. She typed: *You free?*

After a few minutes her phone buzzed and she saw the message: *Yes.*

Want to video chat?

Sure

Teresa started her laptop and pulled up her video chat. It made some noise as it was trying to establish a connection and then the screen popped up with Kelly. She grinned at her, her heart feeling lighter when she saw her. "Hey there."

Kelly returned the grin. "Hey there yourself. A video chat was unexpected."

"I got some good news today and I wanted to share it," explained Teresa. "The editor loved the dog show piece and got some positive comments about it. That means that they decided to offer me a different position. The promotion I was hoping for went through. I get to cover more stories now."

"That's great, Teresa. I'm proud of you. From what you've told me it's long overdue." Kelly applauded a little.

"Well, I think it's overdue, but I'm not sure the editor does. I'm just happy that my write-up of the dog show was good. I was worried the story wouldn't be interesting enough."

"Why not? Dog shows sound like they could be interesting and who doesn't like dogs. You told me as much when we talked."

"At least I won't be covering the city council. I've heard those meetings are really boring. I'm not sure I want to cover those, but I will if I have to."

"Not a fan of politics?"

"More that I've heard they aren't all that interesting. They cover such lovely topics as zoning issues, taxes on gas, and other things like street repair and such. But they do it in the driest manner possible."

"Well, it's still important information for people to know."

Teresa nodded. "True. It is important. I just want to cover interesting stories."

"I'm sure you'll do fine with whatever you cover."

"Thanks. I'm just nervous about what they're going to find for me to do. I don't want to cover simple fluff pieces, but that's likely what I'm going to do, probably for a while. At least it's better than just doing obits and little blurbs about things."

"If I remember correctly, you covering an obit is what led us to getting together. That's not a bad thing." Kelly winked at her.

Teresa smiled and she felt a warmth blooming inside. "That's true. I'm still glad I decided to come to the service to see you. One of the best decisions I've made in a while."

"Same here." Kelly smiled at her. "It was certainly a surprise and not something that I expected when I woke up that day, that's for sure."

"What did you expect?"

"Just to go memorialize my father and bury him. Spend the day trying not to fight with my siblings. You know, the usual." Kelly's smile faded and she looked introspective. "I miss him."

"I'm sure you do. I'm sorry."

"It's okay. There is nothing for it. He passed away." Kelly forced a grin that didn't touch her eyes.

Teresa wanted to change the tone of things but was unsure what she could say. Maybe if she turned to plans for the future, build some anticipation for things to come, that would help Kelly's mood. "So, what sort of things do you want to do come summer?"

"I don't know. Maybe do some more hiking, because that was a lot of fun. And the pool is never a bad idea. There are options we can look at. Hell, we can even take a trip if you have the vacation days. I'm not sure where, but there are places around here that are only a three- to four-hour drive."

"I do have some vacation days coming up that I could use. That could be fun. We'll have to figure out a where to go that's not too far, because I don't want to drive too far."

"That could be a blast and it gives me something to think about besides my classes. We can talk about where to go later, after we've looked into the various options. I'm doing well, and my midterm grades were all good, even in the class I was worried about."

"That's great. I know you were stressed about that."

"I was. Thankfully, I didn't fall behind in my classes, despite there being a few days where I didn't go to classes. It was right after I found out my dad had passed and I just couldn't care about going or doing anything. I was mostly in my head thinking about what I had lost."

"That's understandable. I probably would try to get out of work if that happened to me, at least for a few days."

Kelly seemed to shake herself and offered up a brief smile. "Right. I don't want to get too maudlin. I don't cry as much as I did right after my mom's call but still enough. My grief is getting more bearable, which is good news. The weight doesn't seem as crushing as before."

"That is good news. I've been worried about you." Teresa gave Kelly a gentle smile.

"Really?"

"Yeah. I was concerned your grief might have been too much. I didn't want you to be overwhelmed with no one to turn to."

"I was worried about that as well, honestly. I guess everyone goes through that when they lose someone, because the emotions are just so strong. I'm glad that I had several things to keep me from fixating on my loss, like wanting to keep up with my classes. Life goes on whether or not we want it to. In a way, school and you helped me make it through all that."

"By keeping you distracted?"

"Yes. That certainly helped, but it also showed me that life kept going. In a lot of ways my dad was my best friend. We talked a lot and he helped me through so many difficult challenges. I'm not sure what to do without him, but I'm talking more with my mom and I have you, which is good. You usually have pretty good advice. It's just a lot of adjustment."

"I'm glad. And I'm more than happy to talk with you almost any time about most anything. It's nice." Teresa was serious about that. It was nice to talk to Kelly, about anything. Talking made her feel closer to her and deepened the sense of connection, of intimacy, they were building. "So, anything else exciting going on at school?"

"There've been some good basketball games, but I mostly heard about those as I didn't go. You know I mostly stay in and watch movies when I'm not studying. I'm a homebody for the most part. No wild and crazy parties for me."

"You're no fun. How am I supposed to learn more about you if you don't talk about different things?"

Kelly sighed heavily. "Fine. That's a valid point. Sorry."

"So, you've done nothing fun?"

"Well, the LGBT group on campus met up last Wednesday and it was fun. Ended up going as a group to a restaurant afterward, which was nice. We went to a Mexican place and shared a pitcher of margaritas."

"That sounds fun. Didn't you say that you tried to date people from there?"

"Yeah, none of them worked out because I was a little too focused on school and sort of forgot about them in all the studying. It wasn't a good thing on my part. I can get obsessed over things sometimes and that creates a challenge. I apologized to them and I'm trying to do better now. Thankfully, we were able to remain friends as that might have made going to the group really awkward."

"I haven't felt forgotten. You call me often enough."

"I also have a Post-it note on my desk to remind me to call or text you. This seems to be mostly a school thing, and I hope I get past it when I get out of school. No one wants to get forgotten over a hyper-fixation on something like classes."

"Is this a new development?"

"Kind of. In the military, I was focused on things in classes but was much better about letting it all go after work. I think I'm being so obsessive about my classes because there is out-of-class work that needs to be done and I don't want to fall behind."

"I'm sure it's not bad. Were you avoiding something about your dates and chose to focus on school rather than face them?" Teresa was honestly interested in the answer to that.

Kelly looked thoughtful for a minute, and then nodded. "There may be some truth to that. Things felt off in those other relationships, and I'm not a fan of conflict so I may have hidden in my schoolwork rather than have important conversations. I'm not particularly proud of that."

"That's better to hear than you getting hyper-fixated on things and forgetting people exist. That would be a much more difficult thing to overcome."

"Good point. I will try to let you know if things are bothering me before it comes to that. I don't want to do the same to you."

"Thank you. And I'll try to be aware you might just turtle up if things are going bad."

"What about you? Any bad habits I need to be aware of?"

Teresa thought about it for a moment and realized what one of her bad habits was. She looked down and mumbled, "I stress buy."

"What?"

"I stress buy. Yeah, if I'm overly stressed, I have to buy things so I feel better. I've gotten better about it compared to how I was in college, but it's still not great. Not the best use of money and credit cards."

"What sort of things do you buy?"

"All sorts of things. I used to go to the mall and spend a lot on random things, often times small things that didn't use up all my money. I ended up giving a lot of it away, because they were things I didn't need, like an under-the-bed shoe organizer. I'm not into shoes so there wasn't a lot of need for it and it was just taking up space. It went to a good home though. I also bought cool tech toys, like a laser range finder which I had absolutely no need for. I played with it for one weekend and then never touched it again. I gave that away as well. I try to keep it to stuff I can use, but if things are bad and I'm really stressed, all bets are off."

"Wow…that is not what I expected. I bet Amazon loves you."

"They probably do. I used to binge stuff from there when I first moved back here for work and I didn't really know anybody besides some of our classmates. I'm not proud of it, but almost every paycheck has to deal with some random purchase or another. I even have a section of my budget earmarked for random buys." Teresa blushed. It was embarrassing to admit and something that Kelly should be aware of if they were going to be together. Money issues were never a good thing for a relationship.

"Have you talked with a therapist about this?"

"Yes, and it's helped. I don't buy things nearly as often, which my paycheck appreciates, but it still happens now and again. For all that I enjoyed college, it wasn't exactly stress free which is probably why it was so bad back then."

"I completely understand. It's a lot of work and that's not even considering juggling school and free time."

"I didn't do great with that, but I got better. But there you go, one of my most problematic bad habits."

Kelly laughed before grinning at her. "We are both pretty messed up."

"Like you don't have more issues floating around, and same here. I'm not sure anyone gets out of childhood free of such things."

"Well, so far, our issues seem to be playing nice together. Which is a bonus."

Teresa laughed. "That's one way to put that."

"I'm sure we'll find more things in both the positive and negative categories the longer we stay together. Hopefully, if we stay together long enough, we'll get to see if our issues aggravate each other." Kelly smirked.

"You make living together sound so very comfortable."

"It's supposed to be comfortable from everything I hear. But who knows? Maybe you won't like how I brush my teeth or wear socks in the winter or something."

Teresa cocked an eyebrow and looked at Kelly intently, trying to figure out what she meant. "Do you brush your teeth oddly?"

"Not that I can tell. I just brush my teeth." Kelly snickered. "I just know that our little quirks might not entirely mesh together because that has been an issue in one of my relationships."

"Well, maybe your staying with me for a while over the summer will help with that and we can see if that happens."

Kelly was quiet for a moment, her eyes moving over Teresa's face. "Are you serious about that?"

"Why not? We've talked about it before, and I think we can make it work. I know it won't be for long, since you have to go back to school, but I think we'll both enjoy it. I'll want you to be close to me because I miss you most of the time. Where else can I get this high quality of conversation?"

"Almost anywhere?"

"Not hardly. Being able to have good conversations with someone is one of the big things I look for in a relationship, because you should be friends with your partner as well as lovers. You and I have always had good conversations and that hasn't changed no matter how much you changed."

"We've always connected well, and I've always felt like I could say pretty much anything around you."

"Same. It's one of the things I missed the most after our breakup, the ability to say anything. Some of the women I dated never meshed well into my conversations. That was the reason some of my relationships were one-night stands or several-night stands, because we couldn't just talk. In the end we had nothing in common."

"Glad you had some standards," teased Kelly.

"Well, you were a tough act to follow. The longest relationship I was in was six months. We meshed well, had good conversations, but she wasn't looking for anything long term and I was. We parted as friends, but I missed her for the longest time. She was the best relationship I had in college."

"So, we've both been unlucky in love?"

"You too?"

"Well, yeah. Most of the women I dated before I came out were trying to find military husbands and I wasn't planning on that. And afterward, there were a few dates but nothing to write home about. And like I said, school love just never found me, not that I was really looking. Nothing ever lasted more than three months tops, so you have me beat in that department."

Teresa laughed and shook her head. "What a pair we are."

"Maybe we can manage to break that six-month streak you had."

Teresa smiled brightly at Kelly. That was a lovely thought. "I'm looking forward to that."

"And I think I'll check with my mom to see if she needs me to be there over the summer or if staying with you is workable. You know doing that will make the separation of me heading into my last year harder?"

"True, but after nearly three months with you, we'll know if this can work long term or not. If so, then I think I might find it easier to deal with the distance."

"You think so?" Kelly quirked an eyebrow in question.

"I'm fairly sure of it. We may miss calls and forget to text all the time, but we're still hanging on. I think if we can have the summer together then we'll be able to see if we have what it takes to actually make a longer term go of this. I for one believe we'll make it."

"I am looking forward to that. I am fairly certain my mom will be fine with this new arrangement, and I like this plan. You never know, maybe this will push us to the breaking point?"

"Why? Because of the weird way you brush your teeth?" They both chuckled. Teresa shrugged. "And you know, maybe it'll do that, but either way we'll know how we do in a more serious and intense setting. And I really want to know if we can make this work because I'm starting to fall hard for you, Kelly."

Kelly blushed and lowered her head. "Same here. I hated that we broke up after high school, but I think it was probably for the best. Now we're together as more complete versions of ourselves and I think there may be something there."

"Good, because I want this to work. I'm tired of trying to find love in this little town. We need to get together so you can sweep me off my feet and carry me out of here."

"Carry you out of there? Like something from a movie?"

"You're strong enough to do that right?" Teresa wondered just how strong Kelly was. She was very fit and that was rather attractive in her opinion. Could Kelly lift her and carry her away?

Kelly pondered the question a moment before she said, "Possibly. But I thought you liked living there."

"I think I settled for here because I couldn't figure out any other place to go. I wasn't brave enough to strike out for the unknown. You and I might be able to find a different place to call ours when it comes to it."

"It'll mean starting at the bottom of another paper."

"Yeah, but that whole possibility is also at least over a year away, so I'm not too worried about that. Right now, I'm looking forward to the summer and you coming to live with me. That sounds like it will be amazing." Teresa smiled at the idea of waking up next to Kelly day after day. Maybe she would even be able to learn how she took her coffee in the mornings. Besides just black or was it with a little sugar?

"You know… I won't be completely moving in since I won't have all my stuff with me. I'll probably just bring what I think I need and leave the rest at my parents' house."

"That's good because I'm not sure there's room in this apartment for anything more. I already have a lot of stuff in here and fitting in more things would be really tough."

Kelly snickered. "As long as you're sure there's room for me and some of my clothes, I think it will work out. We can work out the details as we get closer to the summer."

"Great. I'm looking forward to this. This will be a lot of fun." Teresa was almost bouncing in excitement over having Kelly there with her.

"Me too. Well, it's getting late and I have class tomorrow. Are you free this weekend, or do you have another story to cover?"

"I'm free this Saturday so I'm planning on coming up to see you, but I'm covering something next Saturday so that will be a busy weekend."

"Okay. I'll come on down the next Saturday then. That way you have something to look forward to Saturday night."

Teresa smiled at Kelly, happy that things were starting to work out. "I like that idea. See you then."

The chat window closed and Teresa just stared at it. She now had plans for the summer that worked well with her plan to get closer to Kelly. That should be lovely. It would be better than what she had originally thought would be happening over the summer, which was working in the heat with only Baxter to welcome her home. She was starting to fall for Kelly and she was seriously thinking it might be turning into love.

CHAPTER THIRTY-THREE

Kelly was hurriedly packing the last of her stuff so she could get out of there. She'd already confirmed she was getting the same room next year so she was able to put a good deal of her stuff into storage in the basement. The semester felt like it had gone slowly, between schoolwork and talking to Teresa and driving back home each week, the time seemed to drag on forever. But it also felt like it had flown by because she was always busy. Now she was headed back home and to Teresa.

Her mom had been understanding of the plan for her to stay with Teresa over the summer. She told Kelly that she was rooting for them. Kelly had plans to go visit her mother regularly and help out as needed around the house. It should work out well, because she was interested to see how she and Teresa managed to live together. Three months were certainly enough time to make each other crazy with their quirks and ways of doing everything. Kelly didn't think she was too difficult to live with, but then again how would she know?

The room looked like it was supposed to, bare and nearly empty, with just the furniture there. Moving out was always rough, but she felt a sense of accomplishment getting things packed up and away. She could finally head back home. She just needed to get the RA to sign off on things and she could go. The last thing she wanted was to be charged for leaving the room a mess. The RA came to her room, which was mostly cleared out as well. She looked up at Kelly and asked, "Are you done?"

"Yep, just have to take my last few bags down to the car. It's ready for you to check."

The process didn't take long. Soon Kelly had handed in her room key and was riding the elevator to the ground floor. She had done well in her classes and ended the semester again near the top of her class. That made her feel good. While she was excelling in her classes, she was also looking forward to being done with school. Getting out there and going to work sounded good to her. She was still mulling over what she wanted to do when she graduated, and she figured she would be debating it over the summer and maybe into the fall semester. There were options and she wanted to choose the one that suited her best. And she would take the time to gather other people's opinions on the matter as well.

But right now, she didn't have any classes hanging over her and was on her way back home. In roughly two hours she would be at Teresa's apartment. Then her summer would officially begin. She grinned as she walked to her car, the last few bags in her hands. She sat in the driver's seat a minute and thought over the semester, losing her dad, finding Teresa, and starting to date her. It had been hectic and a lot to take, but she'd made it through.

She wanted to get going so she could be back in plenty of time to see Teresa right after she got off work. If she made really good time, she might even drop by to see her mother for a little bit before heading over. It all depended. She sent her mother a text saying she was leaving, and then the same message to Teresa, then she headed home.

The drive was lovely this time of year. The sky was clear and there wasn't a lot of traffic. She had music playing as she drove, making the trip more pleasant. Kelly thought about the coming months where she would be living with Teresa and that made her smile. They had handled the long-distance part of their relationship rather well the last half of the semester. All in all, while they hadn't managed to see each other every weekend, they had managed to see each other for most of them. Talking via text or video chats had helped them share in each other's daily activity and thoughts. They were now about as close as they had been right before the breakup after high school.

Life was going well and she was happy. That was what mattered most to her, the happiness. She hadn't realized it before, but it honestly felt like she'd just been serving time, focusing on work to the exclusion of living. Now she was living and it felt great. Sure, she had to work more efficiently as some of her free time was spent talking to Teresa, but that helped with her classes rather than hindered them. Her thoughts were on these good things as she drove, making the miles roll by easily.

She sang along to the radio, and the mile markers told her how close she was getting. She was only twenty miles from home. Her mood improved. The two-hour trip had flown by and now she could meet Teresa getting home from work. While she didn't need help carrying in her stuff, she wouldn't turn down any help Teresa offered. She hadn't made enough time up that she could go see her mother, but that was fine. She could do that tomorrow. Afterall, there was a whole summer to do such things.

When she got to the apartment complex, she noticed Teresa's car wasn't there yet. With a sigh, she grabbed her bags and headed inside. Baxter ran up and then stopped when he noticed who it was. She smiled down at the cat and said, "Hello, Baxter."

The cat ran into the back of the apartment. Kelly sighed. "Sorry, Baxter."

She took her luggage to the bedroom at the end of the hall, leaving her laptop bag in the living room. There was supposedly some room in the closet and in the dresser for her clothes, so she looked for that. She had another bag in the car she had to bring in and then she could fully unpack. She set that bag on the bed and started unpacking. One bag was finished and she was working on the second when she heard the door open. Teresa called out, "Kelly, are you here?"

"I'm in the bedroom."

Teresa came into the bedroom, with Baxter weaving around her feet. Teresa smiled at her. "I see you got here in one piece."

"Yeah, the drive was easy. Check-out took time, but that meant I got here closer to when you got off work rather than sit around waiting. I haven't been here long."

"Oh good. I didn't want you to be here alone too long, especially on your first day here." She hugged Kelly tightly and kissed her cheek before she let go.

Kelly smiled. This day kept getting better and better. "I'm glad I'm here."

"I figured we could go out to eat to celebrate the end of your semester."

"That would be great. I'm getting hungry. Lunch was a while ago."

"Let me help you put your stuff away and then we can go. But first let me feed Baxter. This is usually his dinner time, and he can get rather impatient if he's not fed." She headed for the kitchen, the cat following behind.

Kelly shook her head at the cat's antics and finished up her task. Soon her clothes were away and she headed back to the living room. Teresa was washing her hands and Baxter was working on his supper. "You ready?"

"Yep. Let me grab my purse."

They headed out to the cars and Teresa asked, "You in a noodley mood or do you want to hit the diner or something else?"

"I could easily be in a noodley mood. I'm often in a noodley mood to be honest. That sounds good to me."

"Then we'll go get some pasta. It's a celebration for you after all so we can go somewhere you want."

"Excellent." Kelly beamed.

"Did you let your mom know you made it here okay?" Teresa asked.

"I called her after I got here. She knows I made it safe." Kelly got in and buckled herself in place.

"That's good. No need to make her worry."

"Nah. She has Carrie for that." Kelly chuckled over how true that was. Carrie was on a new boyfriend and all the drama that brought. She was sure her mother would fill her in on all the details when she went over to see her later in the week, not that she wanted to know. Carrie's romantic choices were rarely something she considered important. Teresa pulled out of the spot and headed toward the restaurant.

"Really? Is she still mad at me?"

"Apparently, she's still pissed that you hurt me because of something she said to you back when we were dating. She can really hold on to a grudge."

"You know I was planning on breaking up with you already when she told me about your plan to propose. It sped up the timetable."

"I know that, since you've mentioned it before, but I don't think Carrie knows that. It's kind of sweet of her in an annoying sort of way."

Teresa laughed lightly and said, "Have you told her that?"

"Are you kidding me. I want to remain alive. She would be super grumpy if she found out I thought that and would find some way to get her revenge. I might tell her when she's calmed down more about me."

"Is the truce still holding?"

Kelly nodded. "So far. Carrie and Tim have been nicer to me every time I've seen them, so that's something. I can tell Carrie is only doing it to please our mother, but it's better than nothing. Maybe if she does it long enough it'll just be the way she acts."

"Good. I'm glad things are getting better in your family. You told me quite a bit about the issues there."

"I'm sure the truce will be tested over the summer, as I haven't been living here for years. I'm sure that means my mom is going to expect family dinners and other fun and exciting plans."

"Like you're going to hate that."

"Are you kidding? I'm planning on dragging you along with me, which will be nice for me but maybe not so nice for you. Especially if Carrie just keeps sniping at you. Besides, my mom will be pleased to see you again."

"I have no problem with that. I like your mom."

Kelly felt herself relax even more. She'd worked hard on her finals and now coming home to this very normal situation made her feel better. They pulled into the parking lot of the Italian place. Kelly grinned, "I think I'm going to go for the carbonara again. That was really tasty the last time I had it."

"You always get that," teased Teresa.

"I do not." Kelly huffed . "Last time we ate here we had the pizza. So there."

"Fine. You and your damn noodles."

"There is nothing wrong with noodles. They're a perfectly acceptable food source. You're just jealous because I get to enjoy such tasty noodles while you stick to eating sauced bread."

"I can't believe you would call pizza just sauced bread. That is sacrilege. Pizza is one of the best types of food there is."

Kelly started laughing and smiled softly at Teresa. She then said, "I love you."

Kelly's eyes snapped wide as she realized that was her out loud voice. Teresa blinked a few times as if she were trying to process what she'd just heard. She gave Kelly a soft smile before she asked, "Did you mean to say that?"

Kelly nodded, surprised at herself. "Well, technically it slipped out, but yeah, I meant to say that. I love you."

"I love you too." Teresa gave her a big hug and a quick kiss on the lips. "I was trying not to rush it too much, but well…"

Kelly felt her cheeks warm and looked off to the side. "I'm sorry it took so long to say."

"No need to apologize. I think we're both taking our time, between us being long distance and our history. Neither of us wanted to get in over our heads too quickly. I think you happened to say it at just the right time."

"Well, we're here now and I love you. I can honestly say that I'm looking forward to this summer and all the fun we're going to have. I'm sure it's going to be tough to leave in the fall."

"That's all part of my cunning plan." Teresa laughed manically. "I want you to lament leaving."

Kelly laughed and shook her head. "Well, we'll see how that goes. I'm okay with that if it comes to it. Missing you might make my last year harder overall, but I'm sure that I'll deal with it."

"I'm sure you will. You're focused on your goal and that's admirable. You'll make a great nurse."

"Thank you. That's what I'm hoping for."

"Well, if I get a summer cold, I expect you to care for me."

"Of course I will, as long as I don't get it as well."

"Oh, well then who would take care of you?"

"You would."

"But if I have it as well…" Teresa trailed off.

"Then we both suffer and try to help each other through it all."

"You have a plan for everything?"

"I try to be prepared. If we're both sick we both need to care for each other as best we can. It's only fair."

"I can agree to that. We'll have to figure out a way to split the chores."

"Since I won't be working, I can get a lot of them. That way I can pay my way through labor. Are you sure you don't want me to pitch in on rent and utilities? It wouldn't be a problem. I can pay my fair share."

"I don't want you to pay because then I would need to put you on the lease. As it is, they're okay with you staying because I explained to them that you're only staying for the summer and there's no reason to put you on the lease for a few months."

"Well, so long as you're sure. If I can help out financially, you'll tell me."

"Absolutely. Ah, the joys of domestic bliss. Deciding over chores and money. It's a glimpse of our future." Teresa smiled and had a drink of her water.

Kelly chuckled a little. "Maybe. So long as we both get to contribute then."

"Well, I'm good with you floating right now because it's summer break and you're still a college student. But as a nurse, I figure you can pay your way pretty easily."

"Since nurses generally get paid pretty well, I can happily do that. Besides, who knows what our situation will be at that point."

"True, but it will probably be lovely." Teresa grinned at Kelly who smiled back at her. "We have plenty of time to get there and see how everything goes. Initially, I wasn't sure we were going to make it, because I'd never had a long-distance relationship. We did it though, and this summer is our reward for making it through."

"This is a celebration of many things, I think. We made it past the first hard part. I'm sure it'll be tough on both of us when I go back to school because we'll both want to see each other more. But we're doing better than I was afraid of early on. I wasn't sure how we were going to do it, but we did. I'm so glad we made it work."

"Me too. And I hope you aren't too tired, because I have plans for you once we get back home."

"I think I can be convinced to follow your plan." Kelly waggled her eyebrows, which made Teresa laugh.

"Goof."

"Yeah, and you get to experience the goof for yourself for three months."

Teresa made her voice sound extra posh. "Hopefully, you won't be too distracting."

"I seriously hope I distract you, at least in a good way."

"You do. I'm glad you're here. I've been counting down the days."

Kelly smiled at Teresa. This was what she'd been looking for, this sort of connection. "I have as well, but thankfully, I'm home now."

"Yeah, you're home. Welcome home, love." Teresa beamed at Kelly who reached over the table and took her hand.

About the Author

Heather K O'Malley is a fifty-plus-year-old transgender lesbian who has been writing stories since fifth grade, lots of stories. Along the way she joined the Army, got injured, traveled the world, learned a number of languages, failed epically, found true love, went to a lot of schools, got a master's in English, was an activist, taught, learned several martial arts, figured out how to cook, tried most everything, and became a proud grandmother. It has been exhausting.

Books Available from Bold Strokes Books

Discovering Gold by Sam Ledel. In 1920s Colorado, a single mother and a rowdy cowgirl must set aside their fears and initial reservations about one another if they want to find love in the mining town each of them calls home. (978-1-63679-786-1)

Dream a Little Dream by Melissa Brayden. Savanna can't believe it when Dr. Kyle Remington, the woman who left her feeling like a fool, shows up in Dreamer's Bay. Life is too complicated for second chances. Or is it? (978-1-63679-839-4)

Emma by the Sea by Sarah G. Levine. A delightful modern-day romance inspired by Emma, one of Jane Austen's most beloved novels. (978-1-63679-879-0)

Goodbye, Hello by Heather K O'Malley. With so much time apart and the challenges of a long-distance relationship, Kelly and Teresa's second chance at love may end just as awkwardly as the first. (978-1-63679-790-8)

One Measure of Love by Annie McDonald. Vancouver's hit competitive cooking show Recipe for Success has begun filming its second season and two talented young chefs are desperate for more than a winning dish. (978-1-63679-827-1)

The Smallest Day by J.M. Redmann. The first bullet missed—can Micky Knight stop the second bullet from finding its target? (978-1-63679-854-7)

To Please Her by Elena Abbott. A spilled coffee leads Sabrina into a world of erotic BDSM that may just land her the love of her life. (978-1-63679-849-3)

Two Weddings and a Funeral by Claudia Parr. Stella and Theo have spent the last thirteen years pretending they can be just friends, but surely "just friends" don't make out every chance they get. (978-1-63679-820-2)

Coming Up Clutch by Anna Gram. College softball star Kelly "Razor" Mitchell hung up her cleats early, but when former crush, now coach Ashton Sharpe shows up on her doorstep seven years later, beautiful as ever, Razor hopes the longing in her gaze has nothing to do with softball. (978-1-63679-817-2)

Firecamp by Jaycie Morrison. Going their separate ways seemed inevitable for two people as different as Fallon and Nora, while meeting up again is strictly coincidental. (978-1-63679-753-3)

Fixed Up by Aurora Rey. When electrician Jack Barrow and artist Ellie Lancaster get stuck on a job site during a blizzard, close quarters send all sorts of sparks flying. (978-1-63679-788-5)

Stranded by Ronica Black. Can Abigail and Whitley overcome their personal hang-ups and stubbornness to survive not only Alaska, but a dangerous stalker as well? (978-1-63679-761-8)

Whisk Me Away by Georgia Beers. Regan's a gorgeous flake. Ava, a beautiful untouchable ice queen. When they meet again at a retreat for up-and-coming pastry chefs, the competition, and the ovens, heat up. (978-1-63679-796-0)

Across the Enchanted Border by Crin Claxton. Magic, telepathy, swordsmanship, tyranny, and tenderness abound in a tale of two lands separated by the enchanted border. (978-1-63679-804-2)

Deep Cover by Kara A. McLeod. Running from your problems by pretending to be someone else only works if the person you're pretending to be doesn't have even bigger problems. (978-1-63679-808-0)

Good Game by Suzanne Lenoir. Even though Lauren has sworn off dating gamers, it's becoming hard to resist the multifaceted Sam. An opposites attract lesbian romance. (978-1-63679-764-9)

Innocence of the Maiden by Ileandra Young. Three powerful women. Two covens at war. One horrifying murder. When mighty and powerful witches begin to butt heads, who out there is strong enough to mediate? (978-1-63679-765-6)

Protection in Paradise by Julia Underwood. When arson forces them together, the flames between chief of police Eve Maguire and librarian Shaye Hayden aren't that easy to extinguish. (978-1-63679-847-9)

Too Forward by Krystina Rivers. Just as professional basketball player Jane May's career finally starts heating up, a new relationship with her team's brand consultant could derail the success and happiness she's struggled so long to find. (978-1-63679-717-5)

Worth Waiting For by Kristin Keppler. For Peyton and Hanna, reliving the past is painful, but looking back might be the only way to move forward. (978-1-63679-773-1)

Flowers and Gemstones by Alaina Erdell. Caught between past loves and present secrets, Hannah and Vanessa must each decide if the other is worth making difficult changes for a shot at happiness. (978-1-63679-745-8)

Foul Play by Erin Kaste. Music librarian Kirsten Lindquist knows someone is stalking the symphony musicians, but can she prove that a string of murders and suspicious accidents are connected, all without becoming a victim herself? (978-1-63679-689-5)

Hollywood Hearts by Toni Logan. What happens when an A-list actress falls for a paparazzo, having no idea her love interest is the one responsible for the photos in a troublesome tabloid scandal targeting her? (978-1-63679-695-6)

Ride It Out by Jenna Jarvis. When the COVID-19 lockdown traps Mick and Katy in situations they'd convinced themselves were temporary, they're forced to face what they really want from their lives, and who they want to share them with. (978-1-63679-709-0)

Scarlet Love by Gun Brooke. Felicienne de Montagne is content with her hybrid flowers and greenhouses—until she finds adventurer Puck Aston on her doorstep and realizes nothing will ever be the same. (978-1-63679-721-2)

The Hard Stuff by Ana Hartnett. When Hannah, the sales manager for a big liquor brand, moves to Alexandra's hometown and rivals her local distillery, sparks of friction and attraction fly. It turns out the liquor is the least of the hard stuff. (978-1-63679-599-7)

The Hunter and Her Witch by Rachel Sullivan. When an ex-witch-hunter falls for a witch, buried pasts are unearthed, and love is placed on trial. (978-1-63679-830-1)

Trustfall by Patricia Evans. Devri and Shiv never expect their feelings for each other to linger, but sometimes what you've always wanted has a way of leading you to who you've always needed. (978-1-63679-705-2)

www.ingramcontent.com/pod-product-compliance
Lightning Source LLC
Chambersburg PA
CBHW032210030726
47494CB00020B/938